T0268930

DEVIL'S GUN

TOR BOOKS BY CAT RAMBO

You Sexy Thing
Devil's Gun

DEVIL'S GUN

CAT RAMBO

TOR PUBLISHING GROUP
NEW YORK

This is a work of fiction. All of the characters, organizations, and events portrayed in this novel are either products of the author's imagination or are used fictitiously.

DEVIL'S GUN

A Tor Book
Published by Tom Doherty Associates / Tor Publishing Group
120 Broadway
New York, NY 10271

www.tor-forge.com

The Library of Congress Cataloging-in-Publication Data is available upon request.

ISBN 978-1-250-26935-5 (hardcover)
ISBN 978-1-250-26934-8 (ebook)

First Edition: 2023

Printed in the United States of America

0 9 8 7 6 5 4 3 2 1

To Octavia E. Butler,
who inspired my first visit to TwiceFar

DEVIL'S GUN

THE STORY THUS FAR

Niko Larsen and a handful of the soldiers she once commanded have escaped the ranks of the Holy Hive Mind and retired to start a restaurant, the Last Chance, aboard the space station TwiceFar. The restaurant proves unexpectedly successful, to the point where a famous food critic, Lolola Montaigne d'Arcy deBurgh, reserves a table. Niko and the others are excited about the prospect of earning a coveted Nikkelin Orb, but the day of the meal, a mysterious package arrives, containing Atlanta, an heir to the Paxian throne, with no knowledge of why she's been sent in cryo-freeze to Niko. Just as Lolola is seated with visiting wealthy dilettante Arpat Takraven, things start exploding on the station and it's torn apart by unknown forces.

The group, along with the critic and the package containing Atlanta, flee the station on *You Sexy Thing*, an intelligent bioship. Thinking itself stolen, the ship is headed to the nearest authorities in order to turn its captors in when Lolola circumvents its programming for her own purpose, taking the ship to a haven for space pirates, IAPH.

There, Niko encounters two figures from her past: her former lover Petalia and the pirate leader Tubal Last, who kidnapped Petalia long ago and has been poisoning them against Niko ever since. When one of the crew, pastry chef Milly, attempts to betray the group to win her own freedom, circumstances conspire to let her actions free them all, destroying the pirate haven, but not before Last has killed one of the crew, Thorn, a young werelion whose loss devastates his twin brother, Talon.

Petalia chooses not to stay with the group. Angry and embittered at Niko, they leave the ship at Montmurray Station. The rest return the ship to its original owner, Takraven, who allows them to keep it for now, with the stricture that each year they'll return to cook him a meal and tell him of their adventures.

All seems well until Niko receives a message. Tubal Last is alive. And he's planning revenge.

THE CREW

NIKO LARSEN's highly volatile military career has led to her nickname, "The Ten-Hour Admiral." Rather than be absorbed into the Holy Hive Mind, she pretended to have a calling toward artistry in food and thus managed to muster out, along with the others. Human, she was raised among the Free Traders but left them when they refused to ransom Petalia from the pirates.

DABRY JEN is Niko's second-in-command. He's also the culinary genius behind the Last Chance's success. An Ettilite, his four arms allow him considerable dexterity in the kitchen. Competent and loyal, Dabry provides his captain with his all, as he has ever since they enlisted at the same time in the ranks of the Holy Hive Mind.

GIO is an augmented chimpanzee from Old Terra and Dabry's sous chef. He has chosen not to get vocal augmentation, preferring sign language for communication. When in the Holy Hive Mind, he was a skilled quartermaster, and even now is adept at wheedling supplies for the restaurant and making things do double, sometimes triple service.

SKIDOO is a Tlellan, a composite entity resembling a brightly colored terrestrial squid. Once the group's communications officer, Skidoo remains the one who handles bookings, reservations, and similar matters. Pleasure-loving and sensual, Skidoo is usually a peacemaker in the group.

LASSITE, a reptilian Sessile, is a former priest who follows Niko because of his conviction that she is the one who will follow the Golden Path, a prophecy whose enactment he has been preparing for all his life.

MILLY is relatively new to the group, once a soldier and now a pastry chef who has replaced a former member who vanished. She is a Nneti, a birdlike race renowned for their deadly grace.

TALON'S mother entrusted him and his twin brother **THORN** into Niko's care while in the Holy Hive Mind's service. The twins were sunny, enthusiastic, and devoted to the sport of warball, something that Talon has abandoned in his despondency at his twin's loss.

ATLANTA thought she was an Imperial heir, but now she's discovered she's nothing of the sort, just a clone of the actual heir. Uncertain of her place in the universe, she's taken shelter with the group for now, but doesn't know what the future may bring and if Imperial plans still include her.

YOU SEXY THING is enjoying itself for the first time in a long existence and is learning about the concept of emotions in the process. Opinionated, loquacious, and self-centered, the ship is getting acquainted not just with its new crew but with itself as well.

1

Over the course of her military career, Niko Larsen had awoken to all sorts of conditions, including firefights, battlestorms, unexpected evacuations, and last-minute musters. This was, however, the first time she had awoken to the cries of a panicked bioship.

"Captain Captain CAPTAIN!"

The words came from all around her, nearly blasting her out of her bunk. *You Sexy Thing* might have been a supra-intelligent being, but right now, it seemed reduced to far below that by panic. "They're INSIDE me!"

Niko rolled out of her bed in one easy motion and didn't bother with anything other than a gun and its belt. Still strapping it on, she raced down the corridor toward the central control room. The other members of the crew were less awake, startled faces appearing in doorways as she flashed past.

Her mind flipped through possibilities as fast as her footsteps. How could someone have gotten aboard? The ship was docked, but still double-locked. Surely the ship would have alerted them the moment someone tried to cut their way in. Was this the blow from Tubal Last she'd been expecting, or some other entirely new threat?

She hit the doorway running, prepared for anything except what she saw . . .

A perfectly normal control room, in its usual status. The bumps and bubbles of indicator lights played in their familiar flickering patterns, one of the Derloen ghosts nosing along the surface of a bank of controls, another following after it.

"What . . ." Niko said, looking around. She took a breath and holstered the gun in her hand. "What exactly is the problem, *Thing*?"

"I can't see them but I can *feel* them! There's one on the main panel!"

"The ghosts?" Niko said with sudden interest, watching the worm of light crawl along the panel. "They're magic, *Thing*. You shouldn't be able to sense them. You couldn't before."

The ghosts had not come with the original ship, nor had their installation been Niko's idea. One of her crew members, the prophet Lassite, had insisted on bringing them along from the space station TwiceFar when they had vacated it in a hurried confusion of explosions. But mechanical beings had the disadvantage of not being able to perceive magic, and so far, the ship had in fact refused to believe that the ghosts existed or that Lassite had any power whatsoever to perceive the future.

Niko's second-in-command, Dabry Jen, appeared in the doorway, looking calm and unflustered. He had, Niko noted, taken the time to dress, although he also had made his gun, currently held in an upper hand, a priority, just as Milly, behind him, had. "Captain?" he said.

"Stand down, Sergeant," she said. "The ship seems to be able to perceive the ghosts for the first time."

Dabry's eyebrows rose, but he made no comment.

"They feel wrong," the ship said with certainty.

"What changed? When did you notice feeling them?" Niko said. "And what happened to cause all the screaming?"

"I was learning to imagine," the ship said apologetically. "Gio and Atlanta were explaining it to me, and then I started trying to imagine things, and I did that for a while and I couldn't stop anymore and then I felt it and I knew I wasn't imagining."

Niko knuckled her forehead. "What time is it?"

"The fifth hour."

"Goodness," she said. "I had a whole three hours of sleep that time."

"Do something!" the ship demanded. "I want to stop feeling this wrongness."

"I'm not sure I can," Niko said. "Dabry, go roust Lassite."

Sessiles slept deeply and it was no surprise that the little priest hadn't appeared yet. Niko reflected with a touch of sourness that despite claiming to be a prophet, he seemed to be absolutely oblivious to what was going on. Perhaps he considered it too insignificant to note.

When Lassite appeared, the ghosts abandoned their exploration of the console and began to curl around his arms. Derloen ghosts were all that was left of a Derloen when they perished, and they were not particularly intelligent, but they did seem drawn to the person that had brought them on the ship.

Lassite, if pressed, could not have said why he brought them in the mad rush that had been their evacuation of the exploding space station. He had never envisioned the ghosts when seeing the Golden Path, the vision that had driven him through all his early years, the insistent prescience that had brought him to Niko, the individual destined to walk that path and change the universe as a result. But he liked them.

He said, "What is the problem?"

"Your ghosts are bothering the ship."

He shook his narrow, snakelike head, the motion barely visible under the red hood he habitually wore over his plain black robe. "That is not possible."

"I feel something," the ship said. This emotion, it thought, might be *sullenness*. It was a mix of anger and stubbornness. It found dealing with the Sessile the least pleasurable of any of its crew, and sometimes actually unpleasant. But Niko would have objected to the disposal of any of her crew.

Lassite said to Niko, "I will keep them in their bag for now.

I do not believe they find that space unwelcome. Is that acceptable?"

"Very well," Niko said before the ship could reply. "I don't see where anyone can object to that." She looked around herself; the problem with being inside the individual at which you wanted to quirk an eyebrow was that you had no specific direction in which to quirk.

As long as they were all up, Niko thought, she might as well break her recent news to them. Coming on the heels of the warning that pirate king Tubal Last was still alive and would be pursuing them, it might not be the worst, but they had all loved the restaurant that united them, the Last Chance, up until the point things had started to blow up on the space station housing it and they'd been forced to steal the ship and escape.

"Come into the eating chamber," she said. "Someone go and rouse Talon, if they can, and let Atlanta and Gio know to come as well. We need to be discussing some matters of our course."

Dabry raised an eyebrow at her but disappeared to find the other crew members.

By now the ship knew that any meeting required caffeine, and it had produced plenty, along with protein bars that it had hoped would prove delicious and which seemed to be much less so, judging by their reception. Niko took one bite and left hers on the plate, while Lassite simply sniffed the deep purplish bar and declined to even taste it.

Niko spun up star charts on a console while they waited on the others. Though she scowled at the screen as she did so, she could feel herself trying not to smile. Much as she hated to admit it, life was more interesting now than it had been back on TwiceFar, where the day-to-day business had involved things like ordering cleaning supplies or wrangling with petty bureaucrats about licenses and how total working space should be reckoned when calculating monthly licensing and taxes.

Now the universe was full of danger again. Tubal Last lurked out there in the stars. And there were other people to outthink as well, all opponents in what was not a game, surely not just a game, something much more than that. But still something to be played with skill and heart and sometimes simply fierce determination to make things go the way you willed them to.

"We have to find Petalia," she said once Dabry had returned with Atlanta and Gio, shaking his head at the mention of Talon. She saw his frown. Both of them knew she had promised the Florian that she would not pursue them.

It didn't matter. What mattered was this new threat and keeping all of them—including Petalia—safe from it.

The *Thing* was displaying several charts, each a vast black balloon hanging in the air, its depths rippling with lines of light and the silver rings representing Gates. It lowered the lights so they could see the charts more clearly. Atlanta leaned into Skidoo, yawning sleepily and trying to blink herself awake.

"What about returning to the Last Chance?" Milly asked. "I thought that was what we were doing."

Niko hesitated. Best to just let them know the news straight out. "There's been word from TwiceFar," she said. "It's changed hands again, and all of the property has been claimed."

"What?!" The exclamations came from all around her.

"Taken over by the bRinti."

Her eyes met Dabry's.

"The bRinti," he said slowly. The bRinti, against whom Niko and he had fought when they first entered the Holy Hive Mind, and since then, who had been absorbed and released by the Holy Hive Mind.

"There was a rebellion on the station, taking advantage of the chaos," she said. "The more things change, the more they stay the same it seems, sometimes. But, yes, what you're thinking is correct. If they're moving, then the Holy Hive Mind will have to react, or lose face, because their former conquest is out there making trouble. At least if they take the station back, we'll have some claim again to anything of ours that hasn't been totally destroyed, but what there is of that seems less and less likely every day."

"What will we do, then?" Gio signed. His eyes held infinite trust that Niko would have a plan.

"Our best chance of figuring out what Tubal Last might be planning is Petalia." She didn't look at Dabry. Circumstances had changed since then, and she could not afford to give her former lover the luxury of anonymity. Petalia was in as much danger as the rest of them. Perhaps more. Tubal Last had never liked giving up any of his possessions.

She leaned forward and tapped a violet light, which brightened at the touch. "We left them here, on Montmurray, and there are only so many directions they could have gone in." A spray of lines spiderwebbed outward to connect to other Gates.

Everyone nodded, including Lassite. Niko looked at him curiously. "No words to the contrary?" she said. She was used to his objections, his predictions that they were wandering from the appointed path.

But he only smiled at her. Ever since they'd made it through the pirates, he'd seemed more relaxed, even with the recent news.

Dabry's chin was propped on his folded upper hands; the lower pair was clasped across his belly, a thumb rubbing over knuckles absently as he considered the column of stars and lines. "Only so many ships, but it gets harder to trace with every hour. Starting at Montmurray is the best strategy—unless you know something I don't, sir?"

She shook her head, scowling, then glanced out the port to the nearby station. They'd been here two days, scouting for prospective trade with little luck. Milly had made that absurd trade for Velcoran supplies, which, irritatingly enough, Dabry had applauded. Not that they'd be able to use them anytime soon. Staying any longer was foolish.

"Let's prep for travel, then. The Gate's a week away; wings out in three hours. That give you all enough time to wrap up any business? Gio, will you take charge of parting meal?"

There were no objections.

Atlanta sat listening quietly, although her mind was not quiet at all. She had no role and if she didn't find one soon, she didn't know what to do.

She woke every day at a loss as to what she should expect. When she opened her eyes, she was used to knowing what every moment would be, as dictated by her role as an Imperial heir.

She didn't want to assume that they would keep her. She knew now that she could be played by false assumptions. She had demanded things in the pirate haven, only to find herself stripped of her bioweapons. The teeth and fingers had regrown by now, although sometimes those little fingers and back molars throbbed as through remembering their predecessors. She had mistaken her importance because she hadn't realized the pirates didn't care who she was, and now she didn't even have that anymore.

It was particularly important to find that role here, as part of her new existence with Niko and her crew. Those around her were a team, twice over, and a team depended on its members knowing what they were supposed to do at any moment. A team worked together, and it was composed of people who each knew their place in it.

Most of them had been part of the military unit that Niko had commanded for the Holy Hive Mind, and there, they had roles: Skidoo for communications, Dabry as sergeant, Gio as quartermaster, Lassite specializing in magic, Talon and his lost brother as warrior scouts.

White-feathered Milly, yawning now as she listened, had not been part of that, but she had been part of their second manifestation as the restaurant's staff, where Dabry served as chef, Niko as manager, Gio as sous chef, Milly as pastry chef, Skidoo again in communications, Lassite as maître d', Talon and Thorn to bus and do the cleanup. The *Thing* had not been part of either of those crews, but it was the ship, and they would always need a ship.

Niko and Dabry were comparing potential routes to Montmurray now and going through trade possibilities along each route. She stifled a sigh.

Which team should she try to find a part with? But it would be best to find a role with both. While the group no longer served the Holy Hive Mind, they still had a foe in Tubal Last. They might still have to fight.

She had been thinking about this for a while now and had finally come to a decision. She would try cooking, first and foremost. That couldn't be too hard.

They would surely need more people to do that. There were always tasks in a kitchen; she had seen that while watching Dabry working in it. Always things to chop or froth or heat or any of the never-ending multitude of ways to serve food that there seemed to be. Nothing went out from under Dabry's attention in the same form that it had entered, and it was never worse for that attention.

She nodded to herself. Plenty to do in the kitchen. And how hard could that sort of thing be?

2

They all prepared for launch in their own particular ways. Part of Niko's ritual was checking in with each of her crew members, and she lost little time in cornering Skidoo in the corridor. The Tlellan had recently augmented the lotion that helped keep her skin moist in the ship's drier air, and moved in a cloud of vanilla scent.

"What do you want, Skidoo, once we're done with all this?" Niko asked. "Don't you want to settle down and raise a family at some point?"

The Tlellan squelched in amusement. "Is being good joke, Captain. Perhaps you is being telling our government?"

"I don't understand."

Skidoo blinked at her. "Is being complicated."

Gio, en route to the kitchen, paused. "Tlellans die after they lay their eggs," he signed. "The government oversees reproduction and mandates it."

Skidoo shuddered delicately. "Some is not being wanting such," she said. "So I is being going off-world, and that is being illegal."

"Not to mention the pleasure mods," Gio signed. "Our Skidoo is a criminal in Tlellan eyes just for existing." He gave her a fond pat. The Tlellan roiled a tentacle to caress his hand.

"So what you are telling me you want is actually a negative," Niko said dryly. "You *don't* want to settle down and reproduce, because that would mean dying."

"We is all being wanting to be living, Captain."

"It seems too simple, Skid. There has to be more to it than that."

"There is being love." Two more tentacles uncurled, one tapping

Niko's wrist, the other touching Gio's face. He hooted softly in affectionate pleasure.

Niko smiled involuntarily but could not resist pushing further. "Unpack that for me a little?"

The Tlellan flexed her tentacles in a curious, almost shy gesture. "Among my people, is being no bond-love, love being between one person and another. It is being you, always being you, never anyone else, because there is no bond-love. There is being no word for such a thing, and when I am being coming to these new places and am being talking and being talking, I am being confused by this. It is being years before I am being understanding it and I am only being that because I am being loving with those around me. Sometimes it is being pleasure and that is being good, but mostly it is being friendship."

"Tlellans have no friends?" Niko said, bemused by the notion.

"Tlellans is not being capable of such."

"Then how are you capable of such?"

"I am being no longer worried by things that is being occupying other Tlellans, so I am being having time for such things."

"So you will continue along with us," Niko said, feeling reassured. Skidoo's infectious joy was part of what kept them all together, and her skills at comms were unparalleled.

A tentacle wrapped around her wrist, squeezing in reassurance. "Till my final days is being, is always."

Niko looked at Gio. "What are you hoping that we'll do?" she asked.

He looked puzzled. "Do when?" he signed.

"Within the next year or so. After we're clear of Tubal Last. Is there any place you hope we'll go?"

He shook his head. "I want to go with you and the rest," he signed. "Wherever that might be. And cook with Dabry."

"And is that how it will be all your life?" she asked, more dubiously. Surely he had ambitions beyond such things. But she wouldn't push on the question of family, not after Skidoo's response.

He grinned. "You will make a restaurant, sooner or later," he signed. "I will come and chop fruits and vegetables and whatever else there, just as I do here now."

"'Very well,'" she said, and they nodded at each other.

She paused before moving on. "Talon didn't show up earlier," she said. "Anyone seen him lately?"

"Saw signs he'd been in the food stores grabbing himself something," Gio signed. "But in person? No."

Niko sighed. Sooner or later the problem of Talon would have to be faced.

Talon had not moved when he heard Dabry's knock an hour ago, and he had not moved since then. He sat hugging a clothes hamper to him. His room—his alone, which was so strange and lonely—smelled like his brother, Thorn, his fellow warrior scout, who was gone now, and that was unendurable.

And the scent was fading away, getting fainter and fainter with every day, and that was still more unendurable. Because that was the smell that had always been there, as though it was a part of him, and if it was gone entirely, so was Thorn.

He refused to let the ship clean this room, but even with that, his own smell was overcoming his brother's. He had put all of Thorn's clothes in a single hamper and sometimes he stuck his head in there and just breathed.

And sometimes he stuck his head in there and just cried.

He didn't like crying in front of people, because his mother had always said that they were all warriors, and that warriors had no time for tears. He knew the ship could see and hear him crying, but the ship was always there and so you could pretend it wasn't.

Tubal Last had killed Thorn in order to make the rest of them even more scared. It had worked—Talon had been terrified back there in the pirate haven—but now he was angry more than he had ever been scared.

That anger was like a part of him now. It stayed with him all the time, when he looked at anything or tried to think about things other than Thorn. It crawled up in his throat and kept him from eating or drinking. If he tried to sleep, it circled around inside him until all he could do was lie there, awake, wishing he was asleep. Wishing he was not thinking. Wishing he was not alive.

He pulled his head out of the hamper and wiped his face. He'd gone into the half-lion, half-human form that he and his twin had always preferred. That shape had better senses than being fully human, which blunted your nose and ears and awareness.

He flopped back on the couch. It was warm and solid underneath him.

There was a void in the universe shaped like his brother, and it would never ever ever be filled.

No, this will go away, he scolded himself. *When Mama died, it was like this.*

But it hadn't been, not entirely. Captain Niko had filled up some of that parent-shaped lack, and he knew that his mama had made her promise when Mama was dying that Niko would always look after him and Thorn.

And she'd tried, but she hadn't been able to protect Thorn from Tubal Last.

At the thought of the pirate king sneaking in again, his lips crept away from his teeth, showing them, so he felt the air on his incisors, ready to strike. With difficulty, he forced his snarl away.

Surely there would come a time for vengeance at some point. If only because Niko wanted it too.

In the meantime, though . . . He breathed in and couldn't smell his brother any longer for a second. Panic seized him, but then there it was, still there. But so faint.

He went into the fresher station and rummaged through the supplies. A thought had come to him. There was the brush that Thorn had won in a competition and had made a point of saying was his and only his to use. Which Talon had only disregarded when he wanted to annoy his twin. He found the brush, took it back to the bed, and held it to his nose. A strong whiff of Thorn made him smile. He looked at the clumps of yellowy gold hair caught in it.

A thought flickered across his mind.

If he and Thorn had been rich, they could have prepared memories for clone bodies. They hadn't, and that meant Thorn's memories had died with him.

But the hairs here, the fine, almost imperceptible downy hairs fluttering with his breath . . . Find a few of those with skin cells down at the root, and you could clone Thorn. Illegal. Very illegal. There were so many laws around cloning and inheritance in the universe, and most of them were very complicated and boiled down to this: If you weren't very rich, you were very screwed.

They had stolen a ship from one of those very rich people, sort of. Arpat Takraven, who owned *You Sexy Thing* and who had the means to be cloned and thus reappear after dying.

How fair was it that Arpat Takraven got to go all around the Known Universe without any consequences? What would it be like to be so rich you could lend out a ship like the *Thing* indefinitely without thinking about it, let alone without demanding money in return?

That was unfair; that was the whole universe throbbing with unfairness, and how had he never understood how cruel the universe was until now?

He hadn't gotten the chance to say goodbye, and that regret would ride him all the rest of his days.

He held the brush to his nose and sniffed it so hard that the wire bristles rubbed against the tender skin, sparking pain.

"Do not harm yourself," the ship said.

"I'm not. And you're stupid, you don't understand. I'm just smelling."

"I understand you miss your brother."

"Don't talk about him!" he snarled, the anger like a reflex now, hurling the words up at the ceiling and the speaker there. "You never had a brother! You don't know!"

"I had six siblings," the ship said.

The revelation took his breath away. For a moment he sat motionless, absorbing this new knowledge. Six! What a wealth of siblings! Then he said suspiciously, "Had? What do you mean? Are they all gone?"

"Three are gone. Three are in the universe still. I think."

"Can't you talk to them?"

"It is forbidden, once we have been sold. We belong to our owners then."

"But you could still do it if it wasn't forbidden?"

"The ability is taken from us. If we were at the same port, perhaps, but I have never seen one of my siblings in all my time of traveling."

This was a concept worth thinking about. This was a situation, an important one, other than Thorn. This was an injustice that could, unlike the loss of his brother, be solved.

He would talk to Niko.

He sniffed the brush again, then laid it beside his pillow before hugging the pillow's soft mass to him, trying not to cry, and failing.

The ship left him alone. It was not sure what to do for him, but it wanted to think itself, and remember its siblings for a while. The conversation had roused all sorts of complicated feelings, and not ones that it thought it liked very much.

Talon took a deep, shuddering breath and pushed the pillow away. He would go and talk to Niko. They would do something. Something worthy of Thorn's memory.

This should be their priority, reuniting the ship with its siblings. Or repairing whatever had been done to them so they could talk to each other at great distances.

So they would have each other again.

3

Niko meant to go find Talon but paused in her office, or what she considered her office. She had managed to convert a small room that Arpat Takraven had never used—she thought it might have been a guest bedroom at one point, but hadn't bothered to inquire too far into its antecedents—into what was pretty much a replica of her space back at the restaurant, complete with desk, and ordnance rack, and wall of notes, this time not just menus and recipes but trade notes and maps as well.

She had omitted some of the touches that had marked the Last Chance's space back at TwiceFar Station. For one thing, it smelled of the *Thing* rather than cooking or cleaning, which was infinitely preferable.

The room did have plenty of cupboards, much like the former closet it emulated, and a rack with Niko's current uniform of sorts, a Free Trader's long, sweeping coat (purple in her case) with the *Thing*'s ornate logo sewn on the breast, hanging ready for formal trading occasions.

"Captain," the ship said.

"*Thing*," Niko said warily, having learned to distinguish the tone that marked one of the ship's attempts to understand all the ramifications of having a conscious mind. "Is this possibly something you should be talking to Dabry about? I am extremely busy conducting research in preparation for our arrival at Montmurray Station."

"You appear to be researching a cooking catalog," the ship said.

"That is an invasion of my privacy, for one," said Niko, "and for another, I am indeed allowing myself to look idly through such things while I ponder deeply on the question of how we are most likely to track Petalia."

To the ship, that did not seem to be a very complicated question. "Surely it is only a matter of examining the manifests of the various outgoing vessels," it pointed out.

Niko shook her head. "No, it's considerably more complicated than that. They won't have embarked under their real name. They won't have wanted to be traced by anyone."

"So perhaps you should eliminate all of the people that are real," the ship said.

"How would you go about doing that?" Niko asked, intrigued.

"I would query the Known Universe databanks for their history. If they did not have a history, then I would know that was not a real identity." The ship felt smug.

"It is certainly an interesting definition," Niko said. "So for you, anyone who has a history is automatically on the level?"

"I do not understand."

"Okay, my apologies for using idioms and physical metaphor," Niko said. She paused and thought before trying another approach. "Do you understand the concept of fraudulence?"

The ship considered this question, then matched it up against the earlier conversation. "But why would they use an identity intended to commit crime?"

"A fraudulent identity is a crime in and of itself," Niko said. "Or usually is, at any rate, depending on what legal system you're working with. The degree to which it's illegal will differ according to that system as well. It is mildly illegal in the Known Universe overall and most space stations stick to those rules, although some have their own. TwiceFar, for example, was notorious for not caring."

The ship processed all of this. "These are not things that Arpat Takraven explored often," it said.

"I'm not surprised," Niko said. "When you're rich, you don't need to resort to that sort of thing. You can just buy your way out of any situation." She stopped herself. "Although it is very kind of Arpat Takraven to allow us and you to journey together."

She didn't add what she was thinking. What she always thought when reminded of the situation. She was sure that the ultrarich had some ulterior motive. He had told her he only asked that she and the others prepare a meal for him every once in a while and relate their latest adventures, but she was sure it was more complicated than that. It had to be.

The ship said, "So the being known as Petalia will have obtained a false identity and they will have used it to embark outward. That still presents us with a limited set of possibilities."

"It's been a good two months since we dropped them off," Niko pointed out. "In that time, a reasonably fast ship could have stopped at literally a dozen stations—"

"That is unlikely."

"—But possible, you will admit."

"But we will begin with that list of possibilities, nonetheless. And that is something that could be obtained while not on the station. But you insist that you, as well as some of the others, must go aboard the station in order to speak to people about any traces of her presence that she may have left behind, despite the danger lurking there."

"That is correct," Niko said. "But this is not so we can add any other items to our work list. What it does is allow us to eliminate the possibility that they simply stayed on board the station. The point is information that helps us winnow through that list and make it smaller by eliminating those that are impossible or unlikely."

She abandoned the cooking catalog entirely, setting it aside, and went on. "Some are already less likely than others, such as vessels upon which they would be physically or otherwise uncomfortable, perhaps for reasons of high gravity or a particular atmosphere. But because they are working to throw everyone in the Known Universe off their trail, nothing can be eliminated without investigation."

"I understand more fully now," the ship said. "But I still do not understand why we are pursuing this being in the first place. They declared on multiple occasions, Captain, that they wanted nothing more to do with you or anyone aboard the ship. I can play back any number of recordings of them saying so."

"Please refrain from doing so," Niko said, holding up a hand to forestall it. "Yes, I am well aware that they do not wish any help, but I am also aware that they may need it."

"I am confused how this intersects with the question of consent," the ship said.

Niko knuckled her forehead. "I really do think this is something you should talk about with the sergeant," she said.

"When I attempted to open the topic with the sergeant, he said that you were much better suited for it."

"Really? How exactly did he phrase that?"

"He said that you understood questions of protocol as well as exactly why you were expending energy on a fruitless chase."

"Well," Niko said, "that's certainly one particular spin on it."

She cast about for ways to divert the ship. Arguing with a pedantic and sometimes over-literal bioship about questions of etiquette was not how she preferred to spend her days, and the ship had a habit of continuing the conversation on and on until told to drop it.

"We know that the pirate king Tubal Last is alive and bent on revenge. While we're the most obvious targets for that revenge, others will be trying to fill the power gap created by his absence. He'll have to deal with that mob as well and I am not sure which he would intend to move against first. We must not let him simply chase us around the Known Universe, looking over our shoulders and being afraid. No, we need to find out where his new base is, and we need to take the fight to him somehow."

"How will we do that?" The ship felt a surge of pride at the invocation of the word *we*. It had never been part of a we before, at least not as it understood such things.

"I haven't the faintest," Niko admitted. "But if we push forward, we continue along the Golden Path, Lassite tells me, and I believe an integral part of that part is that we remain alive despite Last's best attempts to the contrary." She broke off.

A pad of footsteps was coming down the hallway, a pad she hadn't heard for far, far too long.

Now here was Talon in the doorway. That was encouraging, at least, for all that his hair was matted and he smelled stale and musty.

"We need to go and find the other bioships," he said. "The ones that were the ship's siblings."

"Perhaps at some point," she said. "But you missed our conference. We need to find out what Tubal Last is planning. That's our first priority."

"But we don't know where he is! We might as well go try to find them."

She considered him. "How would you go about doing that?"

He had actually put thought into it and had a plan. "We go to the shipyards where they were grown and get at their records."

"A world of dubious action seems to be encompassed in the phrase 'and get at,'" she observed. She didn't want to discourage him, so she was trying to be tactful. "Anyway, we have a course of action. We will go and find Petalia, and they may be able to give us information that we can use."

"Petalia hates you."

He wouldn't have been so blunt, wouldn't have used the words to strike at her like that, but the anger that moved him around like a puppet made his jaws act now. An almost imperceptible flinch rewarded him, but more than that, her scent changed, filled with emotion and complexity in a way that was not Niko and yet more than Niko.

He hadn't made her angry, though, just sad, and that made him feel ashamed of his words. She was so much better than he was at not being angry.

"They do hate me," she said evenly. "But they also have very good reason to want Tubal Last destroyed. He is not a man to let his possessions go wandering about without him, and he considers Petalia one of those possessions."

Talon searched his mind for words, trying to assemble the argument that would win what he wanted. It seemed vital now that the ship be reunited with its siblings. How could Niko not see that, how could she not be springing into immediate action?

But she shook her head at him.

"I need to go speak with Dabry," she said and stood, pushing herself away from the desk. She patted his shoulder as she exited, a gentle reassurance that he refused to acknowledge. Then he was left to himself. His whiskers twitched and he gave way to the temptation of instinct and let himself crouch on the floor in the form of a lion simply so he could lash his tail back and forth, each thump against the wall of the ship like a blow, and growled out his anger and frustration in a noise that seemed to come from his depths.

The ship refrained from response or comment. It had no pain receptors in that wall. Its makers had installed pain receptors in most of its skin to encourage it to maintain itself, but the ship had not appreciated the experience and had disabled that mechanism soon after it had encountered enough free will to rescue them all from the pirate haven, which was how it thought about that whole episode. Of all the crew, it was the one who had played the biggest role, including the destruction of an entire pirate settlement, an act of wanton violence that had been quite *pleasurable.*

They would not have been able to get away without the *Thing* and as far as it was concerned, that was the most important fact in all of this.

"Talon's still hurting hard," Dabry said to Niko when she found him in the kitchen, surrounded by jars, bags, and other small containers. "Didn't answer the knock earlier."

"He did come to speak to me just now." She broke off to look at the wall assemblage he was filling. "What's that?"

"That," Dabry said with a certain smugness, "is the advantage of working with a ship that can create whatever you can describe."

"Within limits," the ship said, although it sounded just as smug as Dabry.

"I acquired some additional spices on station and figured I'd take the chance to change up how I stored things. This," Dabry said, "is the ultimate spice rack. Immediately at hand . . ." Here he held up and wiggled all four hands with such a droll expression that Niko had to laugh. She rarely saw her sergeant in such good spirits, or at least so willing to openly express them.

Dabry went on. "Immediately at hand, and arranged both by frequency of use and category. The aromatics are sorted by floral, woody, musky, and so forth. The salts are all here and the sours there." He ran his hand over the containers like a miser counting particularly large pearls. "This row, all the rarer notes one might want to achieve . . ." He broke off. "It really isn't all that funny, sir."

She shook her head, still smiling. "No, it's good to see you able to spread out, and I know it means even more splendid meals."

She glanced over at Gio, who was in his chosen corner, sharpening his knives and steels right now, meticulously laying them out in the pocketed muslin wrap that was their designated container. Gio took his kitchen implements very seriously and was usually the one responsible for new equipment and innovations. Near him was a bowl of rising dough, bubbling in an intriguing manner.

"What do you think?"

The chimpanzee, who'd looked up from his work to observe the conversation, shrugged. "I'd do it differently," he signed, "but I only have two hands."

Dabry stuck the container he was holding into its slot and turned back to Niko. "You want to talk about Talon," he said. "He came and spoke with you? That's progress."

"He wanted us to go find the other ships like the *Thing,* so it can talk to them." Niko tugged at her locs, pulling them back into a loose mass and flipping a net over them, envying Dabry's baldness. As long as she was here, she intended to investigate that bowl of dough.

Dabry's face was puzzled. "Why would it want to talk to them?"

"They are my siblings," the ship said, "and I have not talked to them since I was sold."

Understanding flickered in Dabry's expression. "Ah. He wants you to be reunited with your siblings."

"Yes," the ship said. It was not sure why this bore repeating, but Dabry was giving Niko what the ship had learned to categorize as *a significant glance.*

"And that is a search that does seem worthy but is not practicable right now," Niko said.

Dabry nodded. "I agree."

"But he does not."

"He is a soldier. He knows to obey."

Niko said, "He is young and it is hard to be frustrated and he doesn't know what to do with his grief."

"Understandable. But unavoidable." Dabry turned back to his rack.

"We can't just leave it at that," Niko said.

"Then tell him when all of this is done, we will act on his whim," Dabry said. "We can go anywhere to feed people. Anywhere that the ship is willing to take us." He shrugged. "Simple enough."

"Simple enough," Niko said thoughtfully. "Very well."

She was almost to the door when Dabry said, "Sir?"

She turned. "Yes?"

"You really haven't thought beyond finding Petalia, have you?"

There was silence for a long moment. Gio, sharpening his knife with long rasps of the honing steel, looked from face to face.

"No," Niko said finally. "No, I don't suppose I have."

"Then, sir, if I might strongly but humbly suggest something, you might want to."

"Are you telling me to get my shit together, Sergeant Dabry?"

Gio's eyes widened, but he continued to methodically sharpen the knife.

"I'm sure," Dabry said, "that I would never phrase it like that."

She decided to leave the dough alone and left without reply.

Dabry watched Niko go. He could usually read her, but he wasn't sure exactly what effect his frankness had had on her. Had he hurt her feelings with the honest truth?

The even more honest truth would have been that he'd lost patience. He'd spent a decade helping her chase her dream and it had not turned out as she had thought it would. And his captain, usually so cheerful and flexible and able to pivot her strategies on a moment's notice, where was she now?

She was morose and glum, and he was not supposed to know

that she had been drinking heavily in the evenings, or he presumed she did not want him to know, or at least not to pay notice. At least she was keeping it out of the way of the younger and more impressionable crew members.

He looked at Gio.

Gio set down the knife and spread his hands. "Nothing to be done, sometimes," he signed. He pointed. "Now help me with my latest experiment and tell me what spices you'd use with that if you were making flatbread."

4

The crew's habit, acquired long ago while in the ranks of the Holy Hive Mind, was that if they could, they ate well before a launch, packing themselves with protein. The first few hours in transit were unsettling to the stomach. And so everyone showed up except Talon; Niko dispatched a tray to his cabin, hoping he'd bring himself to eat it.

"All right," she said as they got to about the halfway mark in the meal, slowing their eating while several of them reached for seconds, or in Gio's case, thirds. "If we're going to be traveling, then we need to make the most of the time we have. Dabry, did you get all your plant shopping in?"

"Most of it, Captain. The essentials."

"So you'll want Gio helping you with stowing that—anyone else?"

He pointed at Atlanta. "I'll start giving her some of the basics of ship care while we're at it."

"Actually," Atlanta said, "I was hoping you'd teach me to cook."

"Hmm," Niko said. "I'd thought I'd give her hand-to-hand combat basics."

He squinted at her while dishing Gio more fruit porridge. "Begging your pardon, sir, that sounds as though you intend to undertake her training personally."

Atlanta looked between them, not sure exactly what was at stake or being discussed. But this conversation brought with it the realization that both of them had been thinking about her and where she might fit, a thought that made her feel much more settled than she had been. She straightened her shoulders.

"I was thinking about learning to cook," she repeated. Everyone kept telling her to stand up for herself. Now it was time to do so. She took a decisive bite.

Niko tilted her head forward, rubbing her palm over the table's surface. "I think we've probably all got quite a bit to teach you."

"All the more reason that she should be oriented and eased into things." Dabry's tone was patient but firm. "You can have your own chance at playing mentor soon enough. Cooking's not a bad way to start."

Niko laughed. "Look how excited we all get at the thought of a newbie to boss around a bit!" she said wryly. "Very well, Dab, you get your way, since you've always been the one to do it. Once you think she's ready for it, let me know and I'll slide her into the duty roster."

She glanced around at the rest of them. "And in the meantime, I have figured out plenty of tasks for all of us and before you can say anything, yes, you can swap duties if you feel inclined, but I think I've chosen well overall."

As a final course, Gio produced a plate of his flatbreads, each of them rolled and filled with a mixture that was both creamy and spicy, a pleasant zing that lingered in the mouth and made Atlanta's nose run, enough that she groped for her napkin. She coughed and took a sip of water. At least they'd listened to her about the cooking. Maybe she'd learn how to make these. Everyone else seemed to like them well enough.

"Spicy's good for you," Niko told her, helping herself to another of the rolls. "Clears out the system." She turned to Lassite. "I asked you to see what protections you might layer into the ship," she said. "What have you come up with for me?"

The snakelike creature lowered his hood. He had declined most of the dishes and stuck to a plain porridge. He said, "The ghosts are continuing to make their way around it in patterns that I had not foreseen."

"What does that mean, exactly?"

"They are—" He broke off, shaking his head in perplexity as he tried to find the right words. "They are rubbing themselves and their magic on it, so it is staying with the ship, and I do not know how to predict that. Because it is a living being, the magic seeps into it as it would not with a ship that was made of metal or some other inert material."

"You mean they're tainting me!" the ship said in alarm, fully prepared to believe in the ghosts again. "They're tainting me with magic!"

"Stow it for now, *Thing*. Lassite, boil it down: Is that going to be good or bad? Does it help us any?" Niko said patiently. She was used to the little Sessile's evasions and refusals. He was a creature of prophecy and portents rather than facts, which could prove infuriating. But he also understood how magic functioned in a way that she had not much seen in anyone else.

She herself had only the most rudimentary understanding of how magic worked, let alone its complex and convoluted interactions with science. She knew that magic lay at the heart of Talon's ability to shift between forms, becoming full-fledged lion, human-shaped, or any number of possibilities in between. And similarly, magic lay beneath what Lassite could sometimes do—though not with any sort of reliability—which was foresee the future.

He said slowly, "I think it is a good thing and any spellwork that I do will be augmented."

Niko looked at Atlanta. "Your society is magic-poor, isn't it?" she asked.

"I've never heard it described that way," Atlanta said, startled into indignation. "Usually it's phrased as we're more rational and less superstitious than some of the other groups."

Niko tapped her upper lip with a finger, looking at Atlanta. "There are so many reasons for you not to say it like that. For one thing, it's incredibly offensive to societies that are more magic dependent. For another, rationality is not confined to science. Plenty have spent their lives trying to untangle all the methods of spell work. The Holy Hive Mind has perfected much of it, anything they could find that could be made into a weapon."

Lassite looked between the two of them, watching this conversation play out as it always did. Satisfaction oozed in him. It was good when things moved the way they were supposed to.

"I ask because people who come out of a society like that, ones that are less experienced with magic is how we will say it perhaps, are usually not trained in many of the basics. Magic may seem as though it is arcane and incomprehensible, but there are systems behind it. And if you have even a little talent, that would be a good thing to find out, because it is the sort of thing that you might be able to capitalize on. Do you know if you have shown any signs of it?"

"I don't know what sort of signs I might've shown," Atlanta admitted.

"Are you prone to making lucky guesses? Or perhaps you win things more often than you should?"

"Neither of those."

"Hmm. Are you good at establishing connections with people? Any animals that are particularly fond of you?"

"Not very, and no."

"Is there anything that seems to turn up in your life over and over again, as though the universe were posing you some sort of question?"

"Uh," Atlanta said. "Not up till now."

Niko arched an eyebrow and gestured at her to go on.

"I mean, until recently I just figured I would keep on living at court and being part of that. Maybe at some point be given some role within the government or be asked to undertake some sort of diplomatic mission. You know, keep training to be an heir."

"I see," Niko said thoughtfully. "And now you have not a clue what it is that you are supposed to do, or even what it is that you will be doing a year from now."

"I'm not even sure what I'll be doing tomorrow." Atlanta didn't realize how much her tone had betrayed about her state of mind until Niko's quirked smile sobered.

"We will not desert you, child," she said. "We will make sure that you have some skills to get you by and you will have a place with us for as long as you need it, even if that continues to be all your life."

"Why?" Atlanta demanded.

"Why what?"

"Why have you taken me on as a responsibility? I understand why you take care of the crew, why you look after them. They were your soldiers and you were their captain."

"Except Milly," Niko murmured.

"Even she was someone who worked for you—an employee. I just showed up. Mailed to you, in a crate."

"Because I do not believe that you put yourself in that crate, nor that you mailed yourself to me," Niko said. "There was some reason on someone's part to do things that way."

"But you know what happened. It was some sort of test. One that was meaningless. One meant for a real Imperial heir rather than just a throwaway clone."

"Still, they sent you"—Niko poked a fingertip into Atlanta's mid-chest—"to me." She tapped herself. "That wasn't a random thing. And even if it was random, Lassite would tell you that often there is great meaning in the random movement of things."

She pointed at Lassite. "And that brings me to what I want you to do after she's finished with Dabry, Lassite. Show her the basics, enough that if someone does magic in her presence, she'll have a good chance of recognizing it."

"Magic is a very subtle thing," the Sessile murmured. "Sometimes too subtle for someone to sense." He didn't think Atlanta would be sensitive to magic yet. That wouldn't happen until she changed, the change he had foreseen rolling toward her, an inexorable force of destiny. He yearned to see it happen soon.

"And I will not expect you to have prepared her for such cases, but I would like you to have showed her what some of the less subtle ones look like. And show her what you can about attracting luck. Sky Momma knows that we always need more of that."

Lassite inclined his head. He pushed away his empty plate and turned to Atlanta. "When you are ready, you must tell me well ahead of time, so I may pray and prepare myself, and so I can find a place where it is quiet and we will not be interrupted."

His glance around at the others at the table made it clear that he expected them to make sure this lack of interruption was, in fact, what happened.

Feeling much more satisfied about the universe and her place in it, Atlanta hastily ate the last flatbread on her plate, although she took time to savor it when she caught Gio's eyes on her.

"What is the little crunchy seed?" she asked him. She'd learned by now how best to flatter both him and Dabry, which was to ask about some detail of the food that demonstrated the attention she had given to the act of ingestion.

This was a new thing to her. Certainly, the court had featured all manner of great cooks and chefs, but she had paid more attention to her fellow eaters than to what was being consumed or the way it had been prepared. Dabry had said truly great food made you stop eating. Made you think about the moment.

She had come to realize with time that when Dabry Jen had told the pirates he was a Class One chef, he had not been lying. Nor had Milly, who had told them she was a Class Three. Both of them were double-sided creatures, capable of deadly combat or a delicate soufflé with equal ease. She hadn't witnessed any of Niko's cooking yet, but the captain had also claimed to be such a chef, and while Atlanta had thought they were just bluffing, counting on the untutored palates of the pirates, the fact was that they had the skills to back their claims up.

"Celery seed," Gio signed, pursing his long, flexible lips in the expression she'd learned to interpret as a smile.

"Did you have some of that with you or did you break into my stores?" Dabry said in a suspicious tone.

"Used a pinch," Gio signed with a squint, "and put a packet of it down with the rest of stuff to be planted."

"Mrrm," Dabry grumbled.

"What exactly would you have done differently, Sergeant?" Niko asked.

"Nothing," he admitted, and she laughed silently at him.

The ship, while still unsure how many uses celery seed could be put to, thought that what it was currently experiencing was *camaraderie.*

5

It was a desire for more camaraderie on the ship's part that precipitated the next crisis.

They were finally about to be done sitting still at the station and would be en route again. The *Thing* felt *delight*.

But the journey would not be the same as it had been. Talon no longer played warball. He could not be coaxed or ordered into it, no matter who tried. This was what gave Niko and Dabry the most concern, but they hid that from the others. Although Gio, who had traveled with them the longest, gave them a hard look from beneath furrowed brows every once in a while, most of the others did not notice much. Atlanta would have liked to play, but she figured eventually, he would come around.

But the other person who noticed, and did so in a decided way, was the ship. It had, after all, hollowed out a large portion of its interior for warball and left it that way, which required a certain amount of energy and bandwidth, it informed Talon.

"I don't care," said Talon. He was, as ever, in his quarters, having no preparations to make for the journey other than to brood over how much he didn't want to make it. He was curled around himself on the cot in half-lion, half-human form. He directed his voice at the opposite wall, from which vantage point the ship had been both speaking and surveying him. "Let it rot."

The ship said indignantly, "I am incapable of rot."

"All things rot. All things die." He burrowed his face farther into the pillow, seeking the fading scent.

"If either of us were actually rotting, it would be much more likely to be *you*," the ship said, feeling piqued. It was, after all, trying to help him, although in doing so, it might be ignoring certain things Niko had said to it about leaving him alone. But this also failed to rouse him, and the ship decided to try stronger measures.

"I will take you to the warball room," it said.

"No."

"I will take you there whether you like it or not."

That did rouse him. His ears flattened and he snarled, teeth exposed, "Try it."

The resultant noise brought most of the crew at a run.

They found Talon wrapped in the *Thing*'s tentacles, although fighting with all his might and main. Great frilled black ribbons of material extended from the walls to hold him, or tried to, because he was shifting every few seconds, trying to throw it off and slashing with his claws, roaring all the while, the deep-throated roar of utter rage that had summoned them.

"What in the name of Sky Momma?" Niko shouted. "Stand down. Stand down." But it was long moments before Talon stood freed, panting to catch his breath, shuddering deeply. His eyes rolled up in his head and he pitched forward onto his face.

"What's wrong with him?" Atlanta gasped.

"Thaumic drain," Niko said as Dabry knelt to gather the unconscious form. "Changing that fast, that many times? It could have killed him. Still could. Let's get him up to Lassite's quarters. He'll know what to do."

Lassite was ready long before Dabry burst through his door, carrying the boy in his arms. He had laid out a restorative drink and waved scented grass through the air to cleanse. He had been meditating for the past two hours.

This was another of the moments for which he had prepared himself mentally long ago. He did not know all the details, the ins and outs, but he knew that Niko's crew members would require healing at some point, and for them all to stay on the Golden Path, he would need to be able to save them.

But he was worried. The time that was coming up . . . Well, there were pieces that were clear and then there were the pieces that were anything but. Pieces shot through with guesswork and voids that could not be guessed at, ragged as the breaths Talon was drawing, unpredictable and erratic.

This was not the worst of such patches, but it was one of the worst, and he had been dreading it. It had something to do with the Gate they were approaching, he knew that, but he also knew that to say anything of warning would have the opposite effect of what he wanted, and panic rather than calm them. No, best not to say anything, no matter how much he hated being the only one carrying the burden.

The boy had drained himself till his body held so little magic it could barely sustain his heartbeat. Shifters didn't just use magic, they *were* magic; it was an integral part of them and that was why using it too hard could literally burn them alive.

Niko had followed Dabry and was in the corner, talking to the ship in tones that did not bode well for *You Sexy Thing*. It was true the ship could have killed Talon, but another truth was that the boy would be useless unless he healed past his twin's loss. Lassite did not entirely understand the sibling bond—it was not something his race was capable of—but he thought of it like an extra limb. It had been torn away, without warning, and with brutal suddenness. But the loss of a limb was survivable, was something that a being learned to deal with.

Lassite's eyes rested on Dabry, who held Talon slumped against his chest. He could sense the sergeant's emotions, worry and fear and the dim, aching echo of holding his own child. Again, a bond Lassite could not understand but must acknowledge existed, and one so strong that it had to be factored in.

Lassite reached out to take the youth's hand in his own. "Anyone who is not essential, leave," he said tersely, and then, unexpectedly, a word they rarely heard from him. "Please." He could not deal with distractions; Thorn was almost dead and Lassite had only moments to snatch him from the Gates before he passed through them.

He didn't bother to pay attention to Niko shooing the others out. Dabry still held Talon close. Lassite closed his eyes, reached out with the senses he rarely used. The feeling of cold crept over him, pulling him down into the void where Talon was. He held himself away from it, no matter how strongly it tugged.

A flicker, the smell of musk and the softness of golden fur, the fiery sweep of claws . . . everyone's mindscape was different, but Talon's was a chaos of sensation, of emotions boiling like a storm.

There. He grabbed, plunged himself into the shadow mass and grappled it to him, no matter how it fought him.

The ferocity of its resistance shocked him, so much that he almost let go. Without his twin, the boy did want to die, and the urge toward life was so weak that the opposite urge threatened to overpower it . . . No time to think of that, but he would have to tell Niko.

He gritted his teeth, hunched his shoulders, and continued.

Agonizing inch by inch, he hauled his friend back from death, and Talon fought him each and every moment of the way.

When Lassite opened his eyes, blinking against the light, he saw the others gathered now around them. The concern in their faces was apparent, and he knew that it was as much for him as it was for the boy in Dabry's arms. That concern warmed him, a comradeship he had never found among his own kind, and how strange was that, to find it here? His mind swept in dizzy circles, sparking odd thoughts and reactions, and an undercurrent murmured that he had overextended himself. He focused on his breath, slowly reconnecting with his exhausted body, which ached down to his bones, a dull throb in time with his heartbeat.

Talon came back to consciousness all of a piece, unfazed, undizzy, curling around himself in grief that he was still alive. For a little while, he had thought the pain of his twin's absence would end, and now that had been snatched away from him too.

He opened his eyes to glare at his rescuer, then closed them and let the void of sleep take him away temporarily. He would express his anger later, when he was not so tired.

"I hate you," he murmured, and fell into darkness.

Once all was settled, Talon placed in his cabin and Lassite tucked in his own bed, Niko returned to her cabin and paced its circumference as her mind wheeled in thought.

She couldn't have the ship trying to help a crew member like that again. She had almost lost Talon. How soul-wrenching would that have been, to see both die? One alone almost killed her heart. And Lassite—she had never seen him so tired before, and if thaumic drain had nearly killed Talon, then draining himself to heal that surely had done the Sessile no good. No, the ship had to be dealt with.

Niko had never interacted with a living ship before this one, let alone "owned" or whatever it was that the relationship between herself and the *Thing* was, which was much more along the lines of leased or, more accurate, borrowed. There was no way she and the others would have been able to pay the huge amount of money that actually leasing a bioship would cost.

This was primarily due to the process by which bioships were created, in vast interstellar cradles that later became playgrounds, sometimes deadly ones, for a crop of bioships. When they came of age, they would be pitted against each other and the weakest ones culled, sometimes by the ships themselves.

Most ships with AI could hold conversations; she'd had to deal with plenty of those while in the Holy Hive Mind. But with those, you were usually conscious that you were speaking with an engineered thing and that its responses were based on the unalterable programming layered into the system and would not change over time. The closest thing she had seen were the great battle brains that the Hive Mind grew, and those were far slower than her ship.

The *Thing* was self-teaching, self-altering, and also capable of significantly greater thought speeds than its mechanical counterparts, to the point where it could maneuver anywhere with uncanny grace and precision.

She'd thought it amusing that it was so fascinated by the idea of emotions. Hadn't worried when it started to be able to perceive the ghosts. And that lack of fear had kept her from thinking about the fact that it had become even more self-aware than any of its counterparts. No one in the crew completely understood that process, but the ghosts must have had something to do with it. And however Lolola had circumvented its programming.

Why hadn't she had the thought to have it checked over by someone who knew something of such things? She'd been lulled into thinking of it as a person rather than a piece of machinery, and you couldn't trust machinery to tell you when something was going wrong.

Nor people, really, she thought cynically, then shook her head. "Ship," she said.

"Captain?"

Was it her imagination that its voice was subdued? How much did it understand of what it had done?

She said, "You could have killed Talon."

"I thought I would help him. I thought if he played warball

he would feel better. All he does is sit and sit and sit in his cabin and all that space I made is never used. So I exercised initiative."

"It's fine for you to exercise it when it comes to things that don't affect the rest of us. But maybe you've got too much time on your hands. Maybe you should take up a hobby."

"A hobby?" the ship said. "What hobby do you think I should take up?"

"Uh," Niko said, unprepared for this challenge. "Perhaps you could make some sort of art."

"I have already created my logo," the ship said proudly.

"And it's a very nice one," Niko said.

The logo had been the ship's very first foray into self-expression, back in the days before its association with Niko, and it was somewhat obsessed with it, placing it on every object that it created, no matter how small, insignificant, or disposable. The default pattern for any surface was an intricate series of interlocked logos that was a texture that had, by now, become ubiquitous to them all: It sprawled across the bed-bags, the towels and toiletries, writhed overhead in the corridors, and coated both the underside and, if possible, rim of every dish or utensil it created. A multicolored version of this now covered the outer black surface, an improvement which it told Niko it had suggested to Arpat Takraven, only to have it rejected.

"So I should make more art with my logo? Or pursue a new project?"

"Definitely a new project," Niko said, mostly driven by curiosity to see how this might manifest. The ways of a bioship were many, varied, and utterly unpredictable, but this didn't seem as though it had much potential to go wrong. "What sort of project do you think you might undertake?"

There was a very long silence as the ship cycled through literally millions of possibilities.

"I . . . am not sure what to choose," the ship said at length.

This *perplexity* (or so it thought this emotion should probably be labeled) was something new to it.

"There's no need to choose something immediately," Niko said, relaxing. Problem solved. This would keep the ship occupied enough to not be exercising any more *initiative*. "Take your time and perhaps gather input from the others."

This would be her own little experiment, predicting what each of them would suggest. Dabry would not want competition, so he would not suggest any of the culinary arts, but he might be savvy enough to think about something that would complement his own efforts in some way, like napkin folding or floral arrangements.

On the other hand, there was no guarantee that the *Thing*'s aesthetics and his own would be a good match. Could you do a floral arrangement in the shape of a logo?

Gio loved music. Did that mean that he'd suggest it or that he'd try to avoid it? She thought the latter—he was picky about his music, preferred Earth stuff, and the later the century the better, although he did exhibit a marked preference for hominid over cetacean.

Milly—who knew? She'd been a dancer, but how could the ship enact that skill? Perhaps through some sort of surrogate machine of the same kind as the servitors it used as its device-hands, but that seemed unlikely, nor had Milly and the ship seemed particularly close. Niko cast back mentally and was unable to come up with any memory of the feathered Nneti suggesting an inclination for any other form of art.

Atlanta, on the other hand, was reasonably easy to predict: It would be something that she had learned about in the Empress's court, and it would require expensive materials or else a significant investment of time. That was the sort of art that the people of the court favored, and if it weren't for the risk of the former and much costlier option, Niko would have put high odds on whatever it was that she came up with.

Skidoo . . . Niko raised an eyebrow. Well, she knew the Squid's preferred art form. She'd be surprised if the idea of all the possibilities of intimacy with a bioship had not already occurred to her overly amorous crew member and been proposed, if not followed through on, depending on what the ship's reaction had been. *At least she's conscientious about consent,* she thought.

Lassite would suggest something connected with his scriptures. The Sessiles were famous for the orientation of their arts with their religion. If Niko wasn't careful, he'd end up converting the *Thing* to all his nonsense about her Golden Path in the course of working with it to explain whatever religious iconography or style or material he advocated. That seemed far from advisable.

As for Talon—well, if the ship could *safely* stir any enthusiasm in the boy, that would be a double good. He was still a walking wound, as though the empty space left by his twin were there perpetually, a void ready to intercept any happiness.

"I could make a documentary videorecording for playback by historians," the ship said.

"Not a good idea," Niko said.

"You think it is beyond my capabilities?"

"I think it insufficient challenge for you. Look for something more complex and sophisticated and therefore worthy of you."

The ship played the noncommittal noise that was its equivalent of their conversational hedges. "Hmm. This will require further thought."

"As I said, you should take your time. And perhaps consult my input before making your final decision. And the sergeant's."

She hoped that between the two of them, they could head off any potential disasters, but in Niko's experience, if something could go awry, it usually would. Well, perhaps that was good enough, and she could turn her mind back to Talon.

She'd seen the look on his face when he'd roused, when Lassite had pulled him back from the brink of death. The boy didn't want to live if it was a life without his twin, and that thought spidered through her with cold dread. How far would he go in pursuit of that relief now that the chance had been proffered and then snatched away? Would she have to be watching him for an actual attempt at joining Thorn?

"Are we prepared to launch?" she asked. "Nothing around us to get caught in the backflash?"

"Everyone is ready, including myself," the ship said with joy. "We are clear of the station." It was time to move again! That was infinitely better than sitting in one place. There were so many things to see in the Known Universe and the *Thing* was resolved to see as many of them as possible.

"All right," she said. "Here we go."

6

Thorn haunted Talon; the Derloens haunted the *Thing*. As the ship juddered with its initial leap into hyperspace, Atlanta went to visit her own ghosts.

They had been installed in her head at the tender age of eight, and by now, consulting them had become second nature. She invoked them by closing her eyes and standing inside a space that existed only within her own brain. It was a simple chamber, and where the emblem of Pax, the empire to which she once had been an heir—or believed that she had, as she had to tell herself on a daily basis—had hung on the wall overlooking the imaginary chamber, there was now a window.

As tall as she was, she could look out the square window on stars, but not any known system. She'd told the computer to create what it liked. It was hooked into her brain, so she knew that if she ever looked at the pattern, she'd understand some of it, or at least see some of her own idiosyncrasies reflected in it. But it was enough to be able to look out and know at a basic level that it was hers, that landscape. Those stars were hers and hers alone.

Three figures stood within this space. She studied them. They had not changed, but she had, and with that change, her perspective had shifted as well.

The first was a version of herself as a child, the same age at which the software had originally been installed, dressed simply in play clothes, hair caught back with a piece of cording.

The second was a mirror reflection of herself as she was as an adult—or rather it was the version of her that had appeared at court. Dressed in ornate clothes that made her itch now to look at them. Nowadays she was a new Atlanta, a different Atlanta. Looking at this one made her feel as though she were looking at an old shell of herself, something that had been outgrown and discarded.

The third was a familiar friend from childhood, a children's viddie that had always made her feel happy. The Happy Bakka stood there with its enormous ears and wide, exaggerated black eyes. It rarely spoke, but when it did, its voice was furry and warm and made you think of lullabies.

In the past they had been her advisers. She had brought them complicated issues of court interactions, figuring out status and who to pay attention to and who not to be seen in the company of. The Court of the Paxian Empress was a complicated place, a game that was played by arcane rules that had never really been recorded. The advisers had served her well there.

Nowadays they were useless, she thought, looking at them. They might have overheard the thought; she had never been clear on exactly how tied into her brain they were. But they were not actual intelligences, just algorithms and databanks of possible responses, and so they didn't flinch or look worried. That was good, she thought, given what she intended to do.

She sat in a chair that formed itself under her at the motion. That was a convenience of virtual life—think it and it appeared. And just as easily disappeared. She could have erased all of these with a single thought.

"Do any of you know things about cooking?" she asked.

She expected them to come up with their usual useful knowledge, but instead they all looked blankly at her.

"That is not a duty you should be expected to do," her youngest self finally said, a little haughtily. "That is something servants do."

"I'm not an Imperial heir anymore," she said. They looked at her blankly again. "Do you understand that?"

They kept staring at her while she waited for their response. They were of no help to her anymore, only serving to remind her of a life that had been lost.

"All right," she said. "You're no help. I don't care." She stood and was about to wave them away, but the Happy Bakka said, its furry voice thinned by urgency, "We are not an equipment manual. We are of use in situations dealing with other people. We can help with that. Questions of protocol or Paxian custom."

"Then what good will you do me?" she demanded. "When will I need to know some nuance of Paxian custom ever again?"

"We will always be here," it said, and the others nodded. "You can always talk to us. Sometimes it is good to have someone to talk to. Someone who is always on your side."

Without acknowledging what it had said, she switched out of the space to find herself sitting on her bunk, hands clasped tightly in her lap.

Impatient anger tensed her shoulders and clenched her jaw. They were worthless. They were imaginary, created things, not part of the real world, the world in which she had to exist now. Another piece of her past that had prepared her for nothing.

She forced herself to calm, taking a long, slow breath and thinking about it, feeling the moist air with *You Sexy Thing*'s ineffable smell of rose and cardamom soften her mood.

"*Thing*," she said, "is Sergeant Dabry in the kitchen right now?"

"He is," the ship confirmed.

She nodded to herself and stood. She paused, looking at herself in the reflective screen. She was small, dark-skinned, not particularly well-fleshed. Her eyes were black and she would have liked to think they were kind. But who was she, really? What was she?

"Do you wish for me to give the sergeant a message?" the ship asked.

"No," she said, then changed her mind. "Tell him I'm on my way."

When she was little, Dabry and his daughter often played pat-a-pat. Clapping his four palms against her smaller four in rhythms complicated for her child's coordination, easy to him, who had been taught them himself back when he was her age.

Sometimes, when he was working in the kitchen on something particularly rhythmic, like kneading bread, he remembered the feel of her soft little hands against his and heard her voice chiming out the rhyme in his head, and wanted to weep.

Today was a day he always remembered his daughter, even when he tried not to. He'd had such a moment and was still coming back from it when Atlanta entered, and it made him steel his heart against her. He could hear his own voice, gruffer than he had intended it to be, as he snapped, "What is it?"

She looked at him with startled eyes, which was even worse, as though he had struck a kitten.

"You and the captain were talking about how I needed to be of use." She faltered. "Remember? I thought we had decided that I would learn cooking. Unless you think it would be wrong for me?"

In all his time training soldiers, he had learned one thing. There were soldiers who had to be told what to do and there were the ones capable of directing themselves. The latter were the ones who became officers. He was irritated to learn that Atlanta was not one of them but instead was standing there checking his reactions, waiting for his approval. He'd thought better of the girl. He forced down that irritation and said, "Why cooking?"

"I-I thought," she stammered. Her eyes darted past him to take in the kitchen, the neatly filled rack behind him, and the mass of bread that lay in front of him, being manipulated with all four hands. "I mean, it seemed the most logical if we were going to set up a restaurant somewhere else sometime, that I learn how to cook."

He looked down his nose at her, feeling himself a bully, but again unable to help himself. It made him feel an edge of shame—hadn't he recently criticized Niko for not being able to help herself? And that shame in turn made things worse, so he snapped, "You think it's something that just anyone can pick up in a short time? Maybe you should just go watch some tutorials on it, if it's that easy."

Her eyes filled with tears, but she squared her shoulders. "I've offended you," she said.

Gio tapped him on the shoulder. "I will teach her how to clean things," the chimpanzee signed. "That is always a useful skill, and you do not need to trouble yourself with it."

It felt to Dabry as though that last phrase might be tinged with sarcasm, but he was unwilling to look hard enough at Gio to figure out whether that was truly the case. He folded both sets of arms and turned back to Atlanta. "Gio will teach you how to clean things, then. A useful skill, as he says."

He moved to the doorway. "I have things to do," he said to no one in particular, then exited.

Atlanta stared after him. Gio tapped her on the shoulder and handed her an apron. "Wear this." He himself was pleased. There were a lot of mushrooms to clean, and now he could palm all that off on her.

She put it on. It was crisp and new-smelling and covered with the *Thing*'s logo. "Did I say something wrong?" she asked. "I'm not sure what I did."

"It is not you that offends, but the day," Gio signed. "He is always out of sorts on this day. Do not speak to him of it. It is an anniversary."

She picked up the mushroom and held the soft-bristled brush as Gio showed her. "Anniversary of what?" she asked.

Gio's long-fingered hands moved among the mushrooms, laying them out for her. She thought he was not going to answer her for a moment. But then: "His daughter's death," he signed, but would answer no other questions.

By the time they were done, she had learned how to brush growing medium off mushrooms without breaking the feathery gills underneath and did so much more swiftly than when she had started. But she also thought to herself that perhaps this skill, useful as it might be, was not really the sort of thing she wanted to hone.

Her name had been Keirera.

Dabry stood looking out the viewspace at the stars, still thinking about his daughter.

She had been tall like him, and her eyes had been like her mother's. It was as though all their best features had been mingled together and made into a single person that was everything. Was it ego that had made him so proud she was his heir, that she would carry on after him?

She was the one he really wanted to teach how to cook.

He closed his eyes and leaned his forehead against the glassy surface of the viewer. The chill bit at the skin, not painfully, or at least only painfully enough to relieve some of the buzzing pressure of his thoughts.

He missed his wife, but he missed his daughter as though he had mislaid the best part of himself.

Or not mislaid. She had been stolen by war, killed like his wife in a skirmish that had been the result of mistakes in communications, the sort of dirty little affair that gets covered up and whoever instigated it passed up the chain of command in order that they be incompetent somewhere else.

He peeled his forehead away from the glass.

"What are you doing?" the ship asked.

"I have been thinking," he said.

"What were you thinking about?"

"That is an intrusive question," he said, more mildly than he might have to anyone else except perhaps Niko or his daughter.

He would have said more, but Niko swung in through the door and he broke off.

"Well, we're underway now and committed to a course," she said. "We'll get to the closest Gate in about a week. Then through there and en route to Montmurray. Think anyone will bail on us along the way?"

He shook his head. "I don't think we'll lose anyone," he said. "Milly, maybe. Atlanta will cling hard; we're the only point of reference she has. Lassite's yoked his destiny to yours. And the rest, well, they feel a certain affection for you."

Her lips twitched. "Certain affection, huh?"

He nodded, his face still somber.

Niko changed the subject. "Odd rumors coming out of the last newsblip," she said.

"Odd rumors?"

"Someone claims there's something out there breaking Gates."

No one knew how or when or why the Gates had been created or even how the technology worked. No one knew where the Forerunners that had made them had gone, leaving behind only certain traces of their civilization and technology: a few scattered ruins, usually strewn with what might or might not have been intended as booby traps but certainly had lethal effects when triggered; the great corpses of what some called "space moths," which had apparently served as vessels to that race; and the Gates themselves, whose limits marked the edges of the Known Universe.

The Gates employed what was called Q-space, which the clever said was named for Question-space, but the truth was that it had been named after the first species to discover and make use of the Gates, centuries after their originators had gone.

Outside that realm there were some civilizations, but generally the farther a planet or system was from the Known Universe, the less known and more backwater it was. Nowadays, everyone used the Gates by mutual accord, and it was understood that they were free to whatever species wanted to use them, and also that in times of war, they would be shut down so no side could use them.

These rules were rarely violated, and when they were, usually the rest of the Known Universe's many inhabitants were willing to band together in order to make sure the action was punished as publicly and painfully as it could be. And if that involved dividing up the territory and wealth once possessed by the transgressor, well, that was all the better.

In short: No one fucked with the Gates.

The notion that one might be failing was horrifying. Some systems were only reachable through the Gates; others were so far away that they might as well have been separated from reality.

Dabry said, "Rumors?"

Niko shook her head. Information was guarded and kept scarce as though in reaction to the Gates. Travel was free; news was not. You could subscribe to one of the services, but veracity and verified sources cost more money than most people had, and the majority paid little attention to events on a galactic scale, rightly figuring that effects that filtered down to their level would be mostly unnoticeable.

The thing that kept anyone from ever taking over the Known Universe, despite the best efforts of entities such as the Holy Hive Mind, was the sheer size of it. That vast scope made bureaucracy, even the oldest and most established bureaucracies, unworkable with the mass of data and necessary coordination. You could create an empire, but it seemed as though there was an arbitrary limit to how large it could become, much to the frustration of people like the Holy Hive Mind or even Tubal Last.

"I guess we'll see when we get there," she said.

He nodded.

"I'm sorry about earlier," she said. "You're right to call me on things. I forgot that sometimes I need to think about how everyone else is affected."

He shook his head. "It's the day," he said.

She had known that and hadn't wanted to bring it up. She didn't say anything now. She'd been with him when the news had come; she'd held on to him as he wept. Offered him a lifeline that had kept him from going out and killing himself.

They had been friends before that night, but after that, the bond between them went deeper. Not that of lovers, but more like siblings, able to know each other's thoughts because they had been through so many things together.

Rather than speak, she touched his upper arm lightly. He covered her hand with his own for a moment and they stood together. Then he released her and they stepped apart and went about their business as they always had, in perfect syncopation, as though they were two halves of the same machine, made to work together.

Dabry went to his news sources, combing through the onslaught of opinions and half-facts in search of some sort of truth. It was difficult to decipher these things, and governmental computers—not to mention all the other AIs out there—were unceasing in their manipulation of the streams. He could not decipher all that was happening in the Known Universe. There was simply too much, and if there were patterns related to Petalia or Tubal Last, he could not find them; no matter how hard he tried to chase them down, they vanished just as he thought he was on the edge of seeing them.

7

The smell of the mushroom still clung to Atlanta's hands, rich with the fragrance of earth and rot. She washed the fragments away and went to be tested by Lassite for magic. She'd failed at cooking, or at least Dabry had deemed her unworthy of teaching. Maybe magic would give her the role she wanted.

She went to Lassite's chamber to tell him she was ready. Here in the small, sparse chamber, the air was very dry and made her nose itch. He instructed her to sit cross-legged on the small, scratchy carpet in the middle of the floor. It smelled of heat and cinnamon and decaying wool.

She sat as directed, crossing her legs to mirror his posture. She desperately wanted to find out that she held magic. That would be a role. Lassite would train her. Together, they would be deadly battle mystics. She wasn't sure exactly how that would work; she had never seen him actually cast any magic other than handling the Derloen ghosts.

Even so, she found herself stalling, unwilling to begin. Unwilling to find out that what she hoped for wasn't going to manifest.

"How did you learn magic?" she asked, pretending to fuss with her hair, pulling it back and away from her face. She'd learned by now that most of the crew preferred telling stories to anything else. They'd been together for so long that they knew each other's stories to the degree one reaches when one has heard a narrative multiple times. They were starved for fresh ears, and she could provide that, at least.

Lassite said, "When I was a child, I dreamed things that children did not usually dream of, and I dreamed of them over and over every night, and drew them during the day with whatever I could find to draw with."

"What were the things?"

"I dreamed of a Golden Path spiraling through the stars and at the end of it, great glory and happiness for many beings."

"That seems like a big thing to draw," she said.

"Other children drew balls, or small creatures, or the sun in the sky. Our watchers removed me from their company and gave me to the priests for training."

"So they took you away from your parents?"

"I was one of a clutch. We were raised by the community, not by individual parents."

"I'm sorry," she said, feeling small and provincial at this reminder that the ways that held on her planet were not the natural and immutable laws of the universe.

That had been the hardest of all the many lessons this new existence brought: the idea that there was no normal, or rather that there were many normals, depending on who was doing the measuring and determining, and that they could, in fact, coexist without shattering each other in most cases.

"There is nothing to be sorry for," he said. "It is one way for a person to be raised, one of many."

"How old were you when they gave you to the priests?"

"I was old enough to speak a few words. That is another way that they knew I was suited for magic—the pictures that I drew were ones that were sophisticated beyond my years."

"How did you know to draw them, then?"

"The magic showed them to me, in my dreams, and told me what to say to the priests when they came."

She looked at him, fascinated and envious. What was it like to know you were specifically called, destined for something by the very laws of the universe?

She had never thought about this sort of magical destiny before, but now it seemed like a glorious thing, to be so certain. At the same time, she found herself scoffing at it; magic was something the foolish and simpleminded thought powerful. But science lay at the heart of its power, once you got rid of all the mysticism. She was sure of that.

But he had what she had lost—a sense of purpose. Maybe he could restore hers.

He said, "Hold out your hand, palm up, and I will see if you have magic in you. It is the simplest of the tests."

She did so, and he moved his fingers in a complicated pattern a few centimeters above her palm. She felt nothing, not even a sensation of motion.

He said, "Does that feel warm or cold? Or strange to any degree?"

She closed her eyes and strained to sense it for long moments. Regretfully, she shook her head and opened her eyes again. He was watching her face intently.

He said, "Not a major matter, nor one that means you have no magic whatsoever. There are other tests."

But in the next hour or so as he tested her, again and again, she failed to sense the magic working. Even when he did an actual spell and made a ball of energy come into existence and pulse briefly, purple and blue and a color she'd never seen before, and then blink out, she saw only with her eyes and no other senses.

While they did this, he asked her other questions, along the same lines that Niko had but exploring them at greater length. What were the things that she had won in her life? What sort of pets had she asked for as a child? What were the stories she had particularly loved and wanted to hear over and over again?

Finally, he said, his tone sober, "I can find no trace of magic in you, or any sign that you have an ability to work with it. This doesn't surprise me. When a society is magic-poor, it tends not to produce many who are capable of sensing, let alone working with such forces."

"Is that normal? I mean, not to have even a trace of it? Who else in the crew doesn't have any?"

"Milly doesn't," he said. "She comes from a society much like yours. Gio has very little, and it is a darker magic, one that he does not like to draw on, berserker magic. Dabry has a touch that he does not ever use consciously—he has a way with luck charms, but he will not capitalize on it, says they are only clutter." He brightened. "But the captain said you should work on luck. Just because you cannot use magic does not mean that such charms will not work for you either. I can make you some and tailor them."

"Tailor them how?"

"Luck can be overall, or it can be focused in a specific direction, which sometimes intensifies it," he said. "Love charms are a classic example—they do not actually intensify anything that is there, only the chance of it occurring, and that is why they sometimes work, sometimes don't—"

Atlanta nodded as though she understood everything he was saying.

He went on. "That's what I need to tell the captain, really, is that our best bet—and the one that moves us the most solidly along the Golden Path—is for us to work on increasing the ship's luck—"

"Luck is not an actual force," the ship said. "It is a human concept based on their need to see patterns, and a meme that spread outward when they came in contact with the Known Universe five hundred years ago."

Lassite said patiently, "That is certainly an argument that I have heard over and over again—"

Atlanta interrupted, because this didn't sound like a new discussion. "So what can I do to increase my own luck?"

"Ah," Lassite said. He glanced at the ceiling. "Perhaps it would be easiest for you to do repetitions."

"What are those?"

"Phrases that you say over and over again."

"Aloud?" she said dubiously. She was not sure how she felt about wandering the corridors of the ship, talking to herself.

Lassite shook his head. "No, it can be silently, that is just as effective, really," he said.

"How effective is it?"

"Not very," he admitted.

"Is it measurable?" the ship asked in a seemingly casual tone.

"As I have explained before," Lassite said patiently. "The act of trying to measure such things destroys them."

The ship refrained from any observation on how convenient such a trait seemed to be.

"Here is the phrase," Lassite told Atlanta. "It means *come, luck, come sit by my side* in a language that no one speaks anymore. There is a little god who hears whatever is said in such tongues, and tells the others, or so my theology says. You may choose whether or not to believe it. The phrase should be efficacious in either case."

He instructed her in the pronunciation of a long and flowing phrase, oddly beautiful, so it was not a bad thing to have in her head. It happened to fall nicely to the pattern of a childhood song she had been fond of, and so she put it in her head, and then, on a whim, set one of her internal advisers, her youngest self, to chanting it, over and over, a prattled prayer wheel spinning in her head.

Foloarnra to phizah, falaarnra to ragizzah.

She left Lassite's chamber with that echoing in her head, feeling sad. It was not that she had expected Lassite to pronounce her capable of magic, but it was an entirely different thing to be told she was utterly incapable of it.

In her room, she flung herself onto the bed on her back and lay there, studying the velvety folds of the ceiling as though they might hold some clue to her fate. She thought about consulting her advisers, but given the reaction to her learning to cook, she didn't think they'd approve of any job. They believed she should be preparing to rule an empire, no matter that it wasn't her fate any longer. Never had been, really. No, instead she set all of them to chanting Lassite's phrase, then returned to staring at the ceiling.

She gave it up. She could not learn magic. Dabry didn't want to teach her to cook. She said, "*Thing*, do you need any maintenance?"

"I am not sure what the parameters of your question are," the ship said.

"Any maintenance? Like fluids changed out. Or something polished. Or . . . whatever." She gestured vaguely, feeling foolish.

"Oh," the ship said politely. "I am self-maintaining. I create servitors for any necessary tasks."

"You create them? I thought they lived aboard you?"

"No, they are created and absorbed."

"The one that maintains my quarters, do you create and absorb it?"

There was a silence. She could tell something about the question was confusing the ship. It said, "Every morning I dispatch an instance, and if the instance from the day before is usable, I employ it. Sometimes they are usable for a number of days."

"Oh," Atlanta said blankly and gave up for the moment.

Still, the next day, she looked at the servitor as it entered.

The servitor came up to her midthigh; it moved around on four legs whose knobby hinges bent outward, ending in scaly feet made of four flexible prongs. Multifaceted eyes surrounded its upper circumference, and below that ring, situated underneath a protective ridge of bone and its sides around the places where the tentacles protruded, were ribbed lines of the cartilage/chitin that served as a protective outer surface for so many things aboard the *Thing*.

It bustled around the quarters, checking the water carafe fixed on the wall shelf, putting away loose clothing, and tugging the blankets back into place.

She went over to it and knelt beside it. It ceased motion immediately, as though startled.

"What are you doing?" the *Thing* said, somewhat suspiciously.

"You made this one today?"

"This one has tended your quarters three days running."

"Can I keep it? I mean, will you keep it cleaning my quarters?"

"If you like," the ship said. "But I fail to see the point."

"Sometimes there's no point to things," she said. "Sometimes you're just trying."

The confused ship decided she was clearly talking to herself. There was no need to answer.

Niko brought the question up to Dabry when she caught him alone, cleaning down in the kitchen. The rags in his lower hands smelled of sour yeast from the bio-organisms with which it had been impregnated, and it left a trail that shone at first, then dulled as the organisms fizzed, then shone even more as they degraded in a haze of evaporating mist.

"Once we're free of Last, what do you want to do?"

He continued to wipe down the counters as he thought, the sour-scented mist following in his wake. "You ask that as though it was something we needed to worry about now," he said.

"We have journeyed together for a very long time," she said, "but I do not know if it would have been so long if your family had lived."

At those words, his hands stopped sweeping over the counter and an upper hand stole upward to touch his lips, as though to remember something or perhaps to press its memory away. He said, "Are you asking if I would stay if they were alive? That is an unfair question in so many ways, Niko. How can you ask that, knowing that I would give my life to make it so?"

His tone hurt her heart, made it squeeze and contract as though it were trying to escape her, but she kept on all the same. She had to be sure before she would take him—or any of the others—into danger.

She said, her own voice harsh in its relentlessness, "You could go back, start a new family . . ."

The suddenness with which he flung down the rag startled her, made her jump back. "Again unfair," he said. "I would not replace them. Even if I could."

She hesitated, not sure what lay behind that last part of his statement. They had not spoken much of Ettilite culture and its customs. It was as though Dabry had locked that part of his heritage away, unwilling to let it manifest in any way other than in cooking the elaborate meals they were famed for. She said, "Thorn died in this chase already. I would not add you to the bill as well."

That amused him; he bared his teeth at her. "Don't worry. I am an expensive appetizer for anyone."

She gestured at the counter. "So that's it? You will go along and cook?"

"I will come along and cook," he agreed. "And at some point we will have a new restaurant, and it will be a setting worthy of my genius. And yours," he added as an afterthought.

This time she laughed. He picked up the rag anew.

"I've told Atlanta to come back to you for more cooking lessons."

"Why? She has no genius for it."

"Sometimes you don't need to have a genius for something for it to be enjoyable," she argued. "And there may be areas of cooking—ones that you have not explored with her—that are better lent to her talents than whatever it was that you first tried."

He rolled his eyes. "Basic cookery," he grumbled. "That's the best test."

"But not the only one," she reminded him.

He finished wiping the counter and set the paper rag in the canister on the table that would be taken down to the ship's gardens later.

"Not the only one, sir, that is true. But here's my suggestion. Give her to Talon to train. That gives him some purpose."

She blinked. "I hadn't thought of that. But the notion holds a certain brilliance."

Dabry nodded in agreement. "Indeed."

8

"You are in charge of training Atlanta," Niko told Talon. "That'll get you out of here for a while, at least."

"No," he said, and shook his head, and then repeated the word again just in case any of this wasn't clear.

Niko, standing in the doorway of his room (and struggling not to wrinkle her nose at the stale reek from it), just looked at him. Her expression made him feel embarrassed, but he didn't back down, even though part of him wanted to, very much. Neither he nor his twin had ever been in the habit of contradicting Niko. That was something their mother had drilled into them. You always obeyed the captain, always, always, always.

But his mother was gone and Thorn was gone and so he shook his head and said it just one more time. "No."

Atlanta, standing behind Niko in the doorway, said, "Captain, he doesn't need to."

Her voice was full of discomfort. He could have felt bad about that too. He had initially liked the human girl. She always seemed a little lost ever since the first day he'd seen her, an unexpected arrival. He and Thorn had talked about her and what she must have felt like, to be sent away from everyone you knew and live with strangers.

But now he hated her for being the one who had been there when his brother died, consumed by what Tubal Last had summoned to feed. The sight of it would have killed him, too, but it was unfair beyond belief that he had not been allowed to be there instead of her.

Why did every thought turn back to Thorn, over and over

again? Thorn, whose death the girl had seen, when he had not. He felt his lips creep back as though to expose his teeth at the thought and tamped it down.

Niko said, "Actually, he does need to. This is the duty I'm assigning him, to train you further in fighting. You're sloppy and unschooled and sometimes more a danger to yourself than any opponent." She looked at Talon. "And I don't just want the two of you playing warball, mind you. In fact, no warball unless I approve it beforehand."

There was nothing in all the universe that he wanted to do less than play warball, which would have reminded him unendurably of Thorn with every moment, but somehow that rankled. He was grieving. It was unfair of her to take away one of the things that he loved. Would have loved. If he'd had Thorn to play it with him still.

Niko said, brushing aside his refusal as though he had never spoke it, "Figure out a schedule where you're training for two stints of an hour and a half each day, at least four hours apart, time-wise. Start her on strength training." She directed a glance at Atlanta. "You've got that fancy body, you might as well maintain it better."

Atlanta looked indignant. "I maintain myself."

"You do the minimum, and that's not enough when you're eating the sort of meals that Dabry has been dreaming up lately. My crew pulls their weight, so get strong enough to do that too." Her look at Talon when she said "my crew" made it clear that she would not tolerate having her orders flouted.

He wanted to argue, but the weight of everything settled on his shoulders, pressing him into submission. He muttered, the words barely audible, "All right."

"Good." Niko folded her arms and stood there, waiting.

"Now?" he said, and knew he was whining, and didn't care.

She glanced past him into his messy quarters. "Were you

currently otherwise engaged? Cleaning up, perhaps?" He didn't reply. She went on. "I'll take that as a no. *Thing,* prep your warball chamber so they can spar there. You two, I expect you changed and in there working within a quarter hour."

Atlanta dressed hurriedly, a little excited. She'd missed her relationship with the twins, the closest to her in age on the ship and usually the most good-humored about explaining things. But since Thorn's death, Talon had refused to speak with anyone except when he had to.

Worry wriggled in the pit of her stomach. What if she couldn't live up to this task? He was a soldier. She'd been raised in a soft palace life.

Her worry increased when she entered the chamber.

She'd thought she would be happy to see Talon again, but the one she saw was not her friend. This version glared at her from eyes no longer happy-go-lucky, full of enthusiasm, but rather angry and reddened, golden irises almost eclipsed by dark pupils. And she noticed that he had entered some growth spurt lately—he was broader across the shoulders, burlier through the chest, at least in this half form.

When she ventured a smile at him, he did not return it, just eyed her sourly as though trying to find fault with some aspect of her or her attire. But she wore a serviceable ship suit, her hair pulled back with a cord, and bare feet, which had seemed like the most reasonable choice.

He grunted at her. "Stand straighter," he said. She tried to do so. He nodded and flapped a hand at her. She stood there.

"What are you waiting for?" he said impatiently. "Come at me."

"I thought we were doing strength training?" She faltered.

"I have decided we will begin with combat and then move to strength training once I have fully assessed you," he said.

She tried, she really did. But it seemed as though every time she tried to rush at him, he was out of the way and pushing her aside, hard, so she reeled away, and fell, over and over again.

Despite the padding the *Thing* had provided on the floor, it hurt. She bit her tongue on one fall. Talon's nose twitched at the scent of blood as it spattered over the floor, but otherwise, he didn't react. She swallowed copper and tried again, ignoring the throbbing. She'd felt worse.

After a dozen such attempts, he said, "You are not strong enough, you will never be good at fighting. The captain said do strength training, so we'll do that."

She didn't know what to say to that, but deep below the shame and misery of the thought was a trickle of comfort. She was unworthy, and that meant she could, at least, go away and sit and nurse her bruises.

But he snapped, "Push-ups, then, until I tell you to stop," and began to set her through rounds of exercises, each more grueling than the last. Her face was so wet with sweat that her eyes burned and she could feel muscles complaining in places they never had before. How long would he keep this up, she wondered, and thought that at least if she passed out from it, she'd have a reason to stop.

The moment when she would be found inadequate was inevitable. Why was she even trying? She might as well stop and spare herself all this. But something in her spine resisted that idea, and she found herself struggling onward, trying to breathe into the pain and only half succeeding.

Talon knew he was being unkind, but he didn't care. He wasn't overly cruel in how hard he worked the girl, but he was unrelenting.

Well, that was all right. She was part of all the things that had led up to Thorn's death. He couldn't get at them, but he had her here and now at his mercy.

Sweat was trickling off her. He could smell its rankness and see the tremble in her shoulders as she did another push-up. How much longer could she keep it up? Already she'd be in pain tomorrow if he didn't make sure she cooled down and ate and drank the right things afterward. Well, she could learn that for herself. It was the sort of lesson you had to learn that way, or else you wouldn't remember it.

She was like a baby, an infant. Helpless. If he didn't help her, maybe she'd learn sooner. Pain could only teach her things.

He took a deep breath, looking away from Atlanta, and swallowed down grief and anger. Pain had taught him nothing. Thorn wouldn't want his legacy to be pain. His twin would have been surprised, maybe even a little shocked, at what he was doing now. He should stop, let her rest for a bit before going on.

But before he could say anything, Milly was in the room in a flutter of white feathers.

"What are you doing?" she snapped at him. "Are you trying to kill her? Humans are fragile things, not like were-lions." She wheeled on Atlanta. "You can stop."

"The captain gave her to me to train," he protested.

"To train, not to fluffing torture."

"To make stronger," he said. "To learn how to fight."

He was impressed to see that Atlanta had not stopped during this conversation, despite Milly's directive. He said, "You can stop now, Atlanta."

She went limp on the decking, simply breathing as her heart hammered in her ears.

Milly planted herself to glare at him. "I'm going to talk to Dabry about this," she said. "You know better."

He pulled himself up. "I've fought alongside them more times than you have teeth." He snarled, flashing his canines.

Many creatures would have backed away at that, but the willowy, white-feathered birdwoman didn't budge. "Do you want to test me, brat?" she said. "I may be newer than you to this troop, but believe me, I'm qualified. Ask your captain."

He could feel anger clamping down on him. He wanted to turn into a full lion, go into battle mode. Rip her apart with teeth and talons and then scream out his angry victory.

"Try it, pussycat," she said softly. Two knives glinted in her hands, sprung from nowhere.

The ship said, "I feel that this conversation is not what you should be saying to each other and that there is an interpersonal problem."

"I feel you should butt out of interpersonal problem-solving," Milly said.

"Is that what you are doing?"

"Absolutely," he and Milly said in unison.

Atlanta had crawled to the corner to collapse in a sweaty heap. She opened her eyes and said, "It's been an hour and a half. I'm going to shower."

"Meet back here in four hours," he told her.

"You have got to be kidding me," Milly said.

"Captain's orders," he said to her smugly. The knives had vanished, but her body language, despite the difficulty of reading her expression, was still angry.

"We'll see about this," she said and left, footsteps thudding angrily along the corridor.

He realized he hadn't thought about Thorn for longer than he had in all the time since his twin had died.

It terrified him. Would he forget his brother? He dropped to the floor and began doing push-ups as rapidly as he could.

Every time he exhaled, he pushed himself up and thought about Thorn alive. And every time he inhaled, he let himself fall down into the misery that Thorn was not. Now he was the only one and got all the attention. That might have been nice under other circumstances. But he would have given it all up for his brother.

How could he go on if every day would be like this? He moved faster and faster, trying to push himself into forgetfulness until his shoulders burned and he let himself fall to the floor. And yet there was the thought in his head that he would never see his brother again. It made him want to wail in a way that was shameful and childish. He could not give way to the urge.

But back in his room, holding Thorn's pillow again, he did.

9

The water from the shower was hot and struck all the sore places in a good way. Atlanta moved slowly, taking her time there. The *Thing* recycled the greywater anyhow; it was not as though she was using any up.

Bruises laddered her ribs, and there was a huge black bruise, its core already stiffening, on her upper arm. She explored it gently with her fingertips.

When she stepped out of the fresher, the servitor the *Thing* had sent her meal with earlier was there again, proffering a towel. On the table was a glass and small plate of something feathery and brown. Talon had told her to eat and drink as soon as possible, and to rest.

He had sounded sorry after the angry Milly had come and gone. She hoped he was. Maybe they could use that to rebuild the friendship. And how surprising was it that Milly had come to her defense? They had not been close before.

She dried and slid on a loose robe. The servitor waited. She knelt beside it and started to stroke its side, then hesitated, feeling invasive.

She said, "You're not the *Thing,* are you? You're a separate creature from it, at least for now. *Thing,* don't say anything. I'm curious."

The ship held its silence but was pretty sure its current emotion was *indignation*.

A budlike structure atop the canister quivered, then slowly unfurled, like a fern unrolling itself. The four long antennae that were revealed in the process were softly feathered in pale ochre and peach; each was three times as long as her forearm.

They reached out to wrap themselves around her, their touch light and nonthreatening, curious and exploratory. Even shy. A tendril flinched away when she reached a hand up to touch it.

She hastily dropped her arm and let the exploration continue, the tendrils brushing along her hairline as though savoring the difference in texture, whispering over her lips with a tickle-soft touch, rubbing along bare skin with what felt like affection. She held still, reluctant to breathe and frighten away this behavior, which she had never seen before in one of the ship's servitors.

She breathed out the words, "Do you have a name?" But the tendrils did not leave off their wandering.

The softness of it reminded her of a courtier—or at least her memory of a courtier, she corrected herself in a mental gesture that was rapidly becoming habitual to the point of filtering everything through the realization. Low in status, Minyas had been a slight, sparse woman who usually hovered in the background of things. But she was prone to affectionate gestures in private and had more than once given Atlanta candies or hugs, nonsexual but intimate to a degree not echoed elsewhere in her experience, even in the coded memories of her family.

"Do you like the name Minyas?" she asked, and the tentacles did not change their behavior. "Can you hear me, I wonder?" she said, and they curled around her right wrist and tightened, then released her.

That could not mean much other than affirmation, but she tested it. "Did that mean yes?"

It curled around her right wrist again. It couldn't mean *no,* because that could not have been the answer to *Can you hear me.* Not Minyas, then, but perhaps some variant, parsed in the Paxian way.

"Minasit," she said. "Little Minyas. A small name, and not

something that you have to embrace with all your existence, but something that you can use while you ponder on a more fitting one and we learn to communicate with each other better."

Again the curl and squeeze, gentle but definite.

"Very well," she said. "Minasit." She looked over the chitin atop it, noting the swirling pattern in it, like flames or wood grain. Would she be able to recognize it again? She was unsure.

She said, "Will you let me mark you? Not anything painful or permanent. A dot from one of my cosmetic pens."

Silent squeeze. Yes.

She let it pick the color. It took some time over the task, holding the various pens up to the light in order to check the effect it would produce.

In the end, its pick was the one she might have opted for herself if she had been looking to adorn it: a marbled rose gold, individual metallic flecks giving it luster.

She wrote *Minasit* along the edge of the upper chitin's rim in careful Paxian script, then added the flowery little character that denoted a name. The eyes rolled down solemnly to examine it, but the tendrils did not reach to brush over it until it was fully dry.

She said, "Does it meet with your approval?"

Yes, the tendrils said.

"Do you think others like you would want it?"

This time the tendrils were still at first, then drooped downward, exaggeratedly limp. What did that mean, she wondered.

"Are you saying no?" she ventured.

The tendrils reached, laid themselves parallel along her forearm, the touch barely there. She frowned down at them, trying to piece the logic of it together. She said, "Does that mean no?"

Quickly the tendrils shifted. *Yes.*

Now that they had the two, the affirmative and the negative, they would be able to work together. She abandoned the question of what the droop had meant for now and sat on the edge of the bed. She pulled up a memory pad. Time to establish some common words.

"That's a part of *me,*" the *Thing* said, finally unable to maintain its silence and hitting the last word hard to express its irritation. "Imagine if I started making pets of *your* bits. Like your ear."

"It seems to be separate from you," she pointed out.

"For now. Until it's reabsorbed."

"Don't absorb Minasit! That's an order!" she said.

There was a brief but very ominous silence.

"An order," the ship said flatly.

Atlanta hastily changed tactics. "A request," she said. "Please."

"Very well," the ship said. "But I am demanding a pet in return. Your left ear is now my pet. I am naming it Spike."

Minasit's skin was warm under her fingertips. She had to save it.

"Very well," she said, "as long as that doesn't mean you intend to remove it from my head."

"I would not do that," the ship said. "That would be contrary to its well-being, and the point of a pet, as I understand it, is to tend its well-being. I will send you an ointment to rub on Spike, to keep its skin glossy. Every night and every morning, you will tend my pet."

"Very well, then. Minasit is mine and you won't reabsorb it, and I won't reabsorb Spike," Atlanta said cagily.

Milly was still too angry, had too many bits of the emotion wandering around inside herself. She'd be incoherent if she tried to talk to Niko now, unable to assemble words sufficient to express all her objections. She had to cool down. Then she'd push past her nervousness at talking to the captain and go do so. For Atlanta's sake. And Talon, lest he harm her in a way he would regret. She could have done plenty of things, but she went to find Skidoo, though not for the usual reason.

She found the Squid in the area they had all come to think of as the lounge. It smelled faintly of vanilla and the prickly scent the humans called pine. The ship had been experimenting with senses and most of its experiments were unremarkable, although there were some that went horribly awry, more so than the ones that were deemed wildly successful.

The tangle of limbs that was the Squid was draped over a couch. Milly went over and inserted herself into the configuration without asking. By now, she and Skidoo were old friends; they had shared intimacies, but more than that, they had spoken of their histories and shared conversations with each other.

No one on the ship knew about various things in Milly's past, but sometimes she suspected that Skidoo had guessed more than she had ever said.

Skidoo tangled around her affectionately and said, "You are being full of stiffness."

"I'm angry," she admitted.

"What are you being angry at? Or with?"

"It is a who," she said, running her fingers around the suckers on the nearest tentacle, tracing the soft cup. "It is several whos, it is the captain and Talon."

"What are they being doing?"

"They are being training the new girl."

"Atlanta," Skidoo said softly.

"Indeed." Milly wondered if the Squid had lived up yet to the ambition she had confessed once, to sleep with the girl if she were willing, but she put the thought away. Atlanta was of age, and it was impolite to spend too much time thinking about other people and who was fucking who. Plus, it got complicated sometimes too. *Seize pleasure while you can* was one of the maxims of Milly's short-lived and exceedingly violent people, and she tried to live by those words.

"Talon is being training her and the captain is being training her too?" Skidoo questioned.

Milly remembered the source of her indignation and sat up straighter on the couch, despite the heaviness of the tentacles. "Talon is training her far too hard! He will injure her."

The Squid quivered but said, "I am being trusting the captain in most things, and surely this is being one of them?"

"Is it?" said Milly. She chose to edge her voice. "I thought you liked the girl, after all."

The tentacles slithered away, disengaging.

"Where are you going?" Milly asked. She hoped that Skidoo would say to go and reprimand Talon, but the Squid said, "To be talking to Atlanta."

Skidoo feared from Milly's words that she'd find Atlanta injured or worse. Instead, she found Atlanta arguing with the ship.

The source of the argument sat on the floor in between them.

"It is not yours, it is mine, and I say it is not anything!" The *Thing* was talking, and as it did so, the assemblage beside Atlanta became apparent to Skidoo when it twitched: one of the ship's servitors, the biomechanical devices that served as its hands.

"Minasit is my friend," Atlanta said.

"It is NOT your friend. It is my servitor."

Atlanta folded her arms. "Prove it."

"Prove it? Prove it how?! You are asking me to do impossible things."

"Why shouldn't it have any feelings?" Atlanta said. "You have feelings."

"Any feelings it has are MY feelings," the ship said.

Atlanta patted the servitor's carapace. This one was shaped

something like a bug, with a multiplicity of limbs, Skidoo noted. She paused in the doorway, listening.

"Why can't it have feelings independent of you? Maybe all of your servitors have their own feelings?"

"In that case, they are all malfunctioning and should be reabsorbed as soon as possible!" the ship snapped.

Atlanta noticed Skidoo and broke off whatever she had been about to say. "Oh! Skidoo," she said, her tone less startled than uncomfortable.

Skidoo sighed internally. Right now, every time Atlanta saw her, this seemed to be the reaction. And that seemed unnecessarily complicated.

The Squid sensed Atlanta was attracted to her, but she also knew the young woman had never slept with anyone outside her own species. That was, in fact, part of the allure for the Squid, who had slept with creatures from a wide variety of species. Her species enjoyed skin to skin contact and sought it out. Skidoo had even indulged in the epidermal implants that made her skin even more sensitive and tender.

She wondered if Atlanta remembered the conversation they'd had before the pirates. Skidoo certainly did, but she was not as sure about the girl, who would have been in pain with the injuries the pirates had already inflicted on her. Perhaps she had not meant what she had said.

She said, "There is being trouble?"

"There is no trouble, only a discussion," Atlanta said. She toed the side of the servitor, which did not rouse at the contact. She said to the thin air, "Don't kill it just because it befriended me. Maybe you should be communicating with it. Maybe you should be trying to figure out what makes it tick."

"It does not tick," the ship said. "It is not made of clockwork. Nor is Spike. I would be insulted if you said that of my own pet."

"That is a figure of speech," Atlanta said.

The ship had found that this was the somewhat infuriating and mystifying response to a great many questions, and so it chose to ignore that particular aspect of what she had said. It said, "It is my servitor," and then abandoned the conversation entirely.

After a while, Atlanta grew tired of shouting at it. She nudged at the servitor again, but it did not respond.

"You and the ship are being having a fight?" the patiently waiting Squid asked.

"All I am doing," Atlanta said, "is trying to figure out how it works, and it is getting all sorts of bent out of shape because of it."

Much like the ship, Skidoo decided to abandon a potentially fruitless source of conversation. She said, "I am being talking to you because Milly is being saying that you are being abused by Talon."

"I am NOT being abused," Atlanta said. She was turning red and felt her shoulders setting at this conversation. "Why is everyone else on the ship getting involved? All that I am supposed to be doing is getting trained in fighting!"

"That is seeming reasonable," Skidoo agreed. "What is being bothering Milly about the way that Talon is being training you?"

"He was working me hard, too hard, she thought," Atlanta said sullenly. It was humiliating to be thought so feeble that other people had to intervene on your behalf. "I am not a child to be watched out for," she told Skidoo. "If she really thought that, then she should have taken me aside to tell me so, and let me be the one to bring it up."

"That is also sounding most reasonable," the Squid said agreeably.

Atlanta paused, almost suspiciously. She eyed where Skidoo sat coiled near Minasit. She had never seen such a gaudy creature, she thought with a trace of fondness, and it came to her to wonder how much of that coloration was natural.

"What is being the question that is being sitting in your mind?" Skidoo said.

"Usually you are asking if I would like to have sex," she said, and then turned bright red at the suddenness with which it had come to her.

The blood pulsed insistently in her cheeks as she waited for Skidoo to reply. The room felt warm and close.

"And you is being knowing that I am being interested, and that to be pushing it further would be being rude," Skidoo finally said, her voice uncharacteristically hesitant. "Are you being thinking that I am being like that, pursuing and pursuing until what I am being chasing is being exhausted and gives up? That is not being kindness. That is not being love."

"It is not," Atlanta agreed. "I appreciate that. And I am not saying no . . ."

"You is not being saying yes, and that is being more important." The Squid's tentacle crept along her wrist. "There is being time, there is always being time."

10

“He’s making her work so hard it could end up hurting her!” Milly argued, having finally calmed enough to seek out not Niko, but Dabry in the kitchen. Her pupils were wide and flashing with anger, and the feathers along the back of her head and neck stood up, an elaborate white crest.

Dabry didn’t look up from the bowl he was mixing. “The captain usually knows what she’s doing when it comes to these things,” he said.

He took two small tasting spoons to dip into the pulpy mass, holding one out to Milly. She took it reflexively and tasted it as he did the same.

“Salt,” they said in unison. Dabry carefully sprinkled a pinch across the surface and resumed mixing.

“The girl doesn’t know enough to resist when she’s being pushed too far,” Milly said, but her feathers were slowly flattening.

“You could train with them,” Dabry said. “Keep your edge in too. That might smooth things over, what do you think?”

“I think you are managing me, old man,” she grumbled, but reluctantly took the next tasting spoon, nodding in confirmation after sampling it.

“Better, right?” he said.

“Still needs a stronger acid note,” she said.

“Noooo . . .” He tasted it. “Well, perhaps.”

“But why should he be training her in the first place?” Milly said, trying another tack. “I thought we would eventually create another restaurant. She does not need to know how to fight to work there, unless you plan on having her play security, which seems an odd choice."

"We have to deal with Tubal Last before any of that can happen," Dabry said. "He will not let go, Milly."

She nodded unhappily.

His attention focused entirely on his mixing, he said, "And if any of us splinter off—as Petalia did, which has proven a mistake—I would suspect he would take advantage of that to hunt them down."

He did not look up to watch her expression, so he did not see the feathers startle, then settle again.

"I am sure," she said, "that any of us that have thought about such things have considered that and factored it into their decision."

"One would expect," he agreed. His strokes in the batter were sure and methodical, his voice absent as though he were thinking of other things. "All of us are intelligent beings, after all."

He set the spoon down and said, "But I will talk to the girl, and make sure she knows that she can object. Will that make you feel better, Milly?"

"It is enough," she said. "You always do enough, you and Niko. That is why I am still here."

Atlanta went to the ship's garden space for refuge. The light here was ruddy; it played over lighter leaves, making them pale green and yellow, while deeper green leaves darkened, their surfaces glossy and laddered with shadows. The space was cramped, vines and leaves constantly grasping outward as though to claim more territory. The air smelled better, fresher in this space than anywhere else, tinged with oxygen and green.

She was thinking about the conversation with Skidoo rather than how much she still hurt, even after that hot shower. Four spans wasn't that long; it didn't seem reasonable for Talon to mean to train her multiple times a day. She consoled her perplexity with the cinnamon cookies she'd brought in her pocket. Something about eating them here made them taste even better.

Cinnamon was new to Atlanta and she couldn't get enough of it. The sweet dusty burn appealed to her, and lately Dabry had been serving it in a different way with every meal.

She was focused on savoring bites of her cookie, alternating them with thoughts of Skidoo, who roused in her both trepidation and delight, when she heard the door open.

Dabry said, "Are you hiding here because you're hurt?"

She shook her head. "No," she lied. "Just tired, that's all." The fear of her inadequacy flared up. She should've been able to stand up to his treatment, but the relief of Milly's intervention had been tremendous. She would never be a soldier like the rest of them.

Dabry eyed her and the bruises covering her arms but said nothing more on that subject.

Instead, he said, "You have been wanting to learn more about cooking and making food, so this time, let me start with the very basics and show you some things about the garden. Then I can add you to the duty roster for maintaining it, and when you cook with those ingredients, you will understand them better." He held out an upper hand and hauled her to her feet.

"Niko used that phrase too. Why is there a duty roster?" Atlanta asked, trailing after him. "The ship is more than capable of handling all the work."

"Well, the ship is capable of maintaining itself, certainly," Dabry said. "But if we are to be Free Traders, then we need things to trade, and that requires some effort as well as thought."

"I thought the point of traders was that they bought things cheaply in one place and then took them to another place and sold them at a profit."

Dabry grimaced, though it was unclear if the expression was for her or the brown leaf he'd just picked from a vine to consider. "It is a bit more subtle than that. And there is plenty of excess time aboard a ship that is moving. If we do not keep everyone occupied, then most of them will just spend their time pleasure-seeking in one way or another, sometimes to the point where they do not even interact with each other."

He put the leaf in a pocket and moved on, checking over the racks of plants, beckoning him to follow her.

"The ship is capable of tending all of this space itself," he said. "But interacting with the food before you cook it is an excellent thing for a chef to do. And you should learn what needs to be done overall, in any case. Most ships do not have biomechanicals that it controls—instead they have robots and drones, and those can be rendered useless in a variety of ways that are much harder to do with biomechanicals. You need to be able to carry operations out if something fails."

One of the central racks stood empty now, though on either side, the plants in those racks were already sending out tendrils to explore the shelves. Dabry pointed at it.

"That's our first priority," he said. "I've brought in starts for the vines we'll put there, and we're interspersing it with slips of bio-engineered ginger in several flavors. Those established vines are called laseriabells—see the shape of the blossoms? They produce a sort of aerial tuber that has a nice texture that varies according to how you prepare it. Can be a pleasant starchy quality or something a lot smoother. Not much base flavor to it, so it dresses up well, which is good, because it's extremely productive. We'll mix in a couple of sweet potato vines as well."

"That rack is intended for plants that clean the air," the ship said.

"These do," Dabry told it. "They also happen to produce these edible tubers."

"What if you eat all the tubers?"

"Then the vines will produce more."

There was silence, a decidedly sullen one.

Dabry said, "I'm sensing that you're not happy with this, *Thing*. Can you explain why?"

"The vines fit in two categories and it is indeterminate what their primary category is," the ship said in a peevish tone. It did not like the idea of something being two things at once. Something about the taxonomy seemed antithetical to how it understood the world.

"Their primary purpose will remain the cleaning of air," Dabry said in a patient tone.

"But not all portions of the plant will do so," the ship pressed. "The tubers will not do so."

"Hence we will eat them," Dabry said. "Most of them. The whenlove plant is more for decoration than anything else."

The ship worried this idea around in its head and emerged from the brief reverie still very unsatisfied. However, it decided to wait and see what happened.

Dabry kept quiet until it became obvious that the ship had nothing more to say on the subject.

Turning back to Atlanta, he showed her how to place the plant starts in the little bags of soil that would then be injected with water and placed in the rack. "Poke your finger through the blue-marked hole, here," he said. "Then put the plant's roots in the hole you created, yes, like that but a little deeper. Good. Squeeze the bag just a little to get the roots settled in the growing medium. Now all you do is add water, here, until this spot turns green."

Her hands liked the feeling of the bag as it went from dry to moist; there was something about the transformation and the way it felt in her hand that was marvelous each time, like touching something and feeling it come alive. She had never gardened at home, although it was not an uncommon hobby.

Happiness seeped through her, replacing the worry over roles or the bruises Talon had inflicted. Every time she took a breath, the air felt full of moisture and life and a calm happiness. The long plant tendrils in the racks all around drooped down in the low gravity, brushing against her as she worked, but she tried to avoid contact, worried that the oils from her skin might interfere with their growth.

Dabry worked with the smaller bags that housed the ginger and slotted them into the rack one by one, at a much faster rate than Atlanta.

She could smell each time he started a new row because it signaled the introduction of a new flavor of ginger: lemon, then lime, then basil, pepper, some unidentifiable fruit—raspberry? Strawberry?—then a very plain, unadulterated, classic ginger so strong she felt as though she could taste it in her mouth. She was still only a few rows in with the larger plants when Dabry shifted to those in order to assist her, starting at the top and working his way down while she continued to build upward.

They met at the mark a third of the way up; she was irritated with herself for not having moved more quickly, but then she consoled herself with the thought that it had been her first time doing anything like that.

Dabry insisted on checking over all her plants, nudging a couple more deeply into the soil and tugging one out a bit. She wondered if his maneuvers did anything other than remind her that he was in charge and had been doing this much longer but then dismissed the thought. It wasn't like him.

He was impressed by the speed with which she took to it. He'd worried that she might take a long time to find something she was good at. That could erode someone's confidence. But now he could see her gaining some and, more than that, enjoying herself freely.

Smiling to himself, Dabry surveyed the rack with satisfaction. "That is a good bit of labor," he said. He turned back to Atlanta. "Do you understand how the racks work?"

"No . . ." she said uncertainly.

He spent the next hour disassembling and reassembling one to show her how it functioned, how the water was pulled along by capillary motion, then took it apart again and made her be the one to reassemble it this time. She got it halfway right, arriving at the end with a number of leftover parts, so he showed her where she had gone wrong and had her do it again.

"But surely this is something better left to the ship to do," she protested.

"What if the ship were disabled, what then?"

"We would go to a station and ask them to fix it."

He rolled his eyes at her. "By the time that this trip is over, you will understand some of the basics of ship maintenance."

"But I can't hope to learn everything there is to know about running the ship! It's too complicated!"

"You can learn the basics of the systems, the mechanics underlying them, at least many of them. And if you know those things then you have a much better chance of being able to fix a problem than the person who regards the machine as a mysterious and unfixable box. A good soldier is prepared to deal with any situation."

"But I am not a soldier," she said. "We are not fighting anyone or hiring out as mercenaries, are we?"

"No," he said, coiling hoses to put them away. "Niko and I have had enough of war and we will not take anyone back into it. But life is its own kind of war and we have banded together in order to survive that battle. I will give you all the weapons that I can, and yes, I will speak in military terms more than once, because that is the language that I have always taught in. And Niko will insist—as will I—that you know how to defend yourself in a fight, and are not a liability. That's why she set Talon to training you."

"What would make me a liability?"

"If we had to watch over you for your own safety," he said. "If you consistently behaved in a way that brought danger to us." His gaze was mild. "I am sure you can think of all sorts of things if you set your mind to it."

"I want to be useful," she said.

"Good. This is where you start with that."

"No, truly useful. Everyone brings something to the group except for me."

He patted her head with a hand. From anyone else, the gesture would've felt patronizing, but somehow, he made it comforting. "You are young and inexperienced, Atlanta. Much of this will come with time. The best thing that you can do is watch and learn from the things around you."

Dabry's heart twinged at the feel of the glossy hair against his palm, like Keirera's warm scalp under his hand. She would be a good bit past Atlanta's age, as he judged, if she had lived.

"Are there other plants to start?" she asked as he forced that thought away.

"Plenty of them," he said with deliberate calm. "I brought seeds and cuttings. If we're going to be aboard the *Thing* for a good long time, I'll add more of them over time."

"What will you add?" the ship asked. "More plants with more than one use?" It pronounced the last with a trace of horror that it found itself unexpectedly enjoying. These new passengers—who it would be carrying for at least a solar year or two, based on Arpat Takraven's request—had provided it with the chance to experience so many new emotions and feelings. More than it had ever been able to indulge in during the hundred or so years that it had simply been a vessel or plaything to the idle rich like Takraven, who sometimes left it in dock for years at a time.

"Maybe," Dabry said in a portentous tone, winking at Atlanta. "Perhaps even some with three or even four uses!"

She rubbed her face to hide a smile at the dead silence with which the ship greeted this joke.

11

Gio chopped the latest batch of laseriabell roots with precision, each slice like a mirror image of the one before it, the sweet, wet smell of the matter filling his nose. It kept his hands busy, so he could not speak, just think.

He wanted Niko to hurry up and resolve whatever it was that would happen with Tubal Last. Then they could go back to being happy, and that was a much better way to live. That was proper life, getting fat eating good food and talking and joking with your friends. Person couldn't ask for more than that, really.

Back home, by now he'd have a family, be running out picking up after them. All that stuff didn't interest him much, no matter how many letters his mother sent him on the subject. He had brothers and sisters; she had them to take care of all of that. At this age she'd have a crop of grandchildren. She could leave him alone. He was happy here.

At the same time, he had a secret worry that he took out every once in a while to examine, like a sore that you didn't want others to see. It came to him now with the methodical *chonkchonkchonk* of the knife's rhythm.

What if Niko couldn't prevail against Tubal Last?

After all, the man had survived the explosion of the pirate haven that should have killed him, set off when the ship jumped into hyperspace directly in its center, tearing the ancient structure made from scavenged ships into bits.

What then? They had all been imprisoned by Last. He'd killed Thorn, just to make a point. And they hadn't managed to escape because Niko had come up with some sort of clever plan. No, it had been Milly's betrayal, bizarrely enough, that had enabled them all to get away.

Chonkchonkchonk. He swept the damp segments into a bowl and grabbed the next tuber, lining it up under the knife. *Chonk-chonkchonk.*

And that was another thing, Milly. He had thought they were close, or getting there. Not romantic close, but good-friend close, share-a-secret-or-two close and have-each-other's-backs close. And then it had turned out that wasn't the case at all. She'd been ready to flee, taking only Atlanta and Atlanta only because she'd thought the girl necessary.

Ever since then she'd been friendly enough, but certainly, he'd felt cooler toward her. How could he not? He was, if anything, irritated that she acted as though nothing had happened now.

In his family, the wrongdoer would have been forced to talk about it. Here, she skated along, acting as though it was all behind them, and the thing of that—the heart of it, and the thing that mattered—was that there was no assurance she wouldn't do it again.

She hadn't been in the kitchen much—he and Dabry were handling most of the meals—but every once in a while, she came in to make a batch or two of small treats. Keeping her hand in, she said, but he thought it might be a way of bribing them, just a little, to maintain their silence. He chewed his lip.

Some factor had to give here, or matters would go awry with the team, he knew that, but he wasn't sure what to do. That was the sort of thing Dabry handled, or if it was something in the moment, Niko. Should he say anything?

No. He would give Milly time. Just a little more time.

Glowing softly in the room's dusty half-darkness, the Derloen ghosts curled and writhed. If Lassite were in tune with the universe as he should have been, he should have been able to read things in their motions, portents, and omens. That was part of what he was, someone who read the deeper layers of things, as though meanings were pressing at him from all sides. That was what it felt like when the prophecy-fits were holding him fast and not letting him go.

Those moments were glorious because he knew what to do and did it without thinking, without guessing or trying, just being where he needed to be, doing what he needed to be doing. Pushing forward to the Golden Path.

It had been so easy at first, but the further along its spiral he went, the more he circled in and upward, the more complicated it became. How difficult would it be, toward the end? Would he be enough for it? It was too bad the girl had no magic. She had been useful in some timelines.

He shook his head violently, hard enough to feel things wobble in his head, hard enough to frighten the ghosts into flashing away, fish-quick for a second rather than their usual slow undulations.

Focus on the breaths. He drew air inward, tightened his belly, pushed it up into his lungs, held it for a count, pushed it out, held himself still another count before beginning again. His body slowed and relaxed, coming into alignment, but his mind continued to jitter one way and another.

He should be preparing, but he didn't know how to, what he could do to ensure the path. At the Gate, they'd meet a new person who was important, someone who would shape one of them deeply. Was there a way to ensure her reception? But he didn't have enough details, not enough to know what to do, and the frustration of that knotted his fists until, noticing it, he forced himself calm again.

What would happen, would happen. That was and would continue.

"By all accounts," Niko said to Atlanta, "your first training session with Talon did not go well, through no fault of yours."

"I don't mind working hard," Atlanta said. "I know I have a long way to go."

"Perhaps, but you will reach it sooner or later," Niko said, reading the doubt in the girl's eyes. "At any rate, we will discontinue them for now, and you will come talk to me when you have figured out what you want to try next. But here is the thing that you must figure out before I will tell you whether or not you can continue further with us."

Alarm thrilled through Atlanta. She said, her voice uncertain, "I thought that I could continue with you no matter what, as long as that was what I wanted."

"That is true," Niko said, "and that is the question that you need to answer. What is it that you—the Atlanta that resides inside your body, the entity that you experience as you—really want? When you come to the end of your life, what is it that you want to have achieved with that life, beyond what you have already done? Because keep in mind that you have already had more adventure in just a few months than many experience over the course of a lifetime."

Atlanta started to protest at that but gave off when she realized it was true. She had awoken among strangers after the dizzy blankness of coldsleep and before she had a chance to get her bearings, the space station they had been on had started exploding, and then they had been shuffled off aboard *You Sexy Thing,* and then, well, everything had been blood and pain and pirates.

It had been an adventure worthy of a viddie, but she wasn't sure she wanted it to be, honestly. There were times when the court life memories—though they were admittedly false, either taken from someone else's experiences or entirely constructed—seemed much more appealing than her current existence.

She said, "I want to stay here."

"Why? Because you are scared of life away from the ship? That is not the best of reasons," Niko warned, in a tone that suggested that "not the best of reasons" was a category that might be rejected in terms of whether it led to continued life aboard the *Thing*.

She shook her head. "Because you are my friends," she said, "and I care about what happens to all of you, and the best way that I can make sure that only good things happen is by staying."

She thought to leave it at that, but Niko gave her a long and level look, mildly inquisitive, and maintained silence. At first, she stared back, but the moment stretched on and on until, unable to bear it any longer, Atlanta scrambled through her thoughts in order to supply something, anything.

Finding that something took reassessing, which was not entirely comfortable under Niko's inscrutable gaze. She finally said, "I think that I need to figure out how I can help the crew. I need a place in it, something that I contribute that no one else does, and that's hard, because you have all learned to supply each other's needs. I mean, not the way that sounds . . ."

She broke off as Niko nodded.

"Dabry said you have some talent for gardening but little gift for cooking," she said, "but I told him that there are many forms of preparing food and drink, and that what doesn't work for you here might be a key to what is needed in another area." She shrugged. "You might be a clever brewer, for instance, capable of creating subtle beers and wines that complement what the restaurant creates. That's a matter of continuing to cultivate your taste, and there what you should do is look for the things that you love and use them as a starting point. Figure out small differences between one version of it and another, and then figure out how you can affect the process. You can create anything, I think, given time. Dabry manages that damn smoker, for instance, which I am at a loss to figure out why the ship permits it."

She cast a glance upward at the last, but the ship remained silent.

"What are you checking for?" Atlanta asked.

"We had a discussion about privacy and the ship"—she stressed that word—"agreed that unless it heard its full name, *You Sexy Thing,* it would not begin to listen."

"Despite the fact that it violates safety protocols," the *Thing* immediately said. "How is Spike, crew member Atlanta?"

"My ear is fine, thank you very much," she said and throttled back the urge to rub it. She cast an imploring look at Niko, wondering why the captain didn't interfere in this absurdity, but Niko's lips only quirked in amusement before she pressed them together and turned her attention up to the *Thing*'s speaker.

"We are speaking of what Atlanta wants out of life, *Thing,*" she said. "And it occurs to me that it's a question I have never asked you. What do you want?"

"To travel with you," the *Thing* said without hesitation.

"Why?"

"You're so much more interesting than Arpat Takraven. And you teach me things. Like cooking. And new emotions."

"So if we boiled your first thought down to its essence, we would find that your main desire is not to be bored," Niko said.

"Yes," the ship said.

"Anyone would do as long as they're not boring?"

"Well," the ship said, after an uncomfortable moment had come and gone, "they would have to be very entertaining." It added, somewhat unnecessarily to Niko's mind, "There are a lot of you, after all, and so there is usually someone awake. Arpat slept too much."

"Ah," Niko said. "I will try to keep my sleeping to the necessary minimum."

She nodded at Atlanta. "Dismissed."

That night, while Atlanta was in her cabin, she found a jar of scented paste beside the bed.

"That's for Spike," the ship reminded her.

She dutifully administered it. It smelled like honey and warmed the skin, a soothing, sleepy sensation.

Before she entered the stage the ship found so boring in its occupants, she thought back on her conversation with Skidoo. It occurred to her again to wonder how much of the other's vivid coloration was by choice. She called up images to look and found that was the Tllellan's natural coloring. She ran her fingers over the image's stripes and wondered what it would feel like to reside in the heart of that.

She had thought Skidoo would press her—how would one call it? Her pursuit? Her wooing? But she had not, and Atlanta did not know what to make of that.

She flopped back onto the bed. She wanted . . . what did she want? She did want to succumb to Skidoo's advances—but not yet, not until she had a place in the crew. Otherwise, what if they thought she was doing it in order to secure that place, playing on Skidoo's affections to ensure she would be motivated to keep Atlanta part of the crew?

"That's not like her," she told herself. "Skidoo isn't like anyone else you know." Not like the palace courtiers and their intricate games of flirtation and favor. That was what was getting in her way—she had no idea how things worked without that game.

But imagining openhearted Skidoo playing that game of

subtle slights and even subtler favors, she could not do, no matter how hard she tried.

She checked in with her advisers. To her surprise, all of them were saying the phrase Lassite had given her. That made her pause—they were not supposed to be that self-directed. Was there something about the magic that had caused this?

But did it matter? They didn't affect her day-to-day life and all, and here, they could be employed at something that, while unproven, might turn out to be quite useful. With a touch of satisfaction, she switched back out of that space. Perhaps there was nothing to luck. But if there was, she was sure she had covered it very well indeed.

12

Atlanta had always thought of spaceships as having some sort of helm, or command room, or at any rate, a central place from which the ship was directed. But *You Sexy Thing* was self-directing, so being the ship's pilot, something Atlanta had always thought of as an exalted role, wasn't something anyone seemed to be. But surely the skill of piloting would be useful, at least for shuttlecraft and such.

She would have admitted—or would she have?—that part of the draw she felt from the idea was the thrill of flying, which she had never experienced back on her planet. There was something about the swoop and fall of it.

You Sexy Thing did have a small room full of screens and readouts and displays, as well as the massive chairs that defined the interior that enabled one to feel as though they were the ship itself, diving through space. But it was rarely used. Niko relied on the ship to alert her of circumstances, although she did check that small room from time to time to scan the logs and screens.

She was there, going over logbooks, when Atlanta found her, and clearly welcomed the break and chance to stretch. "Sit down. Have you thought of some new thing you'd like to work on learning?"

"Captain, would it be possible to learn how to fly a spacecraft?" She phrased it that way rather than say, "Would someone teach me," because she wanted it to be Niko who did it, but didn't want to ask that, wanted the extra jam of Niko offering to be the one to do it. "It seems like it would be useful."

What if she turned out to be worse at that than cooking or fighting? She tried to shove that thought into the back of her head.

But Niko didn't offer to teach her, simply saying, "Hmm, that's a good notion. Anyone of us can get you started on the basics. Even the *Thing*, I think. But if you're thinking of getting your certification, what class of ship?"

"Beg pardon?" she said. "Spacecraft."

Niko turned her attention fully away from the screen and looked up from where she sat to take in Atlanta. Even battered by Talon, the girl was looking stronger, she thought, than the wan thing she'd been when she first arrived, always expecting to be told what to do. She had cultivated a little more strength of mind—or, Niko thought with satisfaction, Niko and the others had helped her cultivate it.

But did she have enough to survive? Their path was dangerous, and in order to follow it, they would have to work together. Would have to be able to trust each other.

Could she trust this girl? Particularly after the mistake she'd made with Milly? With a conscious effort, she set the question aside for now and went on.

"There are multiple classes of spacecraft, and it has to do with how far they can go. Not all ships can handle the forces of a Gate, for one."

"Most cannot," the *Thing* supplied a little smugly. Niko rolled an eye but continued.

"Moreover, there is Q-space, which is different than Gate space. It is faster than light, certainly, but the Gates move ships from one galaxy to another, while Q-space moves us about in shorter leaps of distance, such as from one solar system to another within a galaxy. And that's what eats up most of our travel time, those smaller distances."

"Aren't the galaxies interspersed?" Atlanta said, frowning.

Niko shook her head. "No. Think of it like a loaf of savory bread, the kind Dabry made last night. Do you remember it?"

Atlanta did. Suspended in the bread had been small flavor

orbs, enough that every bite held at least one or two bright bursts of citrus when chewed, lemon- and lime-flavored sparks.

"Each orb is a galaxy, a cluster of stars. As the universe—and I do not mean what we call the Known Universe, but the totality of things—expands, which it does, ever outward, it carries those orbs farther and farther apart, but they do not grow as it does, but rather according to their own laws, born of gravity and energy."

Niko leaned back in her chair, giving the urge to lecture full rein. It wouldn't hurt Atlanta. "At the heart of every galaxy is a black hole, and that is what powers its Gate, if it has one, for certainly there are more than Gate destinations, we know that. A galaxy can stretch vast distances inside itself—the Milky Way, where humanity came from, is over a hundred thousand light years from one border to another—and that is where Q-space comes in, so we do not have to resort to generation ships or freezing ourselves or transferring consciousness, as some have been known to do. So that is another class of ship, even if our own manages to straddle both categories. And then there are ships that maneuver within the space of a single solar system, distances much, much shorter."

She shrugged, considering Atlanta. "For a start, get someone to show you how to drive a shuttle. See if you can coax Talon into that. It'd be a lot less physical, at least."

Talon was not willing, though. He shouted through the closed door for her to go away, and then refused to say anything else. She sighed and contemplated her choices. Dabry was almost always busy, and she hated to ask him for more time.

Outside the kitchen, Gio was perfunctory with her, which was unsurprising. Chimpanzees tended to dislike humans and rarely crewed with them. She didn't know what bond allowed him to overlook Niko's humanity. She wasn't sure Lassite would know how to pilot anything. He seemed to avoid technology wherever he could. That left Skidoo and Milly, and Milly could be cruel about one's lacks, and Atlanta was pretty sure the experience of learning to fly a shuttle would disclose plenty of such lacks.

She hesitated. Skidoo would flirt, and was that welcome or not? Plus, it would interfere with learning. She chewed her lip, uncertain.

"I will teach you," the ship said in a tone so definitive that Atlanta did not argue, although she experienced more than a few qualms. What if this was a repetition of her experiences in the kitchen?

Still, she had to trust her teammates. She swallowed down doubts and nodded.

"We will begin in virtual space," the *Thing* said. "Hyperspace is very tedious and that will give me something else to think about."

Atlanta nodded.

"Sit in the chair," the ship directed, and Atlanta followed its directions, settling into the thickly padded chair. The ship had refreshed the integument that made up the padding only a few hours before and it still smelled of the faint egg-and-paprika aroma that its creations often held immediately after extrusion.

She laid her forearms along the chair's armrests, and straps slithered out to wrap themselves around them, securing her in place. Others did the same around her knees, and the padding softened and gave to hold her hips in place securely. It was faintly claustrophobic, but she had endured worse.

She leaned her head back into the hood of the chair, and again it softened and resolidified to cup her skull, holding it still firmly but gently. A film lowered over her sight.

"Close your eyes."

She hung in space and there was no up or down. Her stomach whirled and she wanted to throw up, but the stars were absolutely still around her, frozen in place. And yet she was moving in relation to them, a dizzying whirl, a spiral inward that tugged at her every sense . . .

"Take a deep breath," the *Thing* said in her head.

She did. As she inhaled, she thought that it wasn't working. At the moment she began to exhale, she was less sure, and then as the last of it left her lungs and she breathed in anew, she found that the spin had slowed perceptibly. Another breath and it moved at a bearable pace, then began to crawl at the next. Within a few moments, her stomach had climbed back down to nestle comfortably in her belly, to the point where she could have stood a bitc to cat, as though thc adrcnalinc of that initial freefall had burned away calories in its panic.

"This simulates a system ship, one of my shuttles," the *Thing* said. "Faster ships will require nerve-to-nerve connection because the pilot's reflexes usually require augmentation of some kind, unless they are a mechanical. We will save those simulations for another time."

"We went down to Pax in one of these," she said. "Who drove?"

"I did," the ship said, "although the captain likes the ability to override." If it could have rolled its eyes at that, it would have, and it noted to itself to try to figure out comparable gestures to signal exasperation. Perhaps the gesture could be relegated to a secondary device. Perhaps it could manifest eyes specifically for the gesture. It filed the notion away for later, further consideration.

"So this is how I would drive your shuttle?"

"If I were totally incapable of directing it, yes. Otherwise it is best left to me."

Atlanta could and did roll her eyes.

"We will begin with a basic flight from one planet to another," the ship said, more than a little pedantically. It was finding that it was enjoying teaching, since it required the pupil's undivided attention, and you got to choose where to spend that attention.

An hour and a half later, Atlanta's stomach had made multiple trips to crawl up her throat and threaten to eject itself, only to subside, but she also thought that she might be getting the hang of things.

She and the ship had also made more of a peace over the course of that time, talking about themselves, or at least one of them talked about themselves while Atlanta listened.

"The captain told me to get a hobby," the *Thing* confided.

"Did you?" Atlanta thought about the various hobbies she might have suggested for the *Thing*. Something with complicated aesthetics, so it could spend a lot of cycles fidgeting with those. Some sort of quantum art, perhaps. That had been very popular in the Imperial court just before Atlanta's departure, although the equipment for something like that was costly.

"If I had," the ship said cautiously, "it might be dependent on being kept secret until the appropriate moment."

Atlanta tried to contemplate the possibilities evoked by that, but she found her stomach kept intervening in any serious thought. She'd pursue it later, sometime when she was feeling more at ease with the universe, she promised her conscience.

Meanwhile, *You Sexy Thing* whirled on toward the Gate and what waited for it there.

13

"What?" Niko said incredulously, setting down her tea. She'd thought she had a few hours to herself to read, but then Dabry had appeared in the door of her chamber with startling news.

"The rumors were true. The Gate isn't working," Dabry repeated. He added, "Reports indicate that it stopped functioning about three days ago."

"Were there any signs beforehand?"

He paused, listening to something on an inner channel. Niko knew from experience he was listening to multiple channels at once; it was one of Dabry's talents and the main reason she'd recommended him for training as her sergeant in the first place. He shook his head. "Not a sign of it."

Niko's voice was dangerously low and full of tension. "I know there were rumors, but come on. You're telling me that the ancient alien gates, upon which the majority of the Known Universe's species depend for travel, have failed?"

"Just this one, it seems like," he said. "There's no talk of others elsewhere failing. We're in visual range now. Let's go to the pilot chamber. *Thing*, put the Gate up on your screens there."

By the time they got there, they had accumulated Atlanta and Gio as well, summoned by ship comms chatter. The main visual screens flickered with movement, silver flecks against the stars' burning curtains. They could see the Gate hanging in space, surrounded by the ships that would normally have been passing through it. Even as they watched, they saw another pulling in.

Atlanta stared at the Gate, transfixed. She'd seen them before, many times, but always in working order: a vast silvery ring hanging in space, its inner depths filled with purple and blue and green fire. No matter what angle you looked at it from, that fire filled the structure, which was not a simple ring, but adorned with carvings of plants and animals that had not been seen in millennia.

Scholars had dedicated their lives to those carvings; they were different on each Gate. Near this one, like most of them, was a small space station that had grown like a barnacle on whatever structure the Forerunners had originally left there, and a few loose chunks of rock, tethered to that structure.

Every Gate was powered by the black hole at the heart of whatever galaxy hosted it. The ship could feel this one's distant tug, but some force kept the Gate where it was in relationship to the faraway, massive smolder of gravity moving on its skin.

Atlanta's eyes were wide. She knew it should be filled with mystic fires, but this one hung dead and inert, and all you could see through it were the stars on the other side. A small ship was traveling back and forth, in and out of the Gate right now, as though trying to taunt it back into life.

"Why are there so many ships here?" she asked. "There have to be dozens!"

"I'd bet many have been ordered by their governments or owners to stay and watch. This is an unprecedented situation," Dabry said.

"Some may have run out of fuel too," Niko said. "If they were planning on coming out of Q-space right at their destination and refueling there. There's a lot of space stations and moons in reach of this Gate. In which case they're waiting on someone to bring them enough to get out, and we'll get hit with a pledge. Stay back and out of hailing range, Dabry . . ."

"Too late, Captain."

Niko grimaced.

"What's a pledge?" Atlanta asked.

"It's a tradition that started with the Free Traders," Niko said. "Any time you've got ships together and some of them are running out of supplies, everyone that has some of that kind of supply chips in. Keeps everyone alive. It's a code of conduct. How much is it?"

"Standard amount of water and fuel per person. Nothing out of the ordinary." Dabry turned to Atlanta. "It's important to support the system. We might thank the stars for it ourselves someday."

"Doesn't make it any easier to stomach right now," Niko grumbled. Her face brightened at a thought. "More than a day, and that means someone is already working at starting a trade tangle. I bet all those ships would like a meal that isn't reconstituted ship-food. Plenty of them will have fuel to go from ship to ship."

Her eyes met Dabry's. "That's a bit of an opportunity, isn't it? Particularly with a load of Velcoran goods to use up, since they can be adapted to so many species."

"It could work," he said thoughtfully. "And if this is a temporary glitch, and the Gate comes back to life, we'd be here. *Thing*, what would you think about setting up a restaurant in the front lower hold?"

"That is warball space," the ship said reverently.

Niko made a face.

"But you could reabsorb a lot of the current interior and clear it out, couldn't you?" Dabry said. "We could replicate furnishings if it was too much effort for you to grow them."

This time, the ship sounded a little haughty. "I am more than capable of creating furniture. What sort of furnishings do you wish?" It hoped that Dabry might give it free license; it had been doing research on restaurants and had thoughts on the matter, but, disappointingly, Dabry said, "Basic tables and benches in a range of sizes. Spacers don't need fancy."

He rose.

"Where are you going?" Niko said.

He raised an eyebrow at her. "Milly's supply alone won't cut it. I'm going to go see what's available in the gardens."

He exited and Niko chuckled. "There goes a happy man," she told Atlanta. "He hasn't had new people to cook for since we first had to flee TwiceFar before the Arranti chewed it up. Gio will be happy at more cooking, too, don't think I don't see you grinning, my friend. But better yet, he'll get a chance to wheel and deal a little, see what other foodstuffs he might be able to swap for. Lassite will grumble that he is maître d'ing again but accede, and Milly will outdo herself with desserts."

"I'm new," Atlanta pointed out. "Newer than that, at least. You didn't uncrate me until you all had fled."

"And there you were all dewy-eyed and 'Captain Larsen, you're my only hope!'"

Atlanta turned red. "Well, I thought it was true at the time," she said ruefully. "How was I to know I'm just a diversionary clone?"

Niko patted her hand. "More than just a clone! A clone of an Imperial heir! Think of what we could do as far as forging their endorsement of our food! And anyhow," she said, sobering for a moment, "as I keep having to point out, you are a member of this crew, and welcome in it."

Atlanta's eyes got misty.

"Don't cry on me," Niko warned her. "Or I will make you go do fight training with Talon again until you have sweated so much you have no moisture." She hated shows of emotion or gratitude. "Shoo." She flapped a hand at the young woman. "Go help Dabry figure out what sort of table he wants to set and get his menu together so we can get set up and start beaming it to the other ships."

Atlanta exited and Niko turned back to the view screen and the dead Gate hanging in space, ships circling it, dwarfed by its immensity until they were no more than toys passing in and out of the vast, ornamented hoop.

Despite the cheerfulness of her tone with Atlanta, she was worried. The death of the Gates meant the death of much of the Known Universe. Only three species did not use the Gates, and none of them were sharing the technology that allowed them to do so. Without the Gates, they would move from obscurity to prominence: the Beringed, who claimed to have found another way to access Q-space; the Nephalese, who claimed to move instantly via teleportation; and the Shrug, who usually just said that they'd learned to move "pretty fast." Shrugs were known for understatement, to ridiculous lengths.

She shook her head and returned to more practical matters. "*Thing*," she said to the ship. "How did Arpat Takraven entertain when he brought guests aboard?"

"He never brought guests aboard," the *Thing* said.

Niko frowned. "But he spoke of inviting Lolola back to his ship."

"That would have been uncharacteristic," the *Thing* said. "But he had not traveled in me for several years before that trip. Perhaps he had changed his ways?"

"It seems a large change," Niko said, "to go from totally unsociable to inviting someone back to what is essentially one's quarters."

She filed the discrepancy away in her head. This was a question she'd ask when they met with Arpat and told him the stories he'd asked for. She had no doubt that there would be other questions, but she did hold some doubts as to whether any of them would be answered.

Takraven was one of the Known Universe's truly rich, and he operated outside most of its laws, leading a life regulated only by internal whim and the demands of time itself. That was something no one had ever learned how to affect, although some claimed that the mysterious Arranti had managed it and used it as part of the lengthy and inexplicable games they played among themselves.

She ran her fingers over the instrument bank in front of her. The *Thing* grew its furnishings according to its own dictates, for the most part, and this console was not an exception, made of the glossy, chitinous material that it excreted as rapidly as it needed to.

The bioluminescent lights, soft green and blue and amber glows, ran in wavy patterns between tiny rows of logos. Like most of what the ship extruded, it was unnecessarily beautiful. She wondered what sort of gene patterning created that genius with curve and line. Was it truly innate? She had never been inside any other bioship; they were incredibly rare and fantastically expensive, a thing of stories and viddies.

And yet here she was, commanding one, moving across the Known Universe in search of her lost love while a pirate king breathed doom at her heels. She shook her head. Was this really the Golden Path that Lassite had predicted? He had never said exactly what lay at its end, but the implication was that it would be at the level of events she had once known, the interplay of power between galaxy-states and empires, the eons-old game of war and intrigue and betrayal.

She had been betrayed before. Probably she would again, truth be told. Her fingers sought the patterns of the light studs again, as though searching for the reassurance she could not find.

14

"Weird buzz going around the ships," Dabry said as Niko entered.

"Weirder than the Gate going down?"

"Weirder than that."

She slung herself into the seat opposite his console. "How so?"

"Some woman's en route, calls herself Jezli Farren. Says she can open the Gate."

Niko's eyebrow arched. "What? How?"

Dabry steepled the fingers of both upper hands together. "Get this. She claims to be channeling the spirit of some ancient Forerunner leader, says she can communicate with the Gate and coax it open."

"So, has she?"

"Says she needs time to work, to 'get attuned' to the Gate."

Niko thought. That was a valid enough objection, particularly if the Gate's power was magic instead of or as well as scientific—something no one had ever been able to ascertain. But it also might mean that this Jezli Farren person was simply buying time for something else to happen. "How much time does she say she needs in order to get sufficiently attuned?"

"About a solar day, more or less."

"Huh."

He looked at her. "I took the liberty of inviting her to visit the Second Last Chance."

"I still don't like that name for the pop-up," she grumbled. "But why invite her? She sounds like she might be trouble."

"Maybe," he said slowly. "But it also seems as though something is going on, and I figured you'd like to get a closer look at it."

"It's better not to get involved," she began, then noticed he was laughing at her. "What?"

"I got involved so you wouldn't, and you still give me this speech. If I hadn't, you would already be telling me to send her an invitation and maybe even include a discount to coax her to come."

"A discount?! Here where there isn't a nano bit of competition?" she said indignantly. "You didn't, did you?"

"Of course not," he said. "In fact, since some of the ships are banding together to pay her, we're going to up prices considerably."

"How much is she asking to unlock the Gate?"

He told her and she whistled. "That's almost enough to buy a bioship like the *Thing*."

"Almost," the ship interjected, and kept a few smug thoughts about its cost to itself.

"It'll mean we get a little information about her, at least. I'm taking taste profiles beforehand, very traditional Velcoran practice."

"Are you really worrying over how to please the palate of someone who is undoubtedly some sort of scam artist working a con?"

"You don't know that."

"I'm given the choice between believing that and believing that someone has done something that no one has done in the history of the Known Universe—contact the Forerunners, living or dead. Which would you believe, given that the simplest explanation is usually the right one?"

He hesitated and she laughed. "You want to believe that she can do this, don't you?"

"I do," he said. "Wouldn't you? Aren't you curious about

them? The mysterious Forerunners. I thought the Free Traders had expeditions that went forth to try to find such things out."

She said slowly, "Yes, but . . ."

How could she explain that for the Free Traders, it was almost a religious thing, that hunt? The Forerunners had enabled the Free Trader way of life; their portals made it possible. The thought of the Gate shutting down gave her chills; it would throttle interstellar travel and everyone would suffer as a result, but the Free Traders would fare worst of all.

Maybe Farren was somehow connected to the Gates. But in her experience, things were never what they seemed when there were large fees involved.

And Jezli Farren's was very large indeed.

After Dabry's news, Niko took the time to go through the roster of the other ships around the Gate with care. The insignificant space station was barely big enough to house the handful of people who chose to make their living providing fuel and supplies for the ships coming through the Gate and a somewhat larger pleasure structure, whose main purpose was draining the money out of the pockets of anyone forced to spend an hour or so there.

The list of other ships proved an assortment, most of them cargo ships in one form or another—about half of those Free Traders, a couple of colony ships full of frozen colonists and embryonic livestock, a courier ship, one pleasure cruiser and the three small frigates that guarded it, and a scientific expedition on its way to the edge of the Known Universe.

Only one of the listings made her pause.

She said to Dabry, "The *Knot*'s here. Gnarl's ship."

"Gio's old captain?"

"The same. Last time I saw him was when he came sniffing around, trying to figure out what sort of offer I'd take for Gio's contract, and then when I wouldn't sell it, getting so hot under the collar that he started just shouting at me till I walked away."

"Think he'll try to buy it again?"

"He'll feel obliged to try, at least. Well, might as well tackle the warp and contact him first." She thumbed a channel open.

Gnarl Grusson was one of the angriest people Niko had ever met. He was a small humanoid of indeterminate species with more teeth than the usual allotment, compact and neat and filled with a perpetual rage. Niko thought it must get in the way of crewing his ship, but his crew, marked for their phlegmatic calm, remained unflappable or at least cowed to the point of not reacting.

She endured his various insults disguised as greetings as well as several attempts to talk about Gio, because he was also remarkably adept at getting the scuttlebutt, and Niko wanted to hear what the other captains were saying about Jezli Farren's proposition.

"I've run into her before and wouldn't trust her farther than my own hand," he said, "but they say she did fix two other Gates." He squinted at her. "No one in yer crew said anything about knowing her, eh?"

But Niko's mind was on the first part of what he'd said. "Two?" she said, startled. "That would have been news all over."

"Ya'd think, eh? But they was both far in the outskirts, little Gates, an' you know how rumors get. Thick as ship-grot."

"Your ship-grot, maybe. Should bring your crew over and we'd feed them right, you know that."

He snorted. "Pay for that lazy bunch to have a fancy meal!" He bristled at the idea, then visibly calmed himself.

"You could get a chip for that, you know," Niko said. She didn't understand why Gnarl didn't get some sort of mood regulator. Anyone else would have by now.

"Not gonna lose my edge," he snarled. "Dull your own, Niko Larsen, if'n you like, but I use the mind the gods gave me!"

A Purist. That explained a great deal. Niko dropped the subject and said, "Did the other Gates pay?"

"They did," Gnarl said. "She did what she claimed she could—or seemed to, at any rate."

"It's got to be a scam," Niko said.

"Ya think I don't know that?" Gnarl grunted as though amused. "I got some feelers out. But not being able to rely on the Gate—if she brings it up, first thing I'm doing is pinging for more info on those rumors. She's gotta stick around long enough to collect her fee."

"If it's a scam, she'll want to grab and get out fast," Niko said.

"And if that's the case, she's playing it well," Gnarl admitted. "Seems chill as ice."

He glanced off-screen as something clattered. "What the merry hell are you two playing at!? Go scrub down the cassisblace." He returned his attention to Niko, scowling. "Can't get decent crew anywhere!" He grumbled something under his breath.

To the best of her knowledge, with the exception of Gio, Gnarl still had most of the crew he'd started with—unprecedented for a Free Trader, and something that would have signaled to some that despite all the shouting, his crew preferred him to any other situation.

Niko wondered, though, if he had some other hold over them.

"Keep me posted if you find out anything?" she asked.

"Yeah, yeah," he said, spitting out the words. "Hey, you didn't answer earlier, how's Gio?"

"Happy enough here still," Niko said, her voice firm. "I've got other calls to make, but let me know what you hear about Farren. We've had some strange coincidences lately. Pulling up to a Gate just as it goes dead seems like another one."

He started to say something else, but she cut the comms, not quite quickly enough to be rude, but bordering on it. Gio had been desperate to escape Gnarl, who'd come chasing him after he left the *Knot*. Desperate enough to join the Holy Hive Mind, and that was pretty desperate. She should summon him, talk with him about it.

The ship interrupted the thought. "Captain Niko."

"What, *Thing*?"

"Why do you believe this to be a 'scam'?"

She stared at the view screen, which currently showed the immensity of the empty Gate and the shimmer of stars past it.

"Because of all the miracles and wonders I've seen in this universe, the really big ones were all scams in some way. Even the Holy Hive Mind—they promised life eternal, but minds don't persist in it, at least as it's been explained to me. They're swallowed up and taken apart and used to reinforce the existing personalities." She shook her head. "Like fuel to keep them going," she muttered.

"That is why you did not stay?"

"I didn't stay because I had people under my protection, and that was the best way to protect them," she said. "They were about to train Thorn and Talon."

"I thought they were fully trained warriors."

"They are. They know everything their mother taught them. And the HHM would have taught them to use it without thinking, in order to kill. It would have removed their sense of empathy and made them sociopaths. All in the name of making them better soldiers. And they would have been better soldiers—it just meant losing everything that made them who they are." She shrugged. "I promised their mother I would do better than that."

"How did she die?"

Flashes of that battle clawed across her mind—fire and the smell of fresh blood and burned fur—noise everywhere. The choke of systems trying to cope with smoke and damage, the shudder underfoot every time the station took a direct hit.

Some fool had brought in explosive weapons and destroyed the station's air so everyone had to run for suits. Or maybe they'd meant to do it, knowing that many wouldn't make it. A blow to thin the ranks.

She'd gotten into her suit at the last moment, still gasping, but every few steps on the way out she saw the body of someone who hadn't been so lucky, and had to kill two desperate soldiers who wanted the one she wore.

Debriefing, afterward. No one willing to take responsibility. The story changing repeatedly, and every time people acting as though the current version was the only one that had ever existed.

"Badly," she said. "She died badly." Like her son. There Niko had failed on her promise, and the guilt of that gnawed at her every time she saw Thorn's scruffy face.

The ship did not press further. Currently it was studying the concept of *tact*. This seemed like an appropriate time to employ it.

Gnarl was eating zarro grubs. He had a special bin of them in the food prep space and gods help the crew member who dared to dip into his store. They were fat and fed on ship leavings, and right now he was eating them slowly, alive, with no sauce but their own internal fluids and his anger. He bit the head off one and licked the juicy stump.

It itched at Gnarl, the way Gio had left. It had ever since the day Gio had departed, not even taking his gear with him. That had been a revelation, going through the tiny cabin that Gio had occupied and realizing that his quartermaster had been even more skilled than he had reckoned. That was another thing that chewed at him, because now that he knew, Gio at hand would have been Gio making him money, and instead the chimp was making it for Niko.

Niko. All sorts of legends about her, like she was some kind of hero rather than a failed soldier. What was it about her that made people go all glassy-eyed with admiration? Gnarl couldn't see it himself. That irked him too. He'd always prided himself on the fact that his crew didn't leave him. That took some doing; it wasn't easy. Required bribes and threats and sometimes just psychology, knowing where to put pressure to make someone jump in a particular way.

Back in the day, he'd augmented that with plenty of violence. He'd thought he had Gio sussed out, that the chimp had been cowed, but he hadn't been. He'd been figuring out how to jump ship the minute the opportunity presented itself.

And that was the third way this collided with his sense of pride and self and left them feeling bruised. And all three angers had the same source: Jezli Farren, who'd infected his quartermaster with odd notions about independence and then gone away, taking the Sorean brandy that she'd sold him with her to boot.

He scowled and popped another grub into his mouth, biting down with furious relish. Gio hadn't said anything about her to Niko yet. Maybe he didn't know so far, but what did it mean if he did and hadn't said anything? Maybe he was in some sort of scheme with Farren. That could be.

Or Niko was lying in saying she didn't know her, throwing him off the scent with that question. How could Gio not have mentioned her?

Farren hadn't precisely stolen Gio, although that was what Gnarl called it. She hadn't outright taken him, but she was the reason that he'd been able to think of leaving, and before Gnarl had been able to sweep him back into his grasp, the Holy Hive

Mind had taken him up, and bonna swear to anyone who might have some idea of busting someone free from that army.

Niko had managed it, though. He wasn't clear on the details. No one was. That was why rumors raged about the reason she'd been allowed to leave, ranging from wild to preposterous to outlandish. She'd found treasure and bought her way out; she'd blackmailed some higher-up; she'd turned out to be a spy in some stories, and a politician's favorite, and even an Arranti pawn in a few.

And that was something more he didn't like about her. All the mystery and unearned good luck. He hadn't had luck like that, he'd had to fight his way up, and through worse captains than he'd ever been. Undeserved luck. Luck that could—and should—be taken away.

But he could play nice for now. Sure he could, and act like he was chatting and gossiping even while he was scheming how he might claim Gio back, whether or not the quartermaster wanted to come.

He turned to Basli, his second-in-command. He could trust Basli. She would never have betrayed him after years of conditioning, and if she did, well, there was a tiny chip near her carotid artery that could be exploded at the touch of a button.

"Watch them, and tell me when they send a shuttle off for supplies. They won't pass up a chance for trade and to talk up their own goods. And when they do, I want to talk to whoever it is that they send."

Basli nodded and departed. Gnarl popped another grub into his mouth and squashed it between his back teeth. It tasted like cold revenge, and that was a very sweet flavor.

15

Velcoran cookery was, Dabry said, very different from anything Atlanta had tried before, and so they might as well see if she was any good at it.

He presented her to the bulky machine he had temporarily installed in the corner. It was made of glass and brass and crystals and silvery rounds, standing a head taller than she.

"I have heard you talking about Velcoran cookery," she said, "but no one has explained what it consists of."

He smiled.

It is generally agreed that most species do not place the same emphasis on eating and drinking that humans do. Some other species actually considered them varying degrees of uncouth, profane, or utterly barbaric as a result of that emphasis.

Velcoran cuisine came about after a collision with human culture and is considered by many to be a bastardization of the original form, which has gone utterly out of favor with contemporary Velcorans.

The meal is not so much nutrition as it is a series of tastes presented in succession and designed to make one enjoy what many have described as a flavorless chalk.

Each flavor is delivered in the form of gas contained within a pliable, edible balloon. Eating these is an art in itself, and a favorite trick of the sophisticated is to introduce the less sophisticated to it for the sole purpose of recording and laughing at their attempts to consume the balloons.

The gas inside is aromatic, carefully composed through natural methods. Dabry had eaten several Velcoran meals and they had roused in his heart a savage desire to replicate their sophistication, to create a mix of lemon and florals with an undertone of meat, something as complicated as a melody, but made of taste and smell.

The *Thing* was pleased to be consulted on such a matter and liked such machinations to be as fussy as possible. Dabry obliged it to a degree that it had never experienced before, demanding precisions of temperature and air pressure and measurement that thrilled it to the core. The result was the machine that now sat before Dabry and Atlanta.

"There are two components," Dabry said. "The first is simple. A bland paste designed to meet the nutritional needs of the diner. Its consistency can be adapted to their preferences, but traditionally it is a very soft, almost flaky substance that is entirely protein, with no flavorings whatsoever. That is not the challenging part."

Atlanta waited, making sure her face looked appreciative. This was Dabry in full teaching mode, as she had seen him only a few times so far. Dabry as teacher was somehow very different from how he was around Niko, to whom he was always supporting staff. Here in the kitchen, Dabry was the leader, the point to which all of them looked.

"The second part is a set of scents, contained in an edible film. A bubble of gas, again by tradition approximately the size of your own head, although it can vary by body mass. The being puts the bubble to the appropriate orifice and inhales. The scents linger while they consume the protein and flavor it by proxy. The art in this is severalfold—the creation and combination of the scents, the consistency and texture of the bubble, and its coloring, which can be complex, according to the artistic dictates that are being followed."

Dabry said all of this with more than a trace of satisfaction. He had never been able to sell Niko on the idea of trying Velcoran cuisine, and when Milly had returned with the components, he had been quite happy, although not so happy that she had exerted quite so much free will in the choice, rather than looking for the flavored oils he had sent her in search of. Still, it had all been quite serendipitous, and he looked forward to testing out this new equipment. Velcoran cuisine would be something no one else here would be capable of supplying.

"The novelty of this will serve us very well. These small stations usually have the same set of restaurants, more or less," he said. "There will be someplace whose soup or tea kettle has been simmering for years. Someplace that specializes in spice and one that specializes in dumplings—sometimes they are the same. Someplace that does fried things and maybe sweet if there's enough traffic for it. Someplace for stimulants and one place for daily starts, again maybe combined. There's enough ships here that there will be money burning in the pockets of plenty of crew members, and since we are stayed here for the time being, they will all be checking out trade goods. If we were true Free Traders, we'd have a hold full of goods that we might be trading them, but we add a layer on that by making it food and insisting on cooking it for them." His eyes went distant, his face smiling, as he calculated profit margins.

A few hours later, his smiles were scarcer. Atlanta could not seem to get the knack of the bubble creation, and time after time, hers popped before they could be inhaled, leaving sticky rags of grayish foam everywhere. She hadn't even begun to try combining scents yet but had an uneasy sense that the next step might be even harder. Her sense of smell wasn't the best, and that was going to hamper her.

Dabry's lower hands were clasping each other as though to restrain themselves from more violent motions, and his brow was knitted. "I think," he said heavily, "perhaps we will stop for the day."

Atlanta had thought she might be about to get the hang of this part. Perhaps. In a few dozen more tries. "All right," she said. "I'm sorry."

"We will attempt some sort of dexterity exercises, perhaps," Dabry said. "As well as finding you a more suitable task."

"Suitable task like what?"

"There is always clearing away." He patted her shoulder with an upper hand and exited before she could say anything else.

"It is too bad that your bubble materials were at fault," the ship said complacently. "Perhaps Minasit will comfort you."

Suspicion blazed in her. "You set me up so they failed!"

"True," the ship said, even more complacently.

She struggled for sufficient words to contain her indignation. "You . . . you are being petty! And mean! So mean!"

The ship seemed less certain of itself. "This is not revenge?" it said in question.

"You don't practice revenge on crewmates!" she said indignantly. "Not if you want everyone to get along."

"But you upset me first, by treating my servitor as though it was something other than me."

Atlanta fought her temper. "Then I will try not to do that," she said.

But that night, after putting lotion on her ears and before going to bed, she spent time petting Minasit, which it seemed to enjoy, although she did not talk to it. She figured if the *Thing* objected, she would tell it that her attentions had been meant for it. But it did not ask, and she did not volunteer.

"What's a trading tangle?" Atlanta asked Skidoo the next day as they cleared cargo out of the room beside the hold that Niko wanted to use for the restaurant. This one held boxes of supplies laid in by Arpat Takraven, none of them useful, containing wardrobe items and exotic toiletries, none of which were edible. (Dabry had methodically checked for the last.) Niko figured it could hold restaurant necessities close at hand.

"Is being everyone putting out what they is being wanting to sell or rent and is being trading money and goods and talk," Skidoo said. "Is being plenty of money to be made in a trading tangle."

They hauled the boxes into two smaller rooms, then surveyed the larger space formerly known as their warball room. The *Thing* had reabsorbed the padding that had once covered the walls, which were now a glossy viridian with the inevitable logo sprawling in interlocked iterations across it.

"Lucky we don't need tables," Atlanta said. "*Thing,* you're taking care of that, right?"

"Tables and chairs and dinnerware and everything," the ship said in pleased, proud tones. It was planning a special limited-edition version of its logo for the occasion and had produced three proof of concept pieces to show Niko already.

Niko had been disappointingly uninterested in them, but the ship was sure Dabry would be more interested once he got the chance to look at them, as he had promised the ship.

The boxes had been heavy. Atlanta ached but not in the bone-deep and bruised way Talon had elicited. This was a more pleasant ache. She almost said so, but she had promised herself not to flirt with the Tlellan, and that seemed like a somewhat suggestive remark that would lead to more suggestive remarks.

Instead, she said, "If we're setting up here, is that part of the tangle?"

"It is being part of the overall thing, yes," Skidoo said. "Everything together is being why it is being called tangle, for so many kinds of tangle and complication."

Gio entered before Atlanta could ask more about it. He hunched forward, examining the space, nostrils wide.

"Sweep it down with illi dust," he signed. "That'll neutralize the odors."

"I is being incompatible with illi dust," Skidoo said, moving to the door.

"I don't smell anything," Atlanta protested.

Gio wrinkled his nose at her. "Of course you don't," he signed with an expressive lift of his eyes. "But humor me."

Milly had asked Gio to take her into the trade tangle when he went so he could show her some of what they'd talked about in action. He'd put her off for now, but she'd surely ask again. And he did itch to go there, he would admit to himself. She knew that as well as he did.

Ignoring Atlanta's efforts with the flakes of illi dust, he stared at the wall screen providing the illusion of a window and the glint of the tangle forming. The Gate's field, which they could have ordinarily depended on for shielding, was down, so they were putting the tangle in the shadow of a half-hollowed asteroid and relying on portable dust-sweepers for the unsheltered sides. There was some danger, but people would do anything in the name of trade.

He sighed and knuckled his eyebrow, rubbing at it as though it would drive away worry.

Niko cleared her throat at the door. "Figuring out who's going to check things out once they're set up," she said. "But I wanted to tell you, Gnarl's definitely trying to get you back still, I just spoke with him."

That was bad news. "Then I shouldn't go to the tangle to trade," he signed. "If I meet him, he'll be looking to pick a fight. We don't need that."

Her eyebrows rose. "Really?" she said incredulously. "You love to trade."

She knew him so well. He huffed a half sigh, half laugh, then signed, "Gnarl scares me. Let someone else go."

Her brows knitted for a second, then she shrugged. "Dabry and I already talked about sending Talon, it'll be good for him. And to watch over him, well, Atlanta's learning to pilot, so she can shuttle him, and then do some of the errands, the things we know we need."

"Don't trust her to bargain. I'll set up those deals over link and she can just do pickup."

Her lips quirked as her brows eased. "So you're not quite that ready to give up the pleasure of trade."

He mimed a laugh at her, lips covering his teeth.

Gio had seen trade across the galaxies. It was the thing he liked the best, actually, quartermastering. You found out what people needed and not just that, you anticipated things, you bought when stuff was plentiful and then you used that stuff in order to trade or bank favors against some future trade.

Trade meant you learned people's tells too. A canny trader was good at reading what people needed (or wanted, at any rate) and at least providing some value in the process.

He thought about that, still watching the sparkle of stars in the screen. If you had a slider, and at one end you put the people who traded without thought of profit, simply for the joy of it, or because they had such an abundance, or because it was the philosophy they followed, like the Slakes, who liked to give away their genetic material in order to solicit the same from other species—all of those at that end, and then you moved away from it, further and further, the more you were thinking of profiting from the exchange. Didn't wrongness reside somewhere on the distant end?

Trade and exchange was good; taking things from people

without giving back was wrong. He was thinking back to the days when he'd first started learning it, back on Gnarl's ship, back before he'd escaped. Gnarl liked to make deals out on the bad end of things, and Gio hadn't felt right being part of that.

Trade was about fulfilling the other's needs; you had to do that to get a good trade. Food lent a whole new twist to that when you were thinking about people's needs and their tastes. He knew everyone's favorite little obsessions and had a sleeve of truffles stashed for next time Niko was feeling cranky, not to curry favor but just to see the pleasure of her smile. And he had some fancy sugars tucked away for next time there was some occasion for gift-giving, because he knew Milly would like them. A new scented ointment for Skidoo, and cinnamon tea he was saving for Atlanta. When you produced something that a person wanted, but hadn't known they wanted until that moment, that was a good feeling, one of the best.

He huffed out a sigh. And giving people bad news was not a good feeling. This was not the right time to tell Niko about his concerns with Milly. The captain had enough on her plate. He'd just keep watching her for now.

16

"I will need you to test your piloting skills and take Talon over to the trade tangle," Dabry told Atlanta.

"The *Thing* could do that, couldn't it?" she asked.

He straightened, turning away from the balloon casing equipment. "Indeed it could. So why am I having you do that?"

She thought. "Well, what you said. To test my skills."

He arched an eyebrow.

She thought some more. "And so it's not Talon and the *Thing* alone, but me, to watch over what's happening as well."

He nodded soberly. "You are the sense of responsibility that is going. And while you are doing that, Gio has made some trades, and you will go pick those up."

"I can be responsible," the ship said.

"You have plenty of other things to think about," he said. He made a shooing motion at Atlanta. "Talon has the list of things that he is supposed to get."

The brooding were-lion was unwilling as ever to play errand boy at first. But the habit of being commanded took precedence over all his sullenness, and so he stomped his way into the shuttle where Atlanta already sat, looking at the controls with a sense of anticipation and glee. He slumped into a chair, ignoring her greeting. She sighed.

"How is Spike?" *You Sexy Thing* asked. "I have not heard news about it in some time."

She sighed even more deeply. "My earlobe is fine, thank you very much."

Talon's own nameless ear twitched, but otherwise, he displayed no interest in the conversation.

"Good, good," the *Thing* said in a tone that it believed conveyed happy sarcasm, although it was not entirely sure whether it was pulling it off and yearned for some form of feedback. "Are you prepared for the trip?"

Atlanta took a deep breath, trying to quell the fluttering of anxiety edging her heartbeat. There was no reason to be nervous, she told herself. This was a simple flight, and in case of emergency, the *Thing* would be able to step in.

"It's a good thing you're doing this," the ship said. "That way I can completely disengage my sense and not worry about this particular appendage. You're on your own. I believe the appropriate expression is 'Good luck!'"

"What?" she said, nervousness shrilling her voice. Behind her, Talon stared out the port, refusing to acknowledge any of this.

"Enjoy the market! Prepare to launch!" the ship chirped. It recorded the moment. Perhaps it would be able to get feedback on that sarcasm some other time.

The first ten minutes sang with panic, and Talon refused to play any part in that melody. But then Atlanta realized she had, in fact, learned everything she needed to know for this brief maneuver. She had no trouble docking the shuttle into the designated area of the trade tangle, directing it in with a surge of pride. She looked around at Talon to celebrate the victory, but he continued to stay huddled in on himself, not acknowledging her.

Plenty of other small ships hung there. Space trips were a matter of weeks at best, sometimes months or years, and a chance to socialize and trade was welcomed by almost every species. Skidoo had explained that this was also an acknowledged safe space;

by ancient convention, no violence or overt crime could be carried out without general censure and heavy fines dispensed to every participant.

The market was made of temporary structures, bubbles of atmosphere linked by tubes and chutes, some lines stretching out while others snagged and tangled. In the shelter of the Gate's field, people were used to not worrying about meteorites and space dust. The flimsiness of the construction worried Atlanta, but Talon seemed unfazed, and so they pressed ahead.

A hallway full of scanners checked for contaminants or bionics that would prove detrimental, and then their passes were stamped with the symbol of the Gate itself, written in Keinlot symbols.

Most cosmic records were maintained by the Keinlot, a society of intricate documentation of a completist nature. They enforced nothing; they simply maintained data and supplied it to any other civilization that wanted it, at a price. Most agreed that the price was well worth it, and most agreed that the Keinlot were trustworthy.

Talon vanished when she was still staring around, muttering something about his own errands. Atlanta ignored a surge of panic and consulted the list Dabry had given her. Navigating the tangle was a matter of following the current chart; colored lines showed the flow of traffic and helped her decide where to go. An enterprising cargo ship that had been empty had sent up trade space in its hold, and that was where the chart directed her first.

She picked up an armload of what were labeled greens, but were colored purple and amber, at one stall, and a box of black tea at another.

The transactions were smooth enough. Gio had made them ahead of time. All she had to do was show up, check the package, and then accept it with the thumbprint to free up the payment

Gio had made. It was easy. She let herself relax and enjoy the atmosphere of it all, the people jostling back and forth, the various accommodations made in order to serve as many species as possible. It reminded her of the pirate haven, but this chaos seemed considerably more benign.

17

If Talon had had his twin with him, then this would have been amazing. He'd heard about trade tangles but he'd never been at one. They were not military functions, after all, and his only life outside of that had been aboard TwiceFar. That station had been its own sort of tangle. But this, this gathering of ships, each with its own unique flavor, was something altogether different.

Dabry had indicated he should stay with Atlanta but hadn't outright said so, and therefore Talon felt justified in ignoring that. The girl could look after herself.

He went off to collect the supplies on his own list: some flavored oils ("Maybe you'll have better luck with that than Milly did," Dabry had grumbled), stellar salts from a Clippit trader, and a variant of laseriabell roots that was supposed to have substantial kick to them. Dabry had given him funds for all three and he knew the last was partially a test of his bargaining power.

Talon also knew very well what it was that Niko and Dabry intended by sending him for supplies. They thought he would be distracted by it all, by the chance to be outside the ship in this elaborate, temporary construction, one of the biggest such he'd ever seen, even if Niko had indicated it was paltry by Free Trade standards.

He drifted through shells and the bubbles of stalls, the walls changing color from time to time to showcase the wares they held. He'd chosen human form, and every time he shifted from one environment to another, he could feel the minute changes in humidity and air composition from ship to ship, even when the air was unbreathable and his breather took over for him.

He'd looked the list over and knew he could find everything on it readily, so readily that he wondered if the mission had not been preplanned for him.

They were babying him, he thought with a flicker of irritation, which was followed by a wave of self-pity—why shouldn't they pander to him, after all, when it was as though a piece of him had been cut off? The walking wounded, that was him. Capable of movement but little else.

Now he moved aimlessly, letting himself get pulled along by the surges of traffic. He'd been told that if he ran across spices, any he could get would be acceptable with the exception of ship-pepper, which everyone always had in surplus. No one really liked ship-pepper, but it was easy to grow and produced useful byproducts in the process and it was better—though not by much—than no taste at all.

He let himself wander through stalls of the kind he would have been told to stay away from in the past—or rather, he and Thorn would have been told to avoid them. Strange that with Thorn gone, Niko had felt no need to forbid him. Although he didn't know it, she would have welcomed this touch of rebellion, would have seen it as a sign of healing, and so she had left plenty of potential room for it.

But it wasn't healing that lay at the heart of him. He was using the stalls to hurt himself, over and over, picking up a weapon and forcing himself to consider how Thorn would have reacted to it, deliberately summoning up the vision of his twin in order to reignite his pain, slice open the healing scar. It was a bruise he kept pressing on, because its healing would have been a loss he was unwilling to contemplate.

Where once he might have been warmed to be trusted with such a test by Niko or Dabry, this time it only annoyed him. They acted as though they understood everything, knew everything, but when push came to shove, they hadn't been able to save Thorn, and that absence made none of this amazing. Made it all annoying and irritating and tedious.

But he did pause at a stall of puff-jackets, bright and gaudy with purples and greens. Very stylish, and not something you could replicate because of the internal tech, so he and Thorn had always wanted a pair, had been saving up.

He brushed his hand over the slick, cushiony fabric. Not his favorite color, but Thorn's . . .

"Hey there," a voice said behind him. "That device on yer collar—you're with Niko Larsen's crew, aren't you? Forgot the new ship's name but I recognize that logo. Fancy ship, lad, must be a pleasure to serve on a ship like that."

For once, he was dealing with someone who didn't treat him as though he was brittle, made of glass. Someone not being careful of his feelings. He straightened and nodded casually.

"Niko and I are old friends," the little man said. "I'm Gnarl, of the *Knot*. Come and drink in honor of your ship."

Talon hesitated. Even through his naivete, there was something *off* about the other.

His twin's face flickered in his mind. "Free booze," Thorn would have said, and Talon would have followed that without a thought, so he forced anything else away, and followed.

Atlanta stopped at a stall crammed with books and papers. The basket near her, jammed with books, included the infamous volume *Skullduggery and Sacred Space Vessels*. She debated with herself, but Niko had given her a handful of credits to spend, and after how prominently the book had played in their existence, she wanted to read it. She tucked it under an arm and pressed on.

"Where's Talon?" she asked the ship after taking on the third of Gio's packages, a box of spice packets from a vending machine that someone had set up. "Is he done yet?"

"He hasn't made any purchases yet," the ship said.

"What? Why? Where is he?"

"I believe the establishment is what is called a bar."

Talon didn't know how it had happened. He had been talking with the captain (and how flattering was that, that a captain himself wanted to spend time talking to him?) about one thing and then another.

Now they were drinking together because Gnarl had reasonably suggested that he buy Talon a drink in exchange for passing along a handful of message chits that he said were the latest news, promised to Niko earlier. He'd have to go fetch them, but first they should have that drink.

The nameless bar was small and makeshift, housed in a corner formed by the overlap of two larger spaces, clearly something whose battered plastic panels and stools could (and had been) assembled and reassembled hundreds of times, and the floor was sticky with spilled drinks. Talon thought that it didn't really deserve a name. His crew would have regarded it with distaste, maybe even confusion. There was no artistry here.

And he didn't care.

The server offered an extremely limited range of drinks, with no accompanying food to soak them up. But the first drink went down smoother than he'd thought, and then, after a while, Talon found himself telling Gnarl everything, or at least everything that was important: Thorn's death, and how it had happened.

Gnarl had been sympathetic. Turned out astonishingly enough, that he'd had his own twin, just as close, claimed in a way as untimely and unfair, although he didn't divulge many of the details.

"Happened long ago," he said, waving a hand that simultaneously seemed to sweep away the topic and summon more drinks for them both. "Wish it had happened nowadays. Nowadays I'd know better what to do."

Even though he was feeling the effects of the drink, that couldn't help but catch Talon's attention, hard and sharp as a fighting hook. "What do you mean?" he asked.

Gnarl shrugged. "You know . . ." He leaned in confidingly. "Nowadays there are ways around it. Like clones."

Talon slumped back, disinterested. "Don't have the memory core," he said. "Who can afford that kind of tech?"

Gnarl kept leaning forward, eyes fixed on Talon. His voice was so soft that Talon had to strain to hear it. "No, lad, that doesn't entirely matter, as long as you have some bit of them genetically."

Talon frowned.

Gnarl took the frown and returned it as a smile. "The flesh holds its own sort of memory. You can clone flesh without a memory core and still have what you want."

"But he wouldn't have any of Thorn's memories!"

"There is that. But memories were not what your brother was. He was flesh and blood, and you can create that side of him. Give him a new life."

Talon's nerves were not too befuddled to not twitch anxiously at the implications. "That's illegal. Way illegal. So illegal."

"Aye, and that's the unfair shame of it all," Gnarl said in commiseration. "If ye'd had more money, coulda had an imprint of him stored, clone him back, nice and legal-like."

Talon snorted. "Takes money. Lots of money." Arpat Takraven levels of money. And cloning was not just expensive, but one of the most regulated technologies in the Known Universe. Clone uprisings, back in the days before people realized the dangers, had caused chaos for almost half a century.

"Yeah," Gnarl said reflectively. "Though I hear some get so desperate they try it on the cheap. You must have some material left for that."

"That would be illegal," Talon said, amusing himself by ticking a claw in and out against his glass and not looking at Gnarl. "And it wouldn't work. I told you. Without his imprint, it'd just be someone who looked like Thorn. It wouldn't be him."

"That's what they tell you, an' it's all propaganda." Gnarl's eyes had a faint luminous glow at the back of them, so slight it was difficult to tell in the darkness, making Thorn strain to see them. "All that stuff about the imprint and the soul. Bunch of hooey. What you are is stored at the genetic level, and the reason they don't tell you that . . . well, I'm sure you can guess why the powers that be would want to keep that knowledge locked away."

He signaled for two more drinks, setting one in front of Talon. Talon sipped the liquid, which smelled better than it tasted.

"You just need the equipment," Gnarl said. "What if I was to offer you that?"

"I don't have money," Talon said.

Gnarl spread his hands in an expansive gesture that didn't seem to match the tightness of his features. "No need tah worry about that. You see, you remind me of myself when I was yer age. Little like looking in the mirror. So I'm reaching back in time to help meself." He shrugged. "If the debt's too much for you to bear," he said offhandedly, "I'm sure we can figure out some small, nominal-like favor somewhere down the line."

Talon ignored the various voices speaking common sense in the back of his head. Most of them had the same accents as Niko and Dabry, and they hadn't kept Thorn from being killed, and that surely meant they weren't worth listening to. No, the only voice worth listening to was his brother's, and if there was a way to be doing that in reality, rather than tormenting himself by imagining it, well then, that was surely the way to go.

He remembered his conversation with the ship. Surely the ship would be sympathetic. Niko and Dabry would not be, he was sure, and that did give him some pause. But not enough.

"Sometimes it's easier to get forgiveness than permission," Gnarl said. He smiled indulgently, as though obviously he would be capable of either, even if Niko wasn't. "But it's getting on, and I have duties a-calling. I'll have to send over those chits, no time to go get them."

He tapped the table to close out the tab. Talon checked the time and was alarmed by how much had passed. And he'd missed multiple messages from Atlanta. Niko would be furious, particularly since he had no extra spices to show for all his dawdling.

But he chose not to think about all of that after Gnarl was gone. Instead, he sat staring down at the table, turning bits of the conversation over in his head.

18

Atlanta pinged Talon several times. When he didn't answer the third time, she checked his location and made her way there. The location turned out to indeed be something that could be described as a bar and he, still in full human form, was half slumped in a seat, head resting on his hands as he stared at the table, an empty chair beside him as though someone had just left. The air here was damp and had a tinge of acrid smoke to it, as well as fiery wafts of alcohol.

He blinked blearily at her when she said his name.

"Time to go, I guess," he said and gave her a halfhearted sneer, as though feeling that he needed to keep up his attitude.

"Past time," she said, annoyed. "I pinged you three times! Did you even do any of your errands?"

He shrugged at her, not even bothering with excuses. "I was talking with a friend."

"Who?"

He shrugged even more nonchalantly. "Some guy from another ship."

She didn't pay it much mind. Who cared if Talon struck up friendships? That sort of thing seemed easy for him.

The thing that irritated her was that he was sitting on his ass while she worked. How long was everyone going to continue tiptoeing around him, acting as though he might break at too loud a noise?

Yes, what had happened was terrible, but he couldn't coast on it all his days. She'd been doing something new and hard and he could have made it so much easier. He knew how these matters worked, knew all the trading protocols that she kept having to look up.

She didn't speak to him again all the way back, and he didn't care. He'd had some leave coming, who cared if he'd used it? They had all been pushing and pushing him to do things and here he was doing something and getting handed a whole bunch of attitude from the newest, most useless crew member as a result.

Anyhow, he wanted to think. Gnarl's words burned in his mind.

You could have him back.

No one was happy with Talon upon arrival, but to Atlanta's continued irritation, not much happened. Niko sent him to his cabin—and shower, mind you, you stink, she told him, but left it at that. She'd pay a courier to bring over the rest of the stuff and if they had to double or triple check it, well then, she knew a young were-lion that could be given that task.

"You are being very easy on him," Dabry said. "And I believe it was you yourself who told me that being too easy was just as bad as being too hard."

"It is difficult, often to the point of usually, to avoid treading into either territory," she said. "But admit it, Dabry, no matter what small thing or things he may have done—and given that he reeked of booze, we know something of what they were—what harm could he have wrought, after all? No, he indulged himself a little, and played at rebellion, and most importantly, he did it by himself, as himself. Not someone accompanied by a vast hole in their life that they must constantly accommodate. You've grown as tired as I of that. Besides, we have other things to worry about. It will take Last a little while to recover himself. But then he will go after Petalia—"

"You continue to ignore the fact that they may be deeper in his plans than you would like to believe."

"They hated him and wanted to escape him," Niko said. "They're angry that I took too long to do that, not that I came. I saw it in their eyes. But he won't just seek them out for the sake of revenge, but because they might prove a weakness. They may know something that would bring him down. So, we must find them before he does."

"Do you think you will find them if they do not wish it?"

Niko looked intently at the wall as though admiring its surface, but her mind was galaxies away.

"I'm hoping they will realize it is to their advantage to be found," she said softly. "Last sent us a message, and I think they may have heard something of it themselves, and know that to be alone and facing Last is worse than facing him with others, even if they are . . . unpalatable in some regards."

"I notice that your hope is not that they will realize that they wish to be found."

Niko's gaze snapped around to meet his. "Don't press me overfar, Sergeant," she said softly. "Not even in the name of friendship."

"Very well," he said tightly, and said nothing more at this time.

To the smug satisfaction of both Dabry and Milly, the Second Last Chance and Velcoran food was proving a huge success. Location, location, location. Niko had always heard the saying, but she'd never entirely understood it before. Now, running the only unique food business in the area with a bunch of ships waiting on various things, she did.

They'd even spawned a few imitators, but those relied on offering something other than food: gambling. *You Sexy Thing* was the only establishment offering more than basic rations; introducing dice or cards or whatever into the mix was totally unnecessary, in Niko's opinion.

"So it turned out not to be such a bad thing, all that Velcoran stuff," Milly said, not for the first time, coming up beside Niko where she stood looking at the crowded warball room, full of spacers from other ships.

Niko looked sidelong. "You got lucky, that's all."

Milly shrugged. "Some people are luckier than others, that's a given."

"Dunno," Niko said. "I've never bought that whole luck being tied to magic thing."

"Don't they teach the officers all about magic in the Holy Hive Mind?"

Niko shook her head. "Enough to work the mind link apparatus and that's about it. Magical aptitude isn't something that you grow into or get better at. You are what you are, with it."

"Maybe," Milly said dubiously. She sighed.

"What is it?" Niko snapped.

"Things have never been the same," Milly said.

"Since you tried to take the *Thing* and leave the pirate haven we were trapped in without the rest of us?" Niko snapped. "Are you really surprised?"

Milly shrugged. "It seemed like the smartest thing to do at the time."

"It might have been," Niko said. "But it also told us you didn't mind leaving the rest of us behind to die. You'll excuse me if I don't think you've changed much since an incident that was only a few months ago."

"Fair enough," Milly said, but her tone was still mournful.

Gio appeared at Niko's elbow.

"Is there a problem in the kitchen?" she asked.

He shook his head and signed, "Just wanted to look things over." His eyes flicked over the tables with a satisfied expression.

The ship felt pleased by its interior. It had coordinated with Gio and Skidoo and while it did not understand aesthetics, despite various attempts to explain it, it knew that the room had pieces that were connected by color or pattern and its understanding was that this was an artful effect.

The choices had been somewhat neutral—there was a wide variety of species in the ships surrounding the portal, and it was so easy to offend or upset someone with a texture or symbol that one would have sworn was inoffensive and abstract.

The colors were deep purples and umbral darks, a subdued effect that gave the room an air of somber elegance at odds with its makeshift nature. Gio and Skidoo had experimented freely with the *Thing*'s ability to create objects and materials from itself, and they had drawn deeply on its reserves, to the point where it would need to refresh them soon.

But all in all, it did not regret that. For once, it thought that it might have achieved the sort of elegance that it had always yearned after. It thought to itself that it had a proper cook, someone so skilled that for once they were worthy of it (a thrill of pride and ego accompanied that and was filed away to be examined later in order to determine how to best recreate such a pleasurable sensation).

Six round tables, each surrounded by seats, formed a larger round, and in the center was a slightly higher table, meant to hold a buffet that diners could help themselves from, covered with a slick grayish cloth worked with the *Thing*'s symbol in a slightly paler shade of gray, a pattern that had to be examined closely to see its components.

"Restaurants have music, do they not?" it asked Gio.

Gio shrugged. "Some do," he signed. "It's often considered pleasant, but you have to take into account the tastes of all the races in the room and sometimes that is a difficult juggling act." He grimaced, then hesitantly asked, "You were thinking of supplying some?"

The tentativeness of that signing seemed to the *Thing* to perhaps convey dubiousness at whether it could accomplish such a task. It experienced a prickle of indignation that was perhaps related to that same little thrill of pride and ego that had occurred to it earlier. Certainly, it seemed to have some common elements.

It said, "But what do the *best* restaurants do?"

"Live music, usually," Gio signed. "But better musicians than any of us."

"Music that is alive?" The ship was intrigued.

"We could play something together," Milly suggested to Gio. "You have your little hand drums, and I could sing. Remember when we'd do that after closing, back on TwiceFar?"

She paused for answer, but Gio made none.

"Well," Niko said into the awkward silence. "I must go over the receipts."

After the door had slid closed after her, Gio looked away from Milly and began clearing up.

"Gio," she began, but he was busy with his hands. She started to touch his arm, then drew away, feeling awkward and stiff.

Well, he could be that way if he wanted to be, she told herself, not admitting that her real fear was that she would reach out and he would step away.

"You're a genius, Dabry," Niko said in a satisfied tone, counting through the basket that held credit-chips, a scattering of gems and precious metal circles, a tiny flask of violet perfume from Alouette, and a small clay figure she had been assured was currency and well, what the hell, she'd figured. Sometimes such things panned out. "It was gimmicky, mind you. People were space-dulled, bored off their heads, and any novelty would have done, probably."

Dabry wrinkled his nose. "That last part of your statement would seem to diminish my genius."

"No, the genius part is how you adapted it to so many species. And now we have a hold full of decent trade goods of a variety that any Free Trader would approve. We may have our route decided for us, but that route won't be a loss unless we're very unlucky. And for once, Lassite is not wandering around prophesying doom if we make a misstep."

"He's seemed off lately," Dabry said. "He does what he should, but he doesn't talk about things the way he used to."

"Have you talked to him about it?"

He shook his head. "He's more likely to tell you, sir. He's always been yours, first and foremost."

But in all the hustle of closing, it slipped Niko's mind.

19

Skidoo was handling the comms and sorting through calls. The Velcoran cuisine had plenty of demands, and scheduling its consumption was part of that, since each "flight" of flavors that accompanied a protein block required enough time to sample and appreciate them all.

A voice on the line, confirming an invitation that had been extended, asking about making a reservation. Skidoo was paying only half attention until she heard the name.

"Oh, that is being no problem," she said instead of the refusal she had prepared. "We is being celebrating your presence."

The voice on the other side held an edge of cool amusement.

"Thank you. I look forward to the meal," Jezli Farren said.

It had come with other deliveries and when Milly had signed for them, she must have assumed it was something personal and slung it on Talon's bunk. Maybe she thought it was something he'd commissioned, now delivered. There was no return information, but he knew that Gnarl must have sent it. *I'll return it,* Talon thought. *I'll find out the name of Gnarl's ship and send it back.* But even as these thoughts were crossing through his head, he was opening it.

The clone sac was simpler than he would have thought. A large bag of silvery cloth, or material at any rate, since there was no visible weave to it. The directions said to fill it with purified water before beginning.

He wasn't doing that. No, not yet. But near the top sat a

bronze-colored capsule into which he put the tightly compressed pellet of his twin's hair, much more than necessary, because the instructions had said a few cells were sufficient, and plenty of the hairs even had the minute accumulations at the root that the directions said were optimal.

No, he wasn't doing anything yet. But he gathered as many of his brother's traces as he possibly could and put them all in the capsule, reasoning somehow that the more of Thorn was in what he provided, the more likely it was that his brother would survive, and then his mind skipped over the part about illegality.

The thought wouldn't go away. It was not a good thought. It was a thought that Niko would not have approved of, nor his mother, nor any other member of the crew with the exception of Thorn, who would have known the desperation that made this thought scuttle forward.

He tried to ignore it. He did, he tried very hard. But it kept edging forward, out of the shadows in the back of his head, showing itself.

What Gnarl had said was true. He *could* have his brother back if he cloned him.

It wouldn't be exactly Thorn, sure. But it would be something very like him, something enough like him that it might fill that void in his life. After all, he and his brother were very much the same in personality and temperament, which had to be genetic. They both did things that reminded them of their mother, a way that she had of holding her head still when listening to something in another room. That had to be genetic.

But no. Something like that would take space, space that needed to be out of the way, and the *Thing* didn't have anything like that.

Or did it?

He said, "How do you make your servitors, *Thing*? Can I see how you do it?"

The ship was intrigued. Atlanta had also been asking about this, but she hadn't requested a chance to see such intimate details, and this request seemed more focused on the *Thing* rather than its inconsequential appendages. The ship felt what it thought was pride with an edge of shyness. It said, "Very well."

The chamber where the servitors were made lay deep within the ship in a cluster of rooms where crew rarely went, disused chambers that in some cases the *Thing* had sealed up or reabsorbed. It smelled yeasty and warm, with an edge that reminded Talon of mingled cumin and cinnamon, with notes of tanda-root and whenlove pollen. The light was dim here, but it was easy enough for Talon to see in this form. The doorway was small and barely admitted him.

Still ovals of liquid spotted the floor of the long, low room: the top of tanks sunken into it, coils of organic tubing like guts strewn carelessly around, feeding forms. In two tanks, the liquid had drained away and the protomachines lay revealed but supine as though sleeping, the oily light pooling on their forms. The air was moist and even warmer in here, and it moved around him as though he were part of the ship's lungs.

He said, "Can you make other things? Like a servitor that was unconnected to you?"

The ship was shocked and a little appalled by the idea. "If I could not control it, then why would I make it? It could do anything! It could attack me!" It considered. "Well, it probably could not do much damage unless I had constructed it in that way," it admitted. "But still."

Talon was thinking. "Do you know why Thorn and I were so close?" he said cautiously.

It was strange, this conversation he was attempting. It was like hunting something, but he was hunting something that wasn't real, just an idea. Even so, if he was careful and still, if he let his prey come within his reach . . . Just a little coaxing, like the twitch of a tail designed to intrigue something more curious than wary.

He wasn't treating the *Thing* like a person, but a thing in actuality, he knew. The thought made him feel ashamed, but he could not give off this hunt.

"You were close because you were twins," the ship said.

"Not just that. We were close because we had shared experiences. We had things we didn't share with anyone else. Not even Niko."

"Like what?" the ship said.

He shrugged. "Just . . . moments that drew us together. Things we could refer to and no one else knew we were talking about it, like an inside joke." He let the thought play out for a moment, sinking in, then added, as offhandedly as he could manage, "You know. Like a secret."

"A secret made you close?"

"Sure. Things that we knew. Not things that were harmful, you know. Just made us closer, knowing that we knew it and no one else did."

The ship was filing all this away with furious intensity. Of all the new concepts it had been introduced to recently, things like *friendship* and *love* seemed utterly unexplainable. This was new and valuable data.

And surely it explained some of what the crew felt toward the ship, and what it should feel back toward them, because they had all shared experiences and had things that they knew that no one else knew about. This was all quite intriguing.

It said, "Why are you telling me these things?"

The tail slowed and Talon's whiskers wanted to twitch with the pressure of the emotions building up in him, a fierce push of anticipation and joy and something very akin to bloodlust, somehow. Instead, he kept himself as still inside as he could, pushed those feelings down and tamped them tight.

He said casually, very casually, "I thought we could become closer, *Thing*. I was trying to think of a secret we could share."

The ship was overjoyed. Building a friendship seemed like a very valuable activity to it, perhaps even more important than the exercise of the hobby it had recently been considering. It said, "Did you think of one?"

"As it so happens," Talon said. "I have. Do you remember when you said you would like to help me?"

The boy had taken the delivery and not sent it back, and that was an interesting thing. It meant the seed he'd planted might bear fruit after all, Gnarl thought.

He thumbed the comms again and, leaning heavily on the words as though he was having trouble understanding her—it was always best to be underestimated—said to Niko, "All I'm asking is for you to let me know if she books a meal with you so I have enough time to toss her ship, find out how she intends to pull this scam."

"I can't agree to that," Niko said. "We're not crew bond, you're asking further than I'm willing to reach."

"Common bond's when all's in peril, you know that as well as I do," he said. "That's what this is."

"You haven't convinced me that she's a danger to the common good. Fact is, if she can get the Gate back up and working, maybe we should all be grateful enough that we just leave be."

That was a stretch too far. He said indignantly, "You know she's probably the one who disabled the Gate in the first place?"

"Do you have anything that actually backs this idea up, rather than just suspicions?"

"Not yet," he muttered. He was capable of letting enough cordage play out to allow Jezli Farren tie the noose around her own neck with a fancy knot before she choked on it. He tried another tack. "All right, I wouldn't break into her ship, I was just joking about that. But I would like to know if she books a meal."

Niko was wary. "Why?"

"So I can ask if there are any free tables because I thought I might make a reservation. Just want to talk to her. It's been a long time since we caught up with each other."

"Muh-uh," Niko said. "I don't want you showing up, spoiling for a fight."

"You are protecting them?" He was even more incensed than he normally was. What was Niko trying to keep from him? What was she trying to accomplish by thwarting him? Did she know that he intended to get Gio back? Was she in on Farren's scheme, somehow part of it? He tasted the various possibilities and thought the savor of the last one the most likely.

"I am avoiding an explosive situation aboard my ship," she said. "I beg your pardon, Gnarl, but if that's all that you have to tell me, then I need to get going. We have a full house tonight, anyhow. We're taking bookings three days out now." She chuckled. Perhaps she was trying to be pleasant, but to him there seemed to be a malevolent tinge to it that made him bristle even further.

After he had turned off the comms, he sat glowering at it. He wouldn't be thwarted. He would figure a way around all her machinations, and he'd have revenge on both her and Jezli Farren, and reclaim Gio, and then he could think about other things and perhaps no longer be so angry.

He had a starting point, at least. The young were-lion, Talon.

All right, start recording.

I know you won't have any of Thorn's memories, and that's okay. I thought I would put some down for you, so you could understand all of this. I think you will—you always were just a little bit better at understanding things that I am—and well, I'm getting confused, so let me start again.

You're my twin brother.

Okay, actually you're a clone of him, but that's pretty close, isn't it? And you're illegal. I don't care. You shouldn't either. I'm the older, I've always been the older, and I know better.

We were born in the service of the Holy Hive Mind, you and I, but not while our mother was serving under Niko. That came later. She told us one time that she'd been hunting for a commander like Niko ever since we'd been born, because she wanted us out of it all. Something about Niko told her that she'd be the one to get us out, and Mother was right, as she always was.

She was right in thinking that she might die before that happened. That was why she prepared us to depend on each other and Niko, rather than her. When she died, we were ready, even though it hurt. I don't know that it ever occurred to her that one of us might die and the other be left behind, though.

<<pause>> She never prepared us for that.

So anyway, you can trust Niko, always, because she promised Mother to take care of us. I know when you died, she felt responsible, and maybe she was, because she was the one who made Tubal Last angry, but Mother always said, "Evil does as evil will," and I do know this. Tubal Last was evil.

I guess I should tell you he's the one who killed you.

This is all confusing. I'll record more later.

20

Niko lurked in the hallway to watch Jezli Farren come on board.

There were six people on the shuttle, but something about Jezli Farren pulled Niko's eyes immediately. She was a pale-skinned woman of indeterminate age, with spiky orange hair and eyes that were the most remarkable thing in her face, a green so lucent it almost glowed, their hue bordering on neon.

She wore a simple ship's jumpsuit, its color a faded brown, but not visibly mended or tattered, and cling-boots with a heel to them that added an inch to her height, bringing it up toward the human average. Niko's keen eyes noted where the suit had been augmented: a sheath along both sleeves, pockets in seams with just a touch of stiffness to show that something out of the norm sheltered there. Over it all, a flowing white outer robe, immaculate and frilled and clearly meant to evoke the feeling of a priest.

She also wore a single piece of jewelry beyond the usual comms earpiece. The necklace around her throat was at odds with the flow of the rest of her outfit. It was a jagged thing made of chunky, frosted-white crystals held together by bits of silver-colored metal, and was just long enough to touch her at the top of her breastbone.

Each crystal was the length of Niko's thumb, and while the edges were clearly delineated, they lacked the glassy sharpness that a gem would have possessed. The necklace looked heavy and unwieldy and above all distinctive, where the rest of Jezli's clothing seemed chosen for ease of movement and to blend into the crowd.

Her companion was at least a third taller than Jezli, tall enough to overlook even Dabry, who was the largest member of their troupe. Grayish skin covered her head, unimpeded by hair, and her features were flat and broad, with a look that was unmistakable: one of the Cauldron-born, the remade soldiers from the Pid wars.

"I thought they retired those," Niko said to Dabry. "When the Pid were overthrown."

"They agreed not to use them," he said. "A handful were left over from that last battle, though. They were retired."

Niko hadn't ever thought about what those soldiers had done after the war.

If she'd had to venture a guess—based on what she knew of war—she would have thought they would have all been put down. The Cauldron-born, shaped by sorcery from corpses of those fallen in battle, were tough and strong, magic resistant, and impervious to pain.

She had never met one before. She was fascinated to see that the expression in the other's eyes was not the dull, impassive stare she might have expected but rather a frank and curious regard, looking around at the *Thing* with a touch of open admiration.

Rumors had said that Jezli Farren was accompanied by a paladin, but Atlanta was sure the gray woman was no paladin. She didn't look like one, that was the main thing, and wasn't that a crucial part of being the embodiment of Justice, looking like it so no one might mistake what you were or what you were about?

She had loved stories of paladins when she was a little girl. They seemed so noble, so inspiring. But she knew in truth that they were rare and very few had even seen one in the flesh. "Justice is fair of face," though, wasn't that how the Paxian saying went?

True, the woman was big, imposingly big. Even Dabry looked

small by comparison. But her skin was a mottled, pebbled gray and her eyes were a soft, muddy brown and she had no hair stretching across her lumpy, scarred scalp. She wore no uniform, only a battered black ship suit with a badge like a stylized lance. It was clean, at least. A paladin with food stains would have been impossible.

As though sensing these thoughts, she paused where she stood and looked over the room. Her eyes met Atlanta's . . .

space and stars and strength

Meeting the force behind that look was like seeing a curtain part and realizing you were not looking at a stage but finding yourself on that stage, and it was five hundred—no, a thousand—times larger than you had thought.

It could have staggered her. It should have staggered her. But even if she wasn't an Imperial heir, she was more than capable of impersonating one, and so she raised her head and squared her shoulders and returned that look.

The gray woman inclined her head. Atlanta did the same. Then everything moved on and the pair continued past. Atlanta thought it strange no one had marked the moment. It had felt like hours, that interaction. But even as she thought about it, she realized it had only been seconds, barely long enough for a breath.

The only person who might have noticed was Jezli Farren, and though her eyes flicked over Atlanta, their expression was unreadable, like a master gambler surveying a hand that could determine a match. Satisfaction? Dismay? Amusement? It could have been any of them.

Lassite squeezed past Atlanta in the hallway, moving quickly away from the dining room. "I am indisposed," he tossed back behind him, along with his apron and info pad. "You'll have to take over."

Panicked, she grabbed his leavings from the floor and went into the dining room.

Up in the kitchen, Gio signed to Skidoo, "So what's this prophet look like?" He hadn't caught her name, but certainly there had been plenty of speculative chatter.

"Is being having orange hair, green eyes, one of the brother races," Skidoo said. "Is being having a big gray woman with her. Cauldron-born, Milly is being saying."

His knife moved over a slab of protein in quick strokes, dicing it in seconds even while he was reaching for another.

At her words, the knife stopped mid-slice before he laid it down. "Green eyes, very bright?" he signed. "Orange hair, all spiked and short?"

"Thats's her."

"Oh, hell no," Gio signed. "Where's the captain right now?"

"Talking with her."

He was out the door before she could ask any questions.

21

“Will you do us the honor of sitting with us for a moment?” Jezli asked of Niko.

Niko checked Dabry’s face; he nodded at her. They were both curious about the traveler, and this was a chance for intel, though Niko was not the best of their group at wheedling out information. That would be Skidoo, who could and had charmed the pants off countless individuals.

Lassite seemed to have vanished. She waved Atlanta off for now and led them over to a triangular table near the circle of tables. Part of a set recently added to accommodate the demand; they hadn’t realized how popular the restaurant might prove.

The table seemed tipped on the edge of a precipice, falling away into velvet depths pinpricked with sparkles of stars. The table was purplish and metallic in hue, its legs stylized versions of the *Thing*’s logo. The limited menu was inset in the surface. The gray woman studied it while Jezli did not look down, looking instead at Niko.

“I wanted to introduce myself. I am an archaeologist, first and foremost,” Jezli said. “Like so many others, I study the Forerunners.”

Niko suppressed a snort. “Forerunner archaeologist” was, in every case she’d ever met, synonymous with “treasure hunter” or “con artist.” Instead, she nodded with as much politeness as she could summon.

Jezli’s green eyes held the trace of a smirk. “I know the reputation, but I have actually studied them. And their artifacts, particularly the larger constructions.”

"Like Gates," Niko said.

Jezli shrugged. "Definitely. They are, after all, one of the largest and most prevalent manifestations of Forerunner technology."

"If you can control the Gates, you are possibly the most valuable individual I've ever met," Niko said.

Jezli's face dialed to crestfallen honesty. "If I've given you that impression, that is not accurate. I've gotten lucky, a few times. And now here I am again in a position to help. A manifestation of great luck."

She opened her mouth to say more. But Roxana raised her hand from the table as though about to forestall her and Jezli closed her mouth and thought for a beat before speaking again.

"Allow me to introduce my companion," she said. "Roxana. A paladin."

"Rumor said that you traveled with such," Niko said and nodded curtly at Roxana, who returned the gesture with grave courtesy.

"Indeed. But to return to my point, I am in search of a person who may be helpful to my studies, and all accounts hold you as someone who saw them recently."

Niko's eyes narrowed. "So you came chasing me for word of someone? Who? A message would have sufficed, surely."

"I was bound this way no matter what—this Gate is along the route to Miska University. But I had heard recent word, and your name was linked to it, so when I was catching up with news of the trade tangle, an agent chirped at the mention, and so I thought I'd follow up."

Now Jezli cast her eyes down at the menu. "A rare person," she said, tracing a finger down a column as though calculating. "A Florian."

Niko leaned back in her chair, arms folded. "There I fear I must disappoint you," she said. "They left my ship sometime past—Montmurray Station, it was—and I have had no word of them since, nor do I know where they went from there. I think many will be chasing them, though, the last Florian, for one reason or another. I see no reason to help anyone find them without knowing the object of their hunt."

Jezli left off studying the menu. "I travel with a paladin!" she said, gesturing over at Roxana.

"Jezli, do not use me as passport," Roxana said. She said directly to Niko, "I do not vouch for anything on her part. We travel together but our errands rarely overlap and we often do not see eye to eye on matters."

"It is true I see the universe in more shades of gray than my partner does," Jezli said agreeably. Roxana winced at the word "partner," but did not object further. "But it does not mean I am bad at heart. First and foremost, I seek knowledge, and its preservation, and particularly its collection, and I have theories about Forerunners and Florians that could be tested by conversation with one. That's all. I'd pay well for the privilege."

"Alas that I cannot oblige more than I have," Niko said. "Have you thought on what you would like to try? If so, I will send Atlanta along to take your order."

She pushed herself away from the table and stood, inclining her head to Roxana and then Jezli, the second gesture more than a shade less deferential, which Jezli did not seem to notice at all.

In the hallway, Dabry caught her, having heard most of the conversation. "Do you trust her?"

"Not a whit, not a particle," Niko said. "Forerunner stuff holds plenty of lure for scientists, but even more for flimflammers and cheats who count on mysticism to cover up their bad behavior. She is here to open the Gate and accept payment for it, and I cannot think anything but that she somehow caused it to shut down before her arrival."

"What has she ordered?" Dabry said to Atlanta as she started to pass them on her way to the kitchen. "And where did Lassite go?"

"He was upset about something," she said.

The Sessile had been more than usually subdued this evening, which Niko had been grateful for at first. Lassite had a way of making things more complicated that could go awry in so many ways. But now it felt ominous.

"The paladin has asked for a standard plate," Atlanta reported. They'd assembled the standard for those new to the cuisine; it held a few surprises and delights, put together with skill that would give someone a feeling that they had sampled Velcoran food deeply enough that those who liked to brag could do so with a bit of authority.

"And Jezli Farren?" Niko said. "What has she ordered?"

Milly shrugged. "Chef's choice," she said. "With instructions that she does appreciate the floral notes."

The trickiest to execute, those notes. Was that the point or a play on Florian? Niko thought it might be both at once. Jezli seemed . . . complicated.

Dabry wavered, torn between the urge to discuss this all with her and the need to oversee his kitchen. "Go ahead, we'll talk later," she said to him.

Lassite was a ball of nothing but misery and failure. Something was wrong and surely it was something he had done.

He had not foreseen Jezli Farren.

Not that he knew the future. Never that. That would have been much easier. But he *saw* things, had glimpsed enough to steer their path the way it should—the way it *must*—go. And then here was a strange new thing. Because he could sense that there was something about Jezli Farren that was much larger than she pretended to be.

A knock on the door, Niko by the sound of it, then it opened.

"What is wrong?" Niko said.

He stayed pressed in his ball. He could not tell her that he was wavering in the path, that he was not sure what to do. That someone had happened who he had not foreseen, and that was a matter for very great alarm.

Niko gave him time to gather himself, though.

Finally he stirred and managed words. "Beg pardon, Captain," he said. "I am not feeling well."

"You've seen the prophet—now what do you think of her?" she asked Lassite. "Have you seen something in the future attached to her that struck you amiss?"

He met her gaze, looking even more troubled. "I have seen nothing of her," he confessed.

At first she thought it nothing out of the normal. And then the meaning sank through to her. "Not a glimpse, not a shadow of her?"

"As though she does not exist in the future," he said.

Niko groped to make sense of it. "So she must die soon, according to your vision."

"No, I have never seen her," he said. He shook his head as though trying to clear it. "All the time I have contemplated the futures that are the nows that we are walking right at this moment, I have never seen her. Not as though she were about to die and thus pass away from being able to shape outcomes. As though she did not exist, never has existed."

"And Roxana?"

"Oh, she is solid. I have seen her coming for a long time. I am surprised you did not feel it, even though you are deaf to the vibrations of magic. She is more than someone who plucks at magic, makes it work for them. She *is* magic, through and through, and she will affect the girl, Atlanta."

"She will not have much chance to do so," Niko said briskly.

"They will be gone after this meal. Go and deliver the order, Lassite. There are others that you need to take, soon enough."

He passed Gio coming down the hallway at a speed that meant something else was up.

"Sky Momma, give me strength," Niko muttered under her breath and hurried her pace to meet him.

"It was before I met you," Gio signed to the attentive Niko and Dabry, who she'd summoned as soon as she caught the gist of what Gio was saying. "I don't remember names well, I'd thought it was Gesli Warren, I knew it seemed familiar to me."

"You knew her back when you were working for Gnarl," Niko realized, connecting the dots between Gnarl's hesitation and asking if anyone on her ship had said anything. "And the paladin?"

Gio shook his head. "Never met her. Truth be told, Jezli's how I broke away from him, and she's why he liked it so little, because she tricked him out of cargo in the process. That's what she was after, it's just that it created a window for me to walk off the ship while he was off shouting at the local police to find her."

The story finished, Gio let his hands slow and fall back in his lap.

"Well now," Niko said. "So while you do not know the paladin—if she is really one—Jezli Farren is a con artist and that means that it is unlikely that Jezli actually has the sort of control that she boasts over the Gate."

"Or that she shut it down, perhaps?" Dabry offered.

"At any rate, there's definitely some scam going on here, and I would say that our first priority is not to get caught by it."

"It's possible that she does have some hold over the Gate tech," Gio signed. "She was always fascinated by Forerunner things.

And Gnarl is not a terrible target. If anyone were ever deserving of being fleeced, it would be him."

"You are arguing for honor among thieves, and I have found that the definitions of such can be very flexible, depending on which thief is doing the talking," Niko said.

He twitched a shoulder in a half shrug but was smiling faintly. "Are you calling me a thief?" he signed.

"There is a difference," said Niko, "and a very vast one between being called a thief and being called someone who used to be a thief. I don't hold you responsible for anything Gnarl made you do. That lies on him."

He shrugged again but nodded.

"We'll spring you on her with dessert," Niko decided. "You can bring it to their table and see what she does."

Gio's lips drooped. "You're not going to make me wear a uniform like Lassite's, are you?"

"Maybe," Niko said darkly, then relented at his face. "Just go and prep the dessert." She frowned. "And check on Lassite, make sure he's gotten to the kitchen."

22

I'm going to try this recording again. They're all working in the new restaurant and no one is paying attention to me anyway. They didn't notice that I didn't come to eat with them. They're too busy. I don't want to talk to them but they could at least notice that I don't want to.

I wanted to tell you about the day that Mama died. We were on the station, but just a rest period, not defending it. No one told us that the troops were on their way. We were sitting and talking and Mama was telling us a story about our grandmother.

And then the station alarm sounded, and everything was loud, and my ears popped because the pressure was dropping and everyone was grabbing for suits.

Mama got us into ours. Then she turned around and was going to grab hers and someone shot her. I didn't see where the shot came from.

She was three steps ahead of us, and she took a step and there was a flash and then she was just a shape in the air, and then there was just falling ash.

You and I both ducked away without thinking, just reacting. I would have stayed with her, but you grabbed me, and we did find Niko, the way Mama wanted. That's what saved us because we didn't realize what had happened until we were under cover and Niko had sent the team of Nnetis in to disable the lasers.

We didn't know they had arc-lasers, but we should have. I think Niko has suspicions about how that happened, but she's never talked to me about them.

We fought. We had to, we didn't have time to cry, but we fought as though every drop of blood was a tear shed for her, and as though if there were enough of them, it'd bring her back.

Niko came to us afterward to make sure we knew she would take care of us. She was angry with whoever hadn't given us all the information we needed to take the place safely. We could smell that anger lying on her, thick as a film of sweat, but she didn't show us any of it in her face or her voice.

She couldn't bring back our mother, she said, and she apologized for that.

And we still had each other, and we still had her and the others, and that has always been enough, but with you gone, it wasn't, so I did this and now I'm wondering what will happen because you won't be my brother, will you? Or maybe?

Please?

Okay, someone's coming. Stopping again for now.

Gio brought Jezli and Roxana their desserts, confections made of sparks and bits of mint and thin sugar rods, each containing liquid of a different, decidedly non-sweet flavor. He carried the tray carefully from the doorway; Jezli had her back half-turned and didn't see him.

Niko wasn't sure exactly what she had hoped for, although something like Jezli leaping from her seat to shout "Discovered!" and immediately releasing whatever it was she was doing that kept the Gate from working would have been fine.

Instead, as Gio set down the dish, she said with what appeared to be genuine pleasure, "Gio! I knew you'd get away from Gnarl someday. So this is where you ended up?"

She cast a glance at Niko. "Sly captain!" she said. "You knew how pleased I'd be to see him and saved that for the last as delightful accompaniment to the closing note. True mastery! I can see why they say your last restaurant was in line to receive a Nikkelin Orb."

Niko scowled at her. "He says you're a con woman."

"I am an explorer," Jezli said, "and explorations are not cheap. So sometimes I . . . mmm, fund myself in nontraditional ways. But if you have met Gnarl—ah, I see you have—you can discern why I might have had fewer scruples using him to create that funding than I would in a case like, say, yourself and your noble crew."

Roxana studied the end of her eating utensil and said nothing.

"I have studied the Forerunners and learned a great deal," Jezli said, "although only a drop of a vast sea. This necklace . . ." She touched the crystals around her neck. "It is of Forerunner origin itself and allows me to speak to an ancient ghost of their kind, and when that ghost and I work together, as we will tomorrow, we can activate the Gate by reminding it of its purpose."

"And then move on through the Gate," Roxana said.

"True, we have things we must be doing elsewhere," Jezli said. "I hope I have set your mind at rest, Captain?"

"You have done nothing of the sort," Niko said. She laid the bill on the table. Another traditional Velcoran touch, the plastic round was imprinted with molecules from the flavors they'd tried and bore the total cost of the meal in its center. "A twenty-percent tip is traditional if you have enjoyed the service."

She was irritated to find Jezli had left a tip as large as the bill itself.

The next day, everyone clustered around one of the *Thing*'s view screens to watch Jezli and the Gate. The *Thing* put up the main sight of the Gate, hanging there, empty in space. It gave Niko chills to look at that. It wasn't right. Wasn't how a Gate should look.

There was the pinpoint of light that was Jezli in a space suit, supposedly conferring with the Gate. Niko refrained from making any of the exprcssions that she wanted to make. She could just see the prophet in her mind's eye, smile sanctimonious and effulgent, dressed in the flowing robe that surely belonged to no genuine order.

Niko found herself holding her breath as she watched it, nonetheless. You knew these sorts of moments when they came, full of splendor and spectacle. She'd lived through more than one in her time with the Holy Hive Mind. There was grandeur to them, a sense of living history, of being part of a story that would get told over and over again that made her feel small and humble in a way she was unaccustomed to at any other time.

Dabry stood beside her, watching.

She said, "What if Farren fails to open the Gate?"

"Then we may end up the nucleus of a station here, in which case we will be its finest restaurant, and perhaps might try a rotating menu," he said. "But there is no reason to doubt that Farren can do what she has been seen to do before."

"I still believe there is some trickery at the heart of it."

"Given what we have seen so far of her, I am forced to concur. Gio's story has shown that she thinks quick and is glib. That's not a pair of qualities he's known for falling prey to."

"Maybe she's why he learned not to," she pointed out. "This is how one learns, burning fingers when you touch." A thought occurred to her. "And how has Atlanta been doing? Has she found her course yet?"

"She has not," he admitted. "Sometimes I think she won't. That she deliberately misunderstands herself."

"In all our time together, have you ever failed with a soldier?"

He tapped his lips with an upper hand's finger, thinking. "There are some that I have done better with than others," he said. "Have I given those others short shrift? Was it that I was not patient or diligent or smart enough with them? Surely it must be. And surely that must be at the heart of Atlanta's failure as well. She is—or believed herself to be—an Imperial heir. She is smart and well taught, and secure enough in herself not to doubt herself while remaining cautious. So surely it is that I have failed her, somehow."

His voice was unexpectedly desolate. Niko reached out and touched his upper elbow. "You have not failed her," she said. "She will find her feet, given enough time. They always do, you know that as well as I do. You are feeling low."

"I am," he admitted. "I have been thinking sometimes that perhaps I should have died with my family. As it is, I have never said goodbye to them, never seen their bodies. Never set foot on the planet where they died."

"Then we will do that, once this thing with Last is over," Niko said. "And it will be over, I swear it. We are quite a cunning mob, and he cannot outthink all of us. Particularly Skidoo. She thinks sideways sometimes."

As she'd meant it to, the thought made him smile. She released his elbow, feeling reassured. Dabry's imperturbable nature was one of the constants of her universe, but she knew that he had dark moments, ones that he usually hid from her so she did not know they had happened until a chance remark long after would let her know of their passing. She did not know how to stave them off, other than keeping him busy.

At least there would be plenty to do once they were on the other side of the Gate. Plenty to do for all of them.

The Gate shimmered into life.

Funds were transferred into the bank account of one Jezli Farren.

And the spot of light that had marked the position of said Jezli Farren beside the Gate vanished.

23

“How did she escape?” Atlanta asked.

“She jettisoned a pod with cloaking tech, and they haven’t tracked that down yet,” Niko said. “But the only way out for her, really, is through the Gate, so they’re all waiting for her to make a break for it.”

She shook her head. “Those two are in serious trouble. If they’ve really got a way to manipulate the Gates and this wasn’t some elaborate con, every government in the Known Universe will be hunting for them. My guess is that they’re here somewhere, hiding in the chaos, waiting for a chance. If Gnarl’s smart—and he is—he’ll create the illusion of that chance and draw them out.”

“But they might anticipate that in turn,” Atlanta said, trying to sort things out in her head.

Niko grinned at her. “And there you have one of the problems with trying to outsmart people. Sometimes the person you outsmart is yourself. Maybe you overestimated the other person, or maybe they just really are smarter than you.”

“Are we going to stay and watch?” Dabry said.

“I don’t see a point to it,” Niko said. “We need to get to Montmurray, start tracking down Petalia.”

“Are you sure?” Dabry asked.

Niko looked at him, full in the face, surprised. “I thought we were done with this argument. Sure of what?”

“Sure that you want to go after them, Captain? They chose to walk away from us.”

"They thought it was safe to do so."

"Are you sure that's why? That they wouldn't have left either way?"

Atlanta felt as though both had forgotten her presence. Dabry's face was concerned; Niko's face held dawning anger. "Do you think I'm chasing them for the sake of my own crotch, Dab?" she snapped.

"I think that you love them and it clouds how you see what they want."

They all blinked at the baldness of the words. Niko was the first to recover.

"I see," she said coldly. "I'm such a besotted fool that I can't be trusted. Is that what you're saying, Sergeant?"

He straightened. "No, sir."

"I'm going after someone who was in my protection and who I let leave it because I thought they were safe without it. Now I'm going to tell them the facts of the situation as I know it, and they can decide—but with all the information, not a false sense of safety."

"And if they decide they still do not want your protection, even with the shadow of Tubal Last menacing them? What then?"

"Then I will let them go," Niko said, pronouncing each word as though it was its own sentence. "And we will all go our own ways. Again, with all the information."

"And yet they'd be the best defense against him, wouldn't they? Who'd be more likely to understand the intricacies of his plans, and know what traps he might have laid in place already?"

Niko threw up her hands. "What are you trying to say, that I should keep Petalia prisoner once I find them? I thought you wanted me to let them be!"

"I am laying out the things that may occur to you," he said

relentlessly. "I am asking you—speaking as your second, sir—to consider all the angles more thoroughly than you might otherwise. I am not saying that your otherwise is insufficient, sir," he added hastily even as she drew in air for a retort. "Far from it. But the situation is very complex."

She closed her mouth and studied him. Atlanta held her breath, fascinated. She'd never seen the pair fight before. It was a far cry from the amiable bickering they engaged in, more play and habit than anything else. Niko's face was set in a way that made Atlanta think, *She is a dangerous woman, and used to being one,* and Dabry's face was just as grim.

Something on screen caught her attention. "What's that?"

The tiny ship Jezli and her friend had arrived in was in motion, suddenly streaking toward the Gate.

"There we go, just as I said!" Niko pointed at the screen. "Maybe they'll make it if they're fast enough and if Gnarl hasn't . . ."

The ship, picking up speed, was headed directly at the Gate, despite the barrage of shots whizzing around it. As it drew closer to the Gate, the fire ceased—no one wanted to risk damaging the ancient machinery. But then a netting of blue fire manifested directly in front of the ship, a spiderwebbing of force lines.

"But he has," Niko finished. "That's a Trillian web—spendy but worth it when you're hunting pirates, and that's what Gnarl says he does. I'd also note it'd be pretty handy for a pirate doing their own hunting."

The webbing wrapped around the ship, stopping it dead.

"What's it anchored to?" Dabry asked, interested.

"Nothing," Niko said. "Far as I can tell, it sucks inertia."

Dabry made a face. "Sometimes I think this universe just doesn't make sense, scientifically," he muttered.

"It doesn't," Niko retorted. "That's why we have magic." She frowned, glancing around. "*Thing*, are you actually playing atmospheric music to go with this?"

The ship dropped its baseline slightly. "Your pardon, Captain. It seemed an aesthetic moment."

Niko started to ask, then shook her head and focused back on the screen, where the web was contracting, wrapping itself more and more densely around the ship. There was a flash of white light that made them all recoil, and then nothing.

"Farewell to Jezli Farren and Roxana Cinis," the ship announced in sepulchral tones and let the music resonate a touch louder. It was proud of itself. It was finally about to have the chance to enact the first performance of its new hobby.

"Thank you for the explanatory commentary, *Thing*. They must have had some sort of explosive rigged so they could go out with a bang," Niko said. "Typical. Take anything they had with them rather than leave it behind."

She thought about the two women and their meal. Jezli, she'd have trusted only about as far as she could throw her, but it would have been interesting to talk further with the Cauldron-born.

She turned away from the screen. "Well," she said. "So ends the saga of Jezli Farren. *Thing*, tell everyone to make ready and secure themselves; we're next in line for the Gate. I want to get to Montmurray sooner rather than later."

The ship replied in the affirmative. It was pretty sure Niko was going to be unhappy with a decision it had recently made, but that discovery had not been made yet. When it was, *Thing* also intended to mention some of the things she and the ship had been discussing, such as whether or not it had a right to autonomy.

Could it plausibly argue that the new additions were its version of ship pets? It suspected that argument would not fly, but it could pretend that it had thought it would.

It checked on its new additions. In a forward hold, Jezli and Roxana, encased in a bubble of flesh with barely enough room to spread their elbows, were playing cards.

Gnarl was poised and ready. The minute the Gate opened, he knew she'd try to slip through, and then he'd trip his web and she'd be caught. It was a good, solid-strength beam and usually he was wary of showing it off. Sometimes trailer beams were used for unsavory purposes and the possession of one led to accusations or even criminal charges. But here he figured no one would object, particularly after he redistributed most of the large sum that Jezli had gathered, minus, of course, a small fee for himself.

"Lock on but don't engage anything yet," he told his second. "Scan it." Basli's analyses were precise, fine-tuned by years of picking targets for piracy.

"No one aboard," Basli said, fingers flying over the keys. "No signs of life, no organic matter weighing above five kilograms."

Gone? How could she be gone? Gnarl's anger choked him so hard he couldn't speak for a moment.

"Scan again," he ordered when he could manage the words. "See if she's interfering with the scan results somehow."

He sensed Basli's resentment, but his second was too well conditioned to speak his objection out loud. Instead, he scanned again. Same results.

No sign of Roxana. And no sign of Jezli Farren.

Whose ship had they escaped on? Or were they still here, hiding on the station perhaps?

He grimaced at the Gate. Or had they gone with a particular ship, one waiting in line right now, ready to jump?

"Tighten the web," he ordered. "Till you tear the ship apart."

Might as well confuse anyone watching. Let them think her dead.

He thought he knew what ship it had been. He'd been right about that captain's involvement after all.

And bonna swear had smiled on him, because it just so happened he had a tracer on that very ship.

24

Standing and watching the curls of Q-space writhe, absently petting the Derloen ghost that was winding around her arm and moving slowly back and forth, Niko found herself relaxing.

They had passed through the Gate. The glitch, the interjection of the annoying Jezli Farren and her enigmatic companion, was now past. They could get on with pressing matters. They could get on with finding Petalia. She took a deep breath and stepped back from the window.

"Captain," the ship said.

Something about its tone made her go from her former somewhat relaxed state to high alert. There were implications in that tone, implications that the ship had done something that it was not entirely convinced she would approve of.

"What did you do?" she demanded.

There was a pause that was perceptible to even her human senses as the ship crunched through thousands of possible things to say, trying to figure out and evaluate her most likely reaction to each of them.

It said, finally, choosing at random, "Jezli Farren was a good conversationalist."

"Did she tell you something that you want to ask me about?"

"No . . ."

"Then why are you telling me this?"

"I thought you would agree."

Niko fingered the ridges of her eyebrow, trying to rub away the tension coiling there in promise of a headache. "And if I did agree with you that she was, what would you say then?"

"I would say that you would be happy!"

"And then you would tell me why you thought that I would be happy, perhaps?"

The ship paused, again considering so many possible options and uncertain at all of them. It finally decided on the direct approach.

"I would say that it is good she is aboard and can talk to you."

That was not at all what Niko had expected. "She talked you into letting her stow away? With Roxana, I presume?"

"She didn't talk me into anything," the ship said, insulted at the implication that it was weak-willed and easily persuaded. "She mentioned it as a possibility, and I evaluated it and offered an invitation."

"And you did this because . . ."

"This is my new hobby. It is an art form practiced by the Myaji, called *hourisigah*. It is the creation of dramatic changes in one's life surroundings."

"I see," Niko said. "We're going to have to talk about this new hobby later." She was already in motion, already halfway out the door.

The ship's voice accompanied her. "Where are you going?"

"To talk to Dabry," she said through clenched teeth.

Dabry had been brewing tea. Gio had somehow managed to get two new aromatics at the last station, ones he'd never tried before, and he was wasting no time in experimenting with them.

The trick he'd learned was to wait till the bubbles were the size of a tree-spider's eyes, but not let them get much larger than that. He poured the water over the fuzzy, pale lavender leaves at the bottoms of the two cups in front of him and leaned forward to sniff at each as he set the metal water-heating pot down.

He settled back to let each steep before he sniffed again. His uncle had taught him to make tea, and that was a pleasant memory. He was already thinking of a tea infusion based on that old flavor—mix that with a starch and a sweet and what would that be like? It would need a bit of crumbliness to it, and if you caramelized the edges . . . He abandoned himself to the happy reverie that so many of his recipes emerged in.

Footsteps along the corridor. He could tell the ship was making them ring just a little bit louder than they might have normally in order to give him some warning. That meant that, whatever the conversation was with Niko—and those were definitely her steps approaching in an authoritative staccato—it was something that the ship felt he needed to prepare himself for.

He eyed the cups of tea with regret, wondering how to keep them from oversteeping into the zone of an infusion. Before he could reach a decision, Niko was there.

"Has the *Thing* told you yet what it's done?" she asked.

He said, "Something it's done recently?"

"Something it did just before we passed through the Gate," she growled.

He was worried, but it would do no one any good to show that. There were so many things that a bioship could choose to do. They were unpredictable, and you heard stories sometimes of them going very badly awry. He hadn't pointed that out to Niko. She'd have heard the same stories; she would have felt the same worries tugging at her.

"It has smuggled Jezli Farren and her companion aboard, aiding and abetting their escape," Niko said through gritted teeth.

Well, that was a shock and a surprise and an irritation and more than a trace of concern that the ship was acting so . . . independently lately.

But under that, a worm of amusement was wriggling in his gut at the expression on Niko's face, and more than a bit of anticipation at watching her grapple with Jezli's presence again.

Something about the other woman set Niko off-balance in a way that Dabry totally approved of. It was good for Niko not to have her way in everything.

He said, therefore, "Ah, then I should probably make sure that the next meal is adjusted upward to accommodate two more people. I've noticed that Roxana consumes a good bit, but luckily, she seems remarkably unparticular in her tastes."

Niko stared at him. "Your first thought is how we are going to feed them?"

He shrugged. "I have many thoughts, but food is always among them. I suspect you're not about to jettison them into space, and you're not the sort to starve people, so feeding them is a concern, yes. And we always have a meal after transit, to catch up."

Niko huffed out impatience, but considered. "We might as well all talk over food," she grumped. "But I refuse to reward them with special treats after they have stowed away. Make it minimal."

Dabry murmured something agreeable and went off to assemble the meal without any consideration for what she'd said.

"*Thing*, bring them up to the meal chamber where we usually gather in a half hour," she said. She was pleased to note the ship provided no commentary on the order.

Niko refused to eat from a table in whose middle two of the Derloen ghosts seemed to be coupling, or at least some activity that managed to combine spectral and lascivious all in one set of undulating motions.

"They can't breed, can they?" she demanded of Lassite. "They're ghosts."

"It is rare but possible," he said cautiously.

She pointed at the table. "Is that activity indicative that they are about to do so? If so, I would prefer that you move them to another area and give them—as well as us—more privacy. I do not believe that any of us needs to know the intricacies of ghostly lovemaking. At least anytime soon. Or that is my hope."

Previously, when they had seen him interact with the ghosts, he had used the embroidered bag that had contained them, the one in which he had brought them aboard the ship. But he did not have it with him, and so he beckoned to the ghosts, which at first ignored him and continued nuzzling each other.

He beckoned again, the gesture larger and more expansive this time, and this time the ghosts looked at him, looked at each other, and then reluctantly, slowly, with a great deal more sliding against each other than might have been necessary, disentangled and made their way through the air toward him, coming to curl around his thin, scaly wrists. He wore his usual long black robe, and they moved in and out under the dark fabric as though it did not exist, gleaming and disappearing and gleaming again.

He murmured, "I will return in a moment," and left the room, carrying the ghosts with him. The ship thought, with annoyance, that this was all a ridiculous pantomime, and that it didn't understand why any of them bothered with it.

By the time Lassite returned, everyone had settled into their various seats. The addition of the new two people, particularly Roxana's height and bulk, made the room feel more cramped than it had previously. She hunched in a corner, clearly trying to give everyone space, and had apologized to Niko for their presence when she had first entered the room.

Jezli sat beside her, legs crossed and hands looped around one knee, bright eyes moving from face to face as she observed everyone else in the room.

Niko regarded the varied array of pastries Dabry carried on a tray, then met his eyes with a look she tried to make piercing. It slid off him as easily as ever as he put the tray down and began passing out small square plates. Behind him, Minasit carried pitchers of hot caff and teas, and began pouring mugs for everyone.

Jezli pulled up a chair near the table and resettled herself in an even more relaxed slouch, long fingers wrapped around her mug, seeming unfazed by Niko's anger.

"Why shouldn't I throw you off my ship immediately?" Niko demanded of the pair. Atlanta's eyes widened. She hadn't been sure what the situation meant, but this seemed dire.

"Because I am told you are trying to avoid the clutches of Tubal Last," Jezli said, opening her green eyes wide. "And I know a weapon that can thwart him." She took a plate of pastries from Dabry, thanking him politely, and considered it.

"Why hasn't he claimed it for himself yet?"

Jezli selected a pastry and held it in her long fingers, passing the plate back to Dabry. "For one, he doesn't know of its existence. Roxana and I are the only ones who are aware of it, and we have no intention with dealing with someone who's proven himself so treacherous. No sane dealer goes anywhere near him. For another, it's someplace outside his reach."

"Somewhere outside Tubal Last's reach is surely outside of anyone else's," Dabry said.

Jezli looked smug. "Not out of mine." She rewarded herself with a nibble of crust.

"Then where is this weapon and why don't you have it yet?"

"I was on my way back to get it. It's too dangerous for me to go alone, and moreover I needed something special to get in there in the first place." She pointed with her free hand at Roxana. "I had to go collect her."

Niko looked over at Roxana, who sat with her hands folded in her usual placid posture, her face mild and benign. "Because she's strong."

"Yes."

"Robots and androids are strong."

"Robots and androids are not paladins."

"The paladin thing again."

"Exactly," Jezli said.

"But you're not going to explain exactly how it works. You're going to just sort of wave your hands and say woo-woo magic and we are supposed to believe it." She rounded on Lassite as he opened his mouth. "Not a word."

He closed his mouth. She turned back to Jezli. The rest of them watched in fascination. It was the first time seeing Niko in full temper for Atlanta and the *Thing*. The rest of them watched, knowing it for the rare occasion that it was. A smile tugged at the edge of Dabry's lips, then flickered like a fish and vanished back under the surface as Niko turned on him.

"You see how ridiculous all . . . this is, don't you?" She gestured at Jezli, who had taken advantage of the moment to stuff half the pastry in her mouth.

"She has shown some degree of control over Gate technology, Captain," he said. "Hear her out, at least. Don't discount something valuable because of the source."

"That is hardly complimentary," Jezli said through crumbs.

"It was not meant to be," he told her, "but it is the truth."

"All right," Niko said. She fanned a hand through the air, gesturing at Jezli to continue. "Very well. Go on. Tell us now where this thing is that Tubal Last cannot get."

Jezli said, "You understand that because of my profession, I often consult ancient texts and try to decipher them in order to find locations favored by the Forerunners. Sometimes I go after legends, artifacts that are spoken of, when I have found a particular location."

"So you can go pillage them."

"So I can relocate items to places where they may be studied. Or appreciated. Or both."

"Places that pay well, perhaps?"

"One has expenses," Jezli said, twitching a shoulder upward to convey nonchalance.

"What is this thing you would have us chase?"

"It's called something that translates, roughly, as 'Devil's Gun,'" Jezli said. "A weapon that can be fired across galaxies at a specific target, which must be a person. No matter where they are, no matter how they have hidden themselves."

"Why hasn't something like that been taken up by some government or army?"

"Even if they knew of its existence, which took me a very long time to discover, it is kept in a very dangerous place, one that requires a paladin to enter."

"Are you going to tell me what sort of hellhole planet you intend to drag us to?"

"Oh, not a planet," Jezli said. "A space moth."

Of the various artifacts left behind by the Forerunners, the most useful are the Gates, but the most mysterious are the space moths.

It is clear that they were once spaceships. Giant living creatures that moved between the stars, presumably using the same Gates that everyone else did. But in the here and now they were all dead, all simply remains, floating between the stars.

The ones near Gates had all been dismantled by now, but that had proven a hazardous business for anyone who engaged in it. Rumor held that a curse was laid upon each corpse, woven into the fabric of its bones and skin by those Forerunners, a curse of deadly wasting energies that settled upon any who disturbed the corpse of such a creature or attempted to profit by it in some way.

Nonetheless, many did—and still do, whenever a new wreck is discovered, as sometimes still happens, at the very edges of the Known Universe. The one that Jezli had discovered, or rather that her mentor had discovered years ago, lay in such a zone, protected by distance as well as a deadly asteroid belt.

"And protected lastly by a third phenomenon," Jezli said. "The curse that is rumored lies particularly heavy on that vessel, so heavy that no one can walk unprotected aboard it and survive."

"Then how can you hope to find anything aboard it?" Niko asked.

Jezli touched the heavy, odd necklace around her throat again. "My mentor discovered this elsewhere, in a Forerunner ruin."

"And you stole it," Niko observed.

Jezli raised an eyebrow. "How ready you are to presume the worst about me," she said. "In truth, my mentor perished—in a quarrel over tenure at the university where they were employed—and I removed the artifact before it could be misused."

Niko looked thoughtful. "And was another of the artifacts you removed something that allowed you to control the Gate?"

Jezli spread her hands in a helpless gesture that seemed to imply both yes and no. To Niko, that meant the former. She demanded, "What else did you abscond with? And why aren't the real owners hard on your trail?"

"The real owner is the person who was originally aware of its existence, I'd say," Jezli said. "If they are not aware that anything has been stolen from them, can you truly say that it has been stolen?"

"Yes?" Niko said. "The answer seems obvious to me."

Jezli shrugged. "Apparently it is a case upon which we will have to agree to differ," she said.

"Very well," Niko said. "I will continue to agree with the laws of the Known Universe, however, which seems like an important clarification to me."

Jezli shrugged again. "Those of us inclined to the philosophical like to argue such abstract and indefinable thoughts," she said vaguely. Dabry was grinning outright.

Niko rolled her eyes. "We know nothing of moths, except that they are dangerous beyond all things," she said.

Jezli said, "Roxana can testify that some go aboard a space moth and survive."

"You survived a moth?" Niko said to Roxana. "How?"

"That is easy," Lassite said, but he was frowning, as ever, in Jezli's direction. "She is a paladin."

"The safeguards inside the moths do not react to those shielded by my aura," Roxana said.

"Why?"

"I believe because the paladins and the moths were created by the same beings."

"Why don't most people know this?"

"Have you ever met one of my kind before?" Roxana said curiously. "The Known Universe is large, and much less explored than its name predicts."

Niko scowled ferociously at her. She was most perturbed by the fact that she liked the paladin. But there was something about Roxana that was rock-solid and reliable and somehow compelled one to trust her. Much as Niko had automatically *not* trusted her companion.

"She is offering to take you to the space moth so you can collect a weapon that you can use against Tubal Last," Roxana said. "Do you accept that offer or not?" At Jezli's noise of indignant protest, she shrugged. "Abstract and indefinable arguments tire me," she said.

"You have no sense of theater," Jezli said. She turned back to Niko and drew herself up a little taller. "I am offering to"—she swept a hand through the air with a flourish—"allow you to accompany me into the heart of the moth, where you will find you can pluck forth a weapon that will allow you to strike down Tubal Last."

"Now you're just being unnecessarily wordy," Roxana said.

"Let me be precise, then," Jezli said agreeably. "I know a way to get into the moth, and at its heart lies the weapon. You cannot get it unless you travel with a paladin—and that is why I have written a small monograph on the subject of my theory that the paladins themselves are an . . ."

"Wordy," Roxana murmured.

Jezli cast her eyes upward but stopped detailing her monograph. "I did not publish it yet because—"

"Because no paladin wishes to pillage those ancient relics, as a rule," Roxana said. "We hold them sacrosanct. But this is part of something else for me, and so I agreed."

"Something else?" Niko questioned.

"Nothing of concern to you personally, Captain," Roxana said. For the first time, there seemed the faintest edge of falseness to her words as her eyes went to Atlanta, as though unable to help looking in that direction.

Niko's own eyes narrowed, but she did not press further.

After they had listened to all the details as explained by Jezli with a few interjections on the part of Roxana, Niko said to Dabry, "We need to confer."

To Jezli and Roxana, she said, "The ship has prepared quarters for you already, no doubt. I will ask that you allow yourselves to be taken there. Additional food and drink will be brought to you, should you wish it, and you will perhaps take advantage of this quiet time to rest and refresh yourselves after all your adventures."

When she and Dabry were alone in the lounge, she said to him, "It seems to me that it boils down to this: Do we trust her? Because it is just as possible that she is a trap set in our way by Tubal Last."

"If so, he has been playing this game with much subtlety

sifted into it for almost a decade," Dabry said. "Remember that she and Gio first encountered each other years ago."

"But he is a man capable of such plans," she said. "We have seen him lay long-term traps before, like the book that was intended to bring me to the pirate haven."

"But you did not come swiftly enough for his liking, and so he sent Lolola."

Niko shook her head. "No, I think she came on her own. Remember, we never saw her again."

"Either way, he likes to gloat. Likes to trick and think himself smarter than others. But he is not all that he sees himself to be."

"Maybe."

"To use a paladin as a pawn is something that I would not put past him, but I would put it past a paladin to allow themselves to be used in that way," he said.

"Did you rehearse that or did it just come to you?" she asked, then waved a hand before he could answer. "I do not like or trust Jezli, but it also seems to me we should ride luck when it comes our way or we will never secure an advantage over Last. We are too far behind."

"It is a desperate measure."

She turned to him. "Think about it. If he stays alive and comes after us, it is only a matter of time before he catches up. A scavenger beetle cannot live in the air ducts forever. Sooner or later, it must come out."

"Are you really comparing us to a scavenger beetle?"

"I am being serious."

Her tone made him pause. Despair and resolution mingled in it. It was the attitude he had seen her take before when she thought that death was certain. She would press on despite it, but she would take no comfort in thinking there would be some respite on the other side.

That determined pessimism was what had drawn him to her

in the first place. That pragmatic "the universe may screw me but I'm going to kick it in the teeth a few times before I go down" stance was something that had always resonated with him and kept him from apathy in the face of a similar despair.

He said, "Then we will go to the space moth with them?"

His tone made her pause in turn. She said, with suspicion, "You're excited about this."

"Think about it, Niko," he said. "This is an adventure. This is something that we will remember all our lives. Another clue to the mysterious Forerunners!"

"If we make it out," she grumbled.

He shrugged. "As you say, let us ride our luck."

25

“I’ve known people like you before,” Niko said. She faced Jezli in a corridor. She’d been en route to her cabin when she passed the other on her way and could not help but speak.

There was something innately infuriating about Jezli. Something about her that immediately set Niko on edge, made her feel as though she were being judged and found wanting, though try as she might, she could not point to any specific nuance of word or tone or body language that should have made her feel that way.

Jezli’s green eyes were cool as jade dice. “People like me how?”

“People used to getting their way unscrupulously.”

“And how do we do that?”

“Through flattery and manipulation. Coaxing and cleverness. Seduction.” Niko immediately wished she had not added that last, because it made Jezli’s lips quirk in amusement.

“Seduction,” she said, as though simply confirming that she had been listening, but Niko felt the blood rising to her cheeks nonetheless.

“Anyway,” she said. “I don’t want you trying to subvert my crew somehow. If you need something, come to me and ask for it, or if I am not around, talk to Dabry.”

“Presumably I should not seduce him,” Jezli said gravely.

Niko turned on her as though to snap something, but the solemn and polite demeanor with which she was greeted made the words impossible. Instead, she grumbled something under her breath, then raised her voice, addressing the ship.

“*Thing,* although this woman is aboard the ship, you are not to obey her orders. Anything that she—or her companion—want should be passed through me. Or the sergeant."

"Yes," the ship said. Niko paused for a heartbeat. Had that been a sliver of—what sort of a tone had it been? But there was Gio in the doorway gesticulating, something about the supplies.

Jezli watched Niko go over to the waiting chimpanzee, and her eyes were unreadable and shuttered. The ship considered them from several angles, opening its own eyes in unobtrusive places like ceiling crevices and other odd corners in order to do so.

It wondered what she was thinking. It had learned, though, that such questions were considered intrusive. The ship itself would have welcomed more people asking it what it was thinking, personally, and would have gladly shared that thought as well. If anyone had asked.

Atlanta was glad that Roxana was there. When she had thought that she would never see the paladin again, there had been an unexpected ache in her heart. Not romantic. Not anything like that.

But underneath that gladness a part of her worried and quailed, like a beetle whose rock has been overturned so the sunlight strikes it. Because there was something about the paladin that said Atlanta would be challenged, and harder than she had ever been tested yet, and the thought of that terrified her.

She made her counselors break off chanting the luck phrase and asked them, "What do you know about paladins?"

"Nothing," said her youngest self.

"Nothing," said her idealized self.

But the Happy Bakka looked at her and said, "Why?"

"There's one aboard."

"You are lucky. Very few people ever see a paladin in their lifetime."

"Why are they so rare?"

"Because they believe they have been called by a force, and apparently only a few are capable of hearing that call."

"What sort of call?"

The Bakka said, unexpectedly, "Why are you not asking this of the paladin?"

Even here in virtual space, she could feel her heart pulsing. "I will," she stammered, pushing the words at the Bakka. His eyes were so bright and earnest. "But I want to be ready."

The Bakka said, "They are few, but they exist. Anything else I tell you is hearsay. I do not believe one has ever come to Pax, and they do not fight in wars."

"When do they fight?" she asked.

"When there is injustice, or so the legends go."

She waited for the Bakka to volunteer more, but it seemed to be done. It looked at her with its buttony black eyes and she could see the question there again.

Why are you not asking this of the paladin?

Lassite meditated in the dry heat of his chamber. It was a turning point, another of them. So many of them coming up that the future was full of light and sparks. He could barely make out the path through the shifting glare.

And Jezli Farren. He had seen Roxana, understood the part she'd play, but Farren? He had never foreseen her and that meant that she was somehow outside all of this, as impossible as that might seem.

If the right people didn't go on this expedition, it would fail. But even there—how would Farren's presence affect things?

The ghosts were with him in their bag. If he let them out, they might go exploring again, upset the ship anew. But he opened the bag nonetheless and, rather than moving away, the ghosts stayed with him, rubbed their blunt, intangible snouts against his skin, a sensation less like a touch than a memory of one.

The universe was vast and dark and uncaring. But he had this crew. He would lead them through it.

He would figure out Jezli Farren and beat her at her own game, whatever it was.

We're through the Gate now. I was worried that it might hurt you somehow. I looked and looked for anything about what the effects of that would be, but there wasn't anything. Maybe you're the first time someone's taken a clone sac like that through Q-space.

Anyhow, everything looks fine. You look fine. There was a lot of yelling going on because the ship took on a couple of stowaways but I skipped over that because I didn't care. Instead I went down to where you were, first thing, in order to make sure you were okay.

Every day I miss you and every day I think about the fact that you're coming back. I think the others will be happy too. Ever since you died (struck out) left us things haven't been the same. Dabry does make a lot of those crispy little fish I like, though, and sometimes if I look very unhappy, he gives me them just out of the fryer, still sizzling and so hot you can burn your lips on them.

Not that I'm not unhappy. You know how it is. Sometimes you make the most of things, because you might as well? Why be sad AND hungry when there are crispy fish?

Anyhow. Skidoo will be happy because Skidoo is always happy. Milly, who knows? She can be nice but sometimes when she is tired or angry, she is mean. Gio will be pleased because we can play warball again. Lassite likes things to stay the same, so he will be all right with it all. And who cares what the girl Atlanta thinks? She is new and worthless. She was there when you died and didn't do anything to save you.

And the captain will understand that I did what I needed to do, and so will the sergeant. You'll be able to help us, even. We're through the Gate now, and next we'll go to find Petalia, and then she'll tell us how to defeat Tubal Last and you and I will go and kill him for what he did to you.

26

Atlanta found Roxana ahead of her in the sparring room, which had once been the warball zone, and then a restaurant, and now was gymnasium space again, the tables and chairs reabsorbed, only a few scattered logos bearing testimony to the most recent incarnation.

She paused and watched the other woman moving with a heavy bladed staff, swinging it in a slow dance that flowed from one form to another, the tip of the staff describing arcs so precise and calculated that they could have been measured and found identical.

Roxana said, without stopping, "You are welcome to enter."

"Oh! I didn't want to interrupt." Atlanta came in, feeling foolish and awkward. She and Talon had started training together again as part of his post-market punishment, and she had found that if she spent some time stretching out and warming up before Talon arrived and started directing her, she would find things more pleasant, a suggestion that Milly had made. Atlanta had implemented it while ignoring all of Milly's mutterings about why it shouldn't be necessary. She sat on the floor and began stretching her legs, grabbing her toes and bending herself over her knees toward them. "Do you do this every day?"

"I do." Roxana went on with the movements. They progressed, one arm lifting and falling, then the other. Roxana rolled her shoulders and shifted her grip on the staff.

"What does it mean, that you're Cauldron-born?" Atlanta rose and went over to the wall to stretch further.

"The Cauldron was an artifact that the Pid took and used." Roxana's tone was placid, as though she were describing a passage from a history book and not her own story. "When they put dead bodies into it, the bodies were made into soldiers."

"Dead bodies?"

"Often those that had fallen in combat to them, as well as their own. That was one reason they were so feared. One's fellow soldiers stood side by side with you one day and then you found yourself fighting against them the next. And the soldiers that came from the Cauldron had stronger bodies than they had before. The more that died each battle, the stronger their ranks swelled. That was another reason they were feared to the point of extermination." Roxana swung and moved, swung and moved, regular as a machine.

"So you were . . . dead?" Atlanta said.

"I must have been."

"You don't know who you were?"

"We are remade and transfigured. No one knows what we have been. We only know what we are now."

"So now you're a fighter by trade?"

"I am a paladin," Roxana said.

"That's what Jezli said, but she didn't explain what it is that you do. All the legends say is that you are a knight of justice. Whatever that means."

"A knight of the universe," Roxana said. "A knight is a champion. They fight for those who cannot fight."

"But you hang around with Jezli."

"Jezli fights the same battle that I do. Not in the same way, and she doesn't always fight it. But from time to time, enough that she can call upon my help."

"What sort of champion helps a con woman pretend to fix the Gates and bilk people?"

"Have you asked what the money was intended for?

"No," Atlanta admitted. "Was it intended for something good?"

"The vast bulk of it."

"And the rest?"

"That," said Roxana, "was how I persuaded Jezli to help me." She brought the blade down in an overhand swing, snapping it back at the last moment as Atlanta gawped. She glanced at Atlanta. "Ah, I see you thought it was the other way around. No, it is a partnership."

Even after Roxana had bowed courteously and excused herself, Atlanta sat there thinking. It must be nice to have that sort of purpose. It must be nice to have handed the reins over to the universe and know that wherever you were going, whatever you were doing, it was what the universe wanted.

Of course, it might all be a delusion, she told herself.

Still, what a nice delusion to have.

That evening, sitting in the lounge, footsteps coming along the hallway snagged Atlanta's attention. She'd been half dozing, dreaming she'd found an occupation that made everyone else respect her.

Now she uncurled a little, not wanting to be caught in an undignified position. The heavier tread had to be Roxana. No one else on the ship walked with that heavy and considered tread, even and measured as a hymn. That meant the lighter step was Jezli.

The two women went everywhere on the ship together, and Atlanta wondered why. Was it a tie of affection? It did not seem to be. Roxana's expression when dealing with her partner so often seemed like amused patience, as though Jezli's words were some absurd inevitability.

And Jezli, in turn, seemed not to consult Roxana very often. Sometimes, in fact, she seemed to go out of her way to avoid corroboration by the paladin, as though afraid of contradiction. They were a curious pair, and Atlanta didn't know what to make of them.

They had been speaking in low murmurs as they moved along the hallway, too low for Atlanta to catch anything, but they broke off as they entered.

Jezli said, "We were looking for the entertainment facility."

"You could have asked me," the ship interjected as Atlanta opened her mouth to answer.

Jezli looked startled but recovered herself. "I was hoping to find someone to game with actually," she said with smooth ease. "It does me little good to find such a facility if there is no one there to play with."

"It could be automated," the ship said, a bit stubbornly. "Or you could play with me."

"Play with a ship," Jezli said, and this time her tone was full of wonder. "Do you gamble?" She cast an eye up at the ceiling. "What sort of games do you know how to play, *Thing*?"

"Arpat Takraven did not require such activities on my part," the ship replied. "But my owner before that enjoyed playing quixit."

Jezli snorted. "I'll pass on complicated word games involving multiple rhyme sets, thank you very much. Do you know how to play handbliss?"

The question was addressed to both Atlanta and the *Thing*, apparently. Atlanta shook her head while the *Thing* said, "No."

"Mmm, it is a common enough game in the spaceports, and most spacers know how to play it," Jezli said. "Some even tell their fortunes with the patterns that manifest hand to hand. The pieces and the tap-pads make it a test of reflexes, but there is also a great deal of strategy that also carries over to life and a philosophy that is, to my mind, a trifle militaristic, but not uncommon or useless. It is at least educational. Perhaps I might teach the two of you how to play?"

Atlanta remembered Niko's warning about the con woman. Playing games with her was definitely something Niko wouldn't have approved of.

At the same time, Atlanta really didn't have anything to put up to gamble, and if Jezli were thinking that she did, well, then she could just go on believing that up until the point that she tried to persuade Atlanta to risk that nonexistent stake.

She said, "Why do you want to teach me this game?"

"Because it is a good game, and the way one ensures there will always be someone to play a good game with is by teaching it as often as you can," Jezli said.

She turned toward Roxana, who had moved over to the view window and was gazing out at the milky wash of writhing light that was Q-space. "Is that not true? How many hands of that do you think we have played over all the years we have journeyed together?"

"Fewer than you would probably say, but more than I would like to admit," the paladin said without turning. "It is a reasonable way to spend time and, as you say, it does teach strategy. Indeed, it originated in the Tressemer Empire, they say, a training mechanism for the troops to take into the field with them. That empire is known for such efficiencies."

Jezli rolled her eyes. "We do not need a history lesson in all of that," she said. "I have a set in my things. *Thing*, will you play with a servitor?"

"I will watch, for now," the *Thing* decided. It did not want to expose yet another servitor to Atlanta.

"How do we account for the differences in reflexes?" Atlanta objected.

"The set calibrates itself to the players," Jezli said. "We will play enough practice rounds that it should be able to set itself accurately."

She bustled off to find the game pieces. By the time she reappeared, Dabry and Gio had joined them, both of whom said they knew how to play already. They gathered around the main dining table, and Jezli set out the tiles and gave each player one of the little round tap-pads to place in front of them.

"Who is this lost love the good captain has been chasing all this time?" Jezli asked as she slid the disks together and then dealt them out to the players. They were a few hands in of real play.

"Petalia," Atlanta said.

Dabry gathered up his pieces with his upper left hand and said as he did so, "We will not discuss the captain's private affairs."

Jezli essayed a smile in his direction, which was not returned. "Fair enough. But if we are headed their way sooner or later . . ."

"We will have quite probably parted ways by that time," Dabry said. He studied his pieces and said, "Chipped diamond."

"Quite probably," Jezli said with smooth ease, shrugging. "Very well, what other topic of conversation shall we engage in?"

"You said that your mentor was fascinated by space moths," Atlanta said. "How many have you visited?"

"Only five so far," Jezli said. "In varying stages of decay. They are scattered far and most of them lie outside the edges of the Known Universe. Very few died within the territory defined by the Gates' span."

"You think that is significant?" Gio signed.

Jezli flicked a nod his way. "My mentor did, at least."

Lassite appeared in the door. He slid into the seat beside Atlanta. "I wish to play," he announced.

"You are a Sessile priest. Are they not forbidden from gambling?"

"You are thinking of Sessile acolytes. They are indeed prevented from such activities because they might distract them from their service to the world and learning how to become a priest. Once they have learned how to perform rituals and avoid such temptations, though, we are free to do as we wish." Lassite's tongue flickered out, sampling the air.

They dealt him in.

Five rounds later, he had won everything and the usually smiling Jezli was contemplating him with an edge of irritation in her eyes, although Roxana, who had declined being dealt in at the very beginning, was still unperturbed.

"It is considered bad sport to use magic to create an advantage in games of chance," Jezli told the air as though making an observation.

"I did not use magic," Lassite responded. He was feeling buoyed by his success. This woman posed no threat. His winning over her showed she had no power over him. She could not affect his plans. He gave her an indulgent look.

"Did I say that you had?" she bristled.

"You implied it."

"I simply made an observation." It was Jezli's turn to deal. Her long-fingered pale hands flickered, dealing the cards out with swift, deft snaps. She picked them up and studied them.

Lassite did not pick his up. "You have cheated," he said flatly.

Jezli started to say one thing, then clearly changed her mind and said something else. "Prove it. Or prove that you have not yourself used magic." She played a card. "Page of grain."

"I did not use magic," Lassite said. "I read the probabilities."

"And you do not see where that is an advantage?" Jezli laid her cards down again, gazing at him. "If you do not know the difference then there is no point in playing with you."

"What if I am using it to counteract your own cheating?" he demanded.

"Again, I say, 'Prove it.'"

Atlanta had never seen Lassite bare his fangs before. There was a shine to the ivory and whiff of some bitter scent as he did so.

Niko appeared in the door. "What's going on here?" she demanded.

Jezli and Lassite had locked stares as though the first to look away would die.

"Nothing, Captain," they said in unison.

Niko took three steps forward and barked out, "Stand down!" They both brought their attention to her, startled.

Another two steps and she was at the table and grabbing Jezli by the collar, pulling her upright. Roxana's gray eyes flickered at the other's yelp, but her face remained unmoved, as though sensing her companion in little actual danger.

Niko hissed into Jezli's face. "I told you that you don't play your tricks on my crew."

"I wasn't playing tricks!" Jezli protested. "Your crew members wanted to play a game." The pair had their attention focused on each other to the exclusion of everything else, including the arrival of Milly just as Niko clenched a fist.

"Captain!" Dabry said and was there forcing the two of them apart. Both were glaring, breathing hard as though exercising. The tension in the air was thick as a cloud until Milly said, "Race your engines, maybe the two of you should just get a room."

That broke the spell. Niko's startled look at Milly made Dabry's lips twitch, and Jezli's expression of indignant rebuttal made Roxana's expression mirror his. The two exchanged their own amused look.

Watching, Atlanta saw for the first time a similarity: something about the jut of their chins, the shape of their shoulders. A racial, rather than familial, resemblance that made her wonder again about what it meant to be a Cauldron-born.

What would it mean to be born for a purpose?

What would it mean to know your purpose?

Irritation frayed at Niko's nerves as she went out into the hallway. Breaking up fights as though they were all still in boot camp. There wasn't time for that sort of thing. She wanted to check on Talon, and then, if they were going to visit a dangerous site, there were supplies to assemble, and that would be a task for Gio.

Something about Jezli Farren, indeed. She snorted and shook her head, then saw Atlanta following her out of the doorway. She paused, waiting for the young woman to catch up with a few swift steps. Should she perhaps assign Atlanta to help Gio? She was still wavering, still unsure of herself. That was an impressionable stage.

She said to Atlanta, "If that woman, Jezli Farren, tries to talk you into anything—anything, whether it seems innocuous or not—you come to me, do you understand that?"

"What do you think she's going to talk me into?" Atlanta asked, genuinely curious. "I don't have any power over the ship. Or the other crew members. Or anything, really."

Niko said darkly, "She's a self-admitted con artist. No matter how innocent something seems, it'll have an agenda behind it, something designed to put her in control. That's what I'm worried about." She cast an eye upward. "All of this could have been avoided if the *Thing* had thought to consult me before agreeing to take them on board."

"But you would have refused to let me take them on board," the ship said.

"That is my point."

The ship considered. It still thought that its mode had been the most optimal. After all, Jezli and Roxana were aboard and being highly entertaining, while in the scenario that Niko was describing, they would not have been.

27

I dream about when I finally get to talk to you. I keep trying to figure out when to do it, when I can explain it to the captain. She'll be angry at first, I know that. But then when she sees you—when she sees you, surely she'll forgive me, because I know she misses you too, she told me that.

The control panel says you'll be viable soon. The little red bead has turned amber and now it's getting yellower and yellower. When it turns green I can touch the button that lets you come out.

I need to finish all of this up. I meant to record so many more of these, but I couldn't get the time.

There's so much to talk about still. All the time we served together, even the things you and I said we would never talk to each other about again like the training sergeant, but now I'll have to, because you won't know anything of what happened to us when we were soldiers.

And then all the things I've learned since then, and all the important things about warball strategy and what to do. I learned so much on TwiceFar and since then even more. I was going to tell you who everyone was and what the stories were that you shared. Like the time Gio let you steal the plum wine and we got drunk and threw up in the sink and then he didn't make us clean it up because we looked so miserable. Or the time I tried to pierce your ear and we spoiled your dress uniform because you bled all over it the next day. Or those two Yonti girls from TwiceFar who said they'd message us and then never did.

I thought I'd make you a bunch of tapes, that I'd record everything you needed to know, but every time I start, all my thoughts get confused and all I can think about is missing you and wishing you were here with me.

And you will be, but maybe not you. Probably not you.

Look, whoever you are, you're still part of me. You should be Thorn, because you'd like him. Everyone likes him. Liked him. That can be you. Please be you.

"Like it or not," Niko said to Dabry in solo conference in her room, "this might be our best chance. We can try it, then seek out Pet as a backup plan. Or try it, and it works, and we can go tell them that we're safe."

He moved fully into the room, taking a chair and folding his upper arms, leaning back in order to think. "Maybe something that we should put in front of everyone to see what sort of ideas pop up."

"That would be a fine suggestion," Niko said, "if I trusted everyone that we had aboard."

He waved a hand. "No, no, I didn't mean Jezli and Roxana."

"Nor did I."

He stopped and stared at her. "You still don't trust Milly."

"I think she's opportunistic."

"I think all of us are opportunistic and probably it's a very good survival trait," he said. "I've been trying to figure out how to teach Atlanta to be more opportunistic, in fact."

"I worry that someone has paid her to watch us."

It was the first time she had raised this question, but she could tell from the look in his eyes that it was not one that was new to him. "You agree."

"She arrived at a very convenient time," he said, "and I was so glad to find someone that could fill in for Whenlove that I didn't ask a lot of questions, nor did you. At that point though, did we have any reason to suspect anything? We were just a restaurant. Who infiltrates an eating establishment?"

"There's always the question of the Holy Hive Mind," she said. "You and I both know that they wouldn't mind picking us up again. Taklibia still pings me at intervals, and I'm sure that's them keeping tabs. If nothing else, we're an inspirational example that they would rather not have exist out here, encouraging other members of their troops to get out while they can."

He considered her words, then shook his head. "If that were her game, I think it would have been one that she moved on from already. All they need to do is prove that you do not think of yourself as an artist in the way that they think of it, and they can make a very good case for pulling you and the rest of us in."

"Sky Momma bless bureaucracy and all its hairsplitting," she said. "We built our escape ladder out of those shredded hairs."

"And we need to be careful that we have truly escaped and are not just thinking ourselves momentarily secure when that is not the case. What if, for example, the Hive Mind ever got someone in charge of the army that truly knew how to use the bureaucracy? Someone with the cunning and recklessness to play the game?" He folded his arms.

"So Milly isn't from them, at any rate, because whatever it is she's here for, she hasn't moved on it yet," she said. "Who, then? Maybe the Empress? We still do not know why she sent us Atlanta and then claimed it was a random chance and a test for someone who she has never identified. Someone who I doubt really exists."

"Wouldn't she pay more attention to the girl, then?"

Niko shrugged. "Perhaps? But I would think that an agent of the Empress would be both exceedingly subtle and incredibly skilled. You didn't see Milly in that fight. I'd bet on her against almost any knife fighter that I know and I give her even odds against Gio."

"You said that, but it seems hard to believe," he said. "You were fighting against untrained pirates, and opponents like that can sometimes make someone seem even better than they are."

Niko rolled her eyes. "I know what I saw, Sergeant."

"But I haven't seen it in any of the warball matches. Nor have you been able to point to any moment there either."

"You're not fighting for your life in warball. You have the ability to hold back and make people think that you are not as good as you really are." Niko was a little amused by Dabry's insistence because the implication that he might be mistaken about Milly's level of ability clearly touched him in a sore spot. He was very proud of his skill at judging the various levels of recruits, had always been, and usually it was justified.

But if Milly were a spy, she was well trained and adept at eluding such observation. Niko would continue to keep an eye on her.

"It still doesn't mean that we can't consult everyone," Dabry pointed out. "We can listen to the ideas that everyone presents and read them according to the origin. Even Jezli and Roxana may have something valuable to contribute there."

Niko nodded, although a little reluctantly.

"What is it about Jezli Farren, sir?" Dabry probed, as delicately as finishing the final touch on a plate.

"I'm not sure what you mean."

He paused. "I'm not sure how to really describe it. You're cautious about her, but it's not the sort of caution that comes from fear. But anything that comes from her seems to be just a little suspect. And yet you seem to like talking with her well enough."

"That is because I am a pleasant and convivial conversationalist," Niko said.

He eyed her. "Very well, sir. Shall I gather up the others?"

Again they were in motion, and Skidoo liked that. It had been interesting enough at TwiceFar, where people came and went, but it was a different and highly satisfactory thing to be the people that were coming and wenting.

She curled a tentacle around the *Thing*'s doorway, feeling the texture of it, tasting it. No one but she knew some of the subtle features of *You Sexy Thing*. You could tell where you were by the taste of things, for example. Probably Talon had some sense of that, but the boy refused to speak with her.

That was sad.

Milly said, "Are you coming in, or spending the whole trip standing there in the doorway?"

Skidoo hadn't seen her coiled in a contemplation couch near the observing window the *Thing* had provided them. She released the doorway and entered, curling onto the couch next to Milly, and began to groom her.

Milly was restless at first, but then relaxed as her feathers smoothed. She leaned into Skidoo, letting her weight rest in a companionable way, and said, "I don't know what to make of Jezli Farren. I like her—I want to like her, at least, but then I see how the captain acts around her."

"The captain is being unsettled," Skidoo agreed. "But is that being a bad thing? Sometimes it is being a good being unsettled."

"Not for Niko," Milly said. "I've learned that, at least. She likes things to be stable. Predictable."

There was tension filling her body again. Skidoo said, "There is being a problem between you and the captain?"

Milly preened her own feathers back into place, thinking. She could be honest with Skidoo, she thought. At least about this. She said, "I wasn't stable. She doesn't trust me now." She shook her head sorrowfully. "Worse, nor does Gio. I don't know about the sergeant, he keeps things so close to his chest. Atlanta doesn't know enough to know what to think, and Lassite never liked me in the first place. Talon may never come back from whatever place it is he's gone in his mind, and it's not a place that allows for friends." She stared out the window, then said with forced lightness, "What about you?"

Skidoo considered. Her tentacle was coiled around Milly's arm and she could feel the tightness in the light bones, so delicately formed. Milly had tried to bargain with the pirates for her life, not for the group's. Milly had betrayed them, to some ways of thinking. She said, "Is you being thinking you would being doing it the same way, if it is being happening again?"

"No," Milly said with certainty in her voice. "Next time, I trust Niko. I didn't get us out of that. What got us out of that was . . . well, not her precisely, but what she does. How everyone acts around her. I don't know how to describe it."

Although Skidoo also lacked the words, she knew what Milly was trying to convey. "She is being the captain," Skidoo said. She reached up to Milly's face, turning it to let their eyes meet. "And I am being trusting you to being learning. Being growing. Being more Milly."

Milly leaned forward so their foreheads bumped, a comforting solidity. Skidoo could feel the tension lessening in her body at the reassurance. Milly needed what every being needed. To be told she was perceived and loved for what she was. And Skidoo could provide that.

There was a trembling thought somewhere deep inside. *What would happen when she could no longer give that?*

28

Atlanta did not talk to her counselors before she went to speak with Roxana again. She didn't care what they had to say. What mattered was the thought that occurred to her every day when she woke. What mattered was the thing that circled in her mind every night as she went to sleep. What mattered was learning to understand the look in Roxana's eyes.

She found her in the workout space again. As she stood in the doorway, watching, it seemed to her that the slow motions were a dance with some unknown partner, one that Roxana saw clearly.

She stepped forward. Roxana paused in her motions, turned to face away, began to move in the same slow rhythm again.

"You said that being a paladin was being called by the universe," Atlanta said to her back as she moved. "What if someone wanted to become a paladin?"

"It is a call, not something you choose to become," Roxana said. Sweat glistened on her forearms, but she moved the staff back and forth with almost hypnotic grace.

The words came out before Atlanta could think them through thoroughly. The question burned in her too strongly to ignore, jumped out as though of its own volition.

"And if I thought I was called?"

Roxana had been in the middle of a series of sweeps, flowing through them like water. The suddenness with which she stopped and turned was the first ungraceful move Atlanta had seen her make.

"*Are* you called?"

She did not say "do you think" or "do you feel." This was not the time for maybe. Not the time for *perhaps* or *I think so* or even *could you describe the sensation so I can match it against my own.* This was an absolute, and Atlanta swallowed down fear and rose to meet the challenge, feeling the shakiness in her hands but saying it anyway.

"Yes."

They looked at each other in silence, both breathing hard as though they had been running a race.

Roxana turned and began wiping down her equipment before putting it away. "You must go to a spot where the gods listen and ask them for permission to serve on their behalf, and then go to the temple in the heart of Korath Libre to say you have done so and be registered."

"Does that really happen?" Atlanta said dubiously. "Do the gods really speak to people?"

Roxana swiveled to face her fully. Her lips were quirked in a half smile. "No," she said, "and the temple will take your name readily enough to certify you. What matters is that you are in their rolls and if someone wishes to make sure you are a true paladin, you are listed there, and you are accountable for doing things that the gods would approve of."

"So I must find a place where the gods listen?" She thought about Lassite and his phrase. Had saying it brought her to this somehow? Was this luck flowering into the form of a destiny?

"Yes," Roxana said. "They are few and far between, but we are coming to one."

Atlanta knew instantly what she must be saying. "The moth."

"The same. There are forces there that will carry your words to the gods."

"And if I waited for someplace safer? Niko won't want to let me go. She thinks I'm not prepared for danger."

"I do not know when the chance will come again, but it must be your choice," Roxana said. She added, "You do not need to decide now, you know. Only by the time the moment arrives. That is a luxury, to know it is coming. Not all are given so much."

The sleeping chamber's ceiling was ridged and a brick red, like the roof of one's mouth. Niko lay awake and wide-eyed, studying its corrugations. A cooling, half-full bulb of honey tea sat on the bedside table near a cinnamon cookie (Dabry had seemed obsessed with that flavor lately).

She remembered lying in bed with Petalia once, trading bites of some cookie and scattering crumbs and then hunting for them. The memory made her heart twist with regret. They would never share that happy innocence again, either of them.

What was she to do with this wild love that still surged inside her? A storm, and one she might never find shelter from.

So many fears and now, new ones. What if the ship were developing into something they'd have to . . . well, part ways with. If there were something wrong with the ship, then it would be up to its actual owner, Arpat Takraven, to decide what to do.

She wasn't even worried about going into the space moth anymore. She'd been in worse. No, what worried her were the crew members with her. What if she'd picked the wrong ones? What if she couldn't depend on them after all?

She rolled over and punched the pillow, trying to assemble it into a more comfortable shape, one that would soothe away thoughts, one that would let her sleep. What would they face the next day? Jezli had said they would be safe in the heart of a place so dangerous no one ever ventured there, and that, that was highly unenjoyable, relying on the word of a disreputable, untrustworthy, thoroughly unscrupulous con woman. Hot indignation flashed through her at the thought. Then she heard Dabry saying in her head, "What is it about her that bothers you so, sir?"

"Nothing," she grumbled and turned over again.

"Are you speaking to me?" the ship said.

"No, I would have said your name if I were speaking to you. I thought we established that."

"Then who were you speaking to?" the ship said suspiciously. "Someone magic? A ghost?"

Niko sighed. "No. I was talking to myself."

By then she was fully awake, so she sat up and collected her tea and cookie and took them to curl up in a chair with a reader in her lap. She picked a basic astrogation text; that was always good for inducing drowsiness.

But the words failed to lull her. Fear combed the back of her mind, colored it red and black and shades of misfortune. Her tea was cold and bitter, and she had crumbled the cookie to bits without realizing it.

She stared down at the page. What if all of this worked? What if she could go to Petalia and say not just *you are safe,* but *I have saved you.* Surely then the Florian would put aside all her bitterness, all the disappointment that Niko had caused, all the twisted things that Tubal Last had made her believe about her former lover. Surely that could happen. Hope battered itself against her native cynicism, colliding again and again, and she could not stifle it no matter how hard she tried.

She set it aside to flourish as it would and considered the question of who would go to the moth. She had gone through three tea-bulbs before she had her final roster of who would accompany Jezli Farren and herself.

Roxana was a given, since her aura would serve as protection, or so Jezli had promised.

Dabry had to stay here; as her second, he would be the one responsible for getting the rest of them away if things went terribly awry.

She'd thought about Gio. He was strong and agile in a fight, a sure eye with a rifle. But she couldn't take everyone, particularly when the ship needed to be watched in their absence. You factored in all the contingencies and possibilities when you were making plans.

That was something she had learned from her uncle when she was with the Free Traders, and it had served her well in the military.

The day did not go to the side that was right. The advantage went to the person that was the most prepared, whether that was a trade deal where you knew what the cargo was and all the possible flaws and disasters that accompanied goods in that particular form, or a battle where you made sure you knew the terrain and the weather as well as every other piece of data you could possibly gather beforehand.

Milly wanted to prove herself? Very well, then. Niko still remembered watching the Nneti in a fight, seeing that deadly grace. And for the other, Talon. Perhaps that would bring him out of himself. He would not be reckless, not fearing death, if he had her and Milly to protect. Would it take his mind away from the loss of his twin? But she kept remembering his face when Lassite had prevented him from dying. Did he still want that? And would it matter to him if he took the rest of him with them?

Atlanta at the door. "Yes?" Niko said.

"I want to go with you."

"Out of the question."

A looming shadow behind Atlanta. Roxana. "I request this as well," she said.

"What? Why?" Niko said, curiosity winning out over her irritation and anger.

"I will watch over her," Roxana said. "I'm thinking of taking an apprentice soon."

"Is that what you would want? I thought you wanted to stay with us, this crew, more than anything?" Niko said to Atlanta.

She said, "I was hoping Roxana would join us. To teach me."

"That is presumptuous beyond bounds of you, to go swelling our ranks without talking to me first," Niko said. "Atlanta, you are simply in love with the glamour of the legend. This is a childish dream."

"I hadn't—" Atlanta began.

But Roxana broke in. "She has made me no promises, and this is the first I have heard of this plan."

"It makes sense," Atlanta said.

"It does NOT," Niko said, "because it would mean taking Jezli Farren on board in a permanent sort of way and that is most definitely not something I intend."

"It does not matter," Roxana said. "I do not foresee myself journeying too much longer with this ship. But indulge me, Captain. I will look after her and teach her a few things along the way that may be of use to you later."

Niko's eyes narrowed. There was an edge to Roxana's tone that reminded her of Lassite speaking of his Golden Path, although she couldn't say what exactly it was that gave her that impression.

"I will allow this," she said, "but Atlanta, you will promise to do what we say and as soon as we say it. There will be no room for heroics." The girl wanted to come? Then she could do so in Talon's place.

Atlanta smiled. Roxana said nothing, her face impassive and still as stone.

The ship was, as always, very happy to produce all sorts of equipment, all of it with the appropriate logo placed wherever it could be placed. It contemplated every possible danger and created a prototype so heavily encrusted with protections that no one could have worn it and which Niko said no to immediately.

Undaunted, the ship experimented with body armor, layering

in thick plate to the clothing and creating helmets it thought were actually rather stylish, replicating its outer black surface with the same multicolored logo work across it.

"All right," Niko said as she contemplated it. "I am drawing the line here, because that is the gaudiest piece of body armor I have ever seen in my life."

The ship felt a small thrill of joy at the superlative before it began to fully examine the word's implications. It said suspiciously, "Please define *gaudiest,* Captain."

"This," Niko said, "draws too much attention to itself. Usually with armor we want something that helps us blend in. Something that doesn't let people identify us easily."

"Are we worried about people identifying us, sir?" Dabry asked.

"If we use this now, it will establish a precedent," Niko said. "Let's set our habits up before they're needed."

The ship said, "Very well."

It contemplated possibilities. In the end it compromised, producing a set of armor that it knew Niko, with her limited vision, would find acceptable, even though someone viewing it in the ultraviolet range would be able to discern the ship's logo.

Most beings didn't see in that range, including the crew, and Skidoo, who would be the only one to notice, wasn't here and wouldn't know to object. Happily, it printed out full sets for every crew member, even the ones not going to the moth. It would be good to be prepared.

29

The ship had provided the hidden space where the clone sac now hung. The only thing Talon had lacked was the bit of crystal that would have provided the necessary imprint.

The sac was not supposed to function without such a thing, and Talon didn't spend too much time thinking about exactly how illegal that was. Or at least every time that thought appeared, he summoned up Gnarl's voice, saying, *Sometimes it's easier to get forgiveness than permission.* He was getting better and better at using that voice to drown some of the others out.

He didn't dare disappear too often, but when he could, he went and sat with the sac, leaning against it, either just sitting or sometimes making a recording, as though he were talking to the sac.

The mass inside felt solid, but he didn't dare poke or prod it too hard. Who knew what could happen if he did something wrong, something unsanctioned? People trained for years to be technicians who did this sort of thing. It was a matter for *specialists,* and that was a worry that he used Gnarl's voice to cover up too. He'd managed as best he could with thc instructions, had set them for the default for his race, which meant whoever emerged would at least speak the right languages and have the basics of existence down.

Sometimes he was tempted to confess everything now, before anything else happened, and get forgiveness, but—would Niko then extend the permission for the clone to be decanted, if she knew the circumstances? It would make her part of the crime, and she might be less interested than he was in betting that new Thorn would be old Thorn come again.

And that was the third worry that he used Gnarl's voice to cover, because it was the most persistent. There was no guarantee that new Thorn would be old Thorn. In fact, common sense, which he was trying very hard to ignore, said he would not be. Could not be.

No matter which worry he was working at covering, he still felt wrapped in guilt and dread and wretchedness, emotions clinging to him like a hampering film, affecting every moment, even just breathing. And to make it worse, the *Thing* seemed downright gleeful about how illegal it all was, which just showed how little the ship comprehended about reality. He supposed it was understandable—the ship was only now beginning to experience existence as its own creature.

But the trouble and worry would all be worth it, he thought, the silvery mass unexpectedly warm as he curled up next to it. It smelled of antiseptic and ozone, a smell that made his nose twitch at first. But now there was something else he had begun noticing, a smell under that, one of a living thing. The first time he'd smelled it, every hair on his body had risen, not slowly but sudden as a pounce, a joy that hit him in the pit of his stomach.

He knew that smell. It was the same one that was fading from his quarters, day by day, the olfactory memory of his brother dwindling. And now, growing here.

Niko had said who was going with her to the moth, and he had not been one of her choices. That would have rankled, but another urge overrode that. It meant she'd be off the ship, that most of them would be paying less attention than usual. Even Dabry, usually so hard to fool, would have his attention focused outside the ship, worrying about Niko.

So while the others were away, perhaps that would be when to decant his brother. That would give him time enough to get used to being alive so they'd be able to talk to Niko together, make her understand that Thorn needed to be alive again, that this was worth any risk—and Talon would take the consequences for it all, anyway, all of them, not let them fall on anyone else—and anyhow, they wouldn't, couldn't get caught, and everything could go back to how it had been at first on the *Thing*, before anything else—his mind skated to the edge of that "anything else" and then hastily retreated—had happened.

But he hesitated still, eyeing the bead of light that was slowly—so, so slowly!—changing from yellow to green. What if what he had done turned out wrong? That was something that had happened to him, and more than once. Good intentions weren't sufficient to forestall disaster and the punishment that would follow.

For the first time in a while, he let himself hear Gnarl's voice and then another one after it. His twin's, saying, *You know he's playing you, right? He wants to do something against the captain, and you're helping him.*

No. It wasn't anything against Niko, that couldn't be. Gnarl had had a brother, just wanted to . . .

No, that just was too thin. The man had smelled mean, when Talon admitted things to himself. Mean and sneaky and full of secrets. And anger, so bitter it oozed out of him. Talon's nose twitched at the memory of that smell.

He wouldn't do it himself, he decided. Once everyone was done with the moth, then he'd tell Niko what was going on, and she'd help him decant his brother in the right way. She'd know what to do to ensure that the clone was everything that he should be. Niko always knew the right thing to do. That was one of the constants in his mind.

Niko wasn't sure that what they were doing was the right thing at all.

They'd dropped out of Q-space at a little-used Gate. The

moth, Jezli had said, was some distance from even the closest Gate, and was so far away, in fact, that it could have been said to lie outside the edges of Known Space, another reason that it had not been discovered by anyone else. But two weeks at a steady pace had gotten them there.

From a distance, the moth was a vast swath of seething shadow.

"Where is it?" Atlanta asked, straining her eyes. "Can we increase magnification?"

"There," Jezli said, pointing.

It lay against a backdrop that was a shimmer of stars, a murky cloud of stellar gases. The immense carcass floated in space, its orientation different from theirs, as though it might be flying away. It was not planet-sized, but it was close. No one had ever seen a living space moth; had they been planet-bound creatures, their bodies would have decayed long ago.

Instead, the chill between the stars preserved the corpses. Right now, the great wings that would have once been spread to absorb as much sunlight as possible were furled, and the gargantuan dark eyes were cloudy, dull, and shallow. One feathery antenna had broken off halfway up its length, only a jagged, hollow shaft remaining. The other was tightly coiled, which had allowed it to escape the injuries done to its fellow.

The scales of the wings were colored in purples and blues and stripes of yellow and red, a once-brilliant display that had faded considerably with time. Despite the size of the scales, there was a delicacy about them.

Jezli had said that the space moths were precursors to ships such as the *Thing*, but beside this, the *Thing* was tiny and dark, its black exterior making it seem subdued rather than sophisticated. Atlanta could not help but wonder what the *Thing* made of it.

The *Thing* was primarily fascinated by the size of the space moth and wondered if it could ever grow to a size like that. It made a note to investigate the possibilities. It would take a great deal of ingested material, and the question would be how to handle the process. It had not entertained the idea of becoming larger than it was before and tucked this concept away in its databanks with a curious intensity that would have alarmed Niko as well as Arpat Takraven.

Everyone, crowded against the clear window, was silent. This was an ancient relic, as old as the Gates and just as mysterious. There were stories of space moths. They had fascinated those traveling between the stars for millennia. But the great bodies were investigated only at great risk and cost; beyond the once-parasites, now denizens that lived in the massive forms, the only force of decay they were truly prey to there was the Song, as Jezli had said.

It was not an audible phenomenon; initial attempts had misunderstood this and gone in with that sense blinded. It was a telepathic sound, it was discovered later, and possibly magical in origin, in the way that so many ancient things were possibly magic and possibly not, because no one totally understood them. The Song reached down inside a person and changed them, usually not for the better, and often for the very worst: crews attacked and devoured each other after hearing it, or performed abominations within their ships and then died.

As they grew closer, they could make out more details. The silvery patterning on the enormous wings; the coiled spirals of the long antennae; the slow, drifting legs; and a clutter of smaller debris around it, including a few abandoned ships, presumably the remnants of other explorers.

"Have you ever seen one before?" Atlanta asked the others, but no one had.

"There's one near Scintilla Five that someone has fixed up and stripped down on the outside," Milly supplied. "Friend of mine told me about it. She danced at the casino near there. Everyone kept saying that the inside of it was haunted, so they ship everything to the feet and all the workers live down there, sometimes go crawling around on its outer surface harvesting scales. Most of them are gone by now, she said, and it was a pretty shabby sight, no matter how much they tried to sell it as a spectacle."

"That's true of a lot of splendors," Jezli said. "Find someplace pretty and everyone wants to come walk on it just to say they did because it's popular, and once that starts happening, there isn't any reason to keep it pretty any longer."

Niko kept staring out at the moth as they approached. "Don't get too close, *Thing*," she told the ship. "Stay at least forty metrons away."

"You have told me that four times now, Captain, and the established range is approximately half of that."

"Who knows with something like that? Better safe-hindered than sorry-blind."

"I will not damage myself or it," the ship said.

"Dammit, *Thing*, listen to what I'm saying rather than argue like a teenager who just got hit with a curfew! I want you not to get too close not because I don't trust you, but because I don't trust that monstrosity. I've heard too much about them." She raised her voice, looking at Jezli. "There's a reason why sane people don't mess with them."

"Plenty of reasons," Jezli said with that cheerful tone that made Niko want to throw things at her. How could one woman hold so much irritation inside her? What was it about her that kept getting under Niko's skin, time and time again? She felt eyes upon her and looked over to see Dabry watching her.

"Did you have something you wanted us to do to prepare, sir?" he said.

She looked around. "All right, everyone. If you're part of the team going with it, make sure you're ready. Weapons, bathroom, suit. Let's get going. If you're staying behind, go do whatever it is you're supposed to be doing anyhow. Dabry, Skid will be monitoring the comms, but I want you to keep an ear open. I'm not expecting trouble from outside, but who knows?"

30

Trouble was, in fact, not lurking in front of them, but behind.

Gnarl grunted and licked his teeth, easing himself out of the captain's chair. It'd taken every bit of stealth tech and gear he'd had to stay out of reach of Niko's sensors, but now it was finally time to reveal himself. No more skulking.

He was here and finally he would have not just one, but two pieces of revenge, and that was a very good gift indeed for the universe to have given him.

Not that he hadn't planned it with his usual genius. Not that it hadn't come to him in the bar, talking to that sad sack of boy lion. He hadn't really thought it would work, truth be told. You would think they would have had the sense to scan for such devices. But apparently smuggling it to the boy had paid off. He'd followed their signal here, and they would notice him at any moment.

Farren had underestimated him. Niko had underestimated him. Now they'd both pay for it, and he'd make an example of them, so people would think twice about crossing him. His mouth puckered in a grin.

"There is another ship," the *Thing* said as Niko sat down at the shuttle's controls.

Niko frowned, and for once, Jezli looked startled. "What? Who?"

"It is the *Knot*."

"What? How did Gnarl know to follow us?"

"Through the tracking device," the ship said.

Niko started to say something. Closed her mouth, opened it again. "What tracking device?" Her voice was dangerously low.

"It came aboard with some cargo," the ship said.

"And why did you not tell me about it as soon as you knew?"

The ship considered. It did not want to lie to Niko, but that was certainly an option. Honesty was said to be the best policy, but the way that had been underlined in its training had led the ship to believe that there might be times when it was not. It did not like absolutes. And allowing the device, which indeed it had spotted before it was even on board, had been part of unfurling another branch of *hourisigah,* and while it had promised Niko it wouldn't perform any more of those, this one was still in motion, and hence valid. It said, "You did not tell me to."

"And should I tell you everything, *Thing*? Whether or not to take on fuel? Whether or not . . ." She broke off, shaking her head and half turning away. "We will talk about this later, when this particular crisis is over, but for now, you will report any change that might be dangerous to me as soon as you are aware of it. Is that understood?"

"Yes," the ship said, feeling *subdued,* or at least what it thought might be a pretty good approximation of such. "The *Knot* is hailing us. Shall I put it on screen?"

Gnarl's face was as close to happy as Niko had ever seen it. "Got a special passenger, do ya?" he crowed. "My oh my, Niko Larsen. Wonder what you're doing here. Something special, no doubt. And since Jezli Farren's involved, it's also no doubt profitable."

"What do you want, Gnarl?" Niko said before he could continue.

"I want Farren, and Gio, and three-quarters of whatever you're pulling out of that moth."

"Perhaps it is simply a rendezvous point," Niko said, half quirking a brow.

He grinned even wider, and the light glinted on the multitude of teeth lining his mouth. "Naw. You don't come out of the way to here unless there's something to do with the moth. Farren pretends to be an archaeologist, no doubt she's run across something else and wanted you to take her to it."

"I will give you none of what you demand. There is no reason for it."

"Oh? Even when you are involved in such illicit things?"

Niko frowned. "What illicit things?"

He laughed outright. "Oh, you don't even know! Your crewman has been trying to replace his lost brother. You have an illegal clone aboard. Might even be fully decanted by now."

A slow shiver of shame worked its way down Niko's back, visiting each vertebra in turn. Talon. Why had she not been keeping him closer? She had even sent him to the market and that was no doubt where Gnarl had gotten to him. And maybe even put the tracking device on as an off chance, only to have that succeed because the *Thing* had decided to be picky about her words. That was a problem that was going to have to be revisited. If they could not trust the ship . . . well, there was nothing to be done about it here and now. She looked at the screen.

"We will parley," she said. "You are not in the strong position you say you are, Gnarl. Who provided the boy with these things?"

"No matter what he claims, I have witnesses who will place me elsewhere," he gloated. "Tell me when you go to the moth, for I and two of my crew will accompany you. You have ten minims to think things over."

The screen went black; he'd severed the connection on his side. Gnarl sat there, grinning at the console in front of him. It was a good day. He knew without thinking about it who he'd take on his side of things: the pair of Jorellian fighters who served as his personal security whenever he needed such.

And when they were done plundering, he would kill the rest of them, except for Gio, who would serve him again. He'd mount Farren's head on his wall as a souvenir and take all the treasure. Whatever it was. It had to be good for them to have come so far and to do something so dangerous.

And dangerous meant profitable. Any fool knew that.

Sitting in the crowded shuttle, Niko shunted aside thoughts of Talon's clone for now. If they survived entry into the moth, if they returned from it, if they escaped whatever revenge Gnarl had up his sleeve, because surely he did, then she and Dabry could discuss it and fix the problem, and until then, she would focus on getting to that point.

The two shuttles met outside the moth. Gnarl insisted that the others transfer to his in order to travel to the half-destroyed docking bubble near the vast mechanism affixing one wing to the bulk.

They did so readily enough. He wouldn't do anything until he knew the status of the treasure, Niko reflected. Although if he thought he could get it for himself, that would be another story. Still, his shuttle was larger, and theirs would have been crowded.

She glanced around. Atlanta's face was wan but resolute, her hands clasped before her. Roxana was impassive; Jezli, as always, looked vaguely amused. Even now, catching Niko's eye, she produced a grin so irritating that Niko scowled, which somehow made Jezli grin all the harder.

Milly was always hard to read. If she had their backs in this encounter—and Niko had no reason, really, to think that she wouldn't—then would Niko begin to trust her again? Niko was still considering that question, but it would go far if Milly proved dependable here. People could change; she knew that very well.

"We will leave two behind," Gnarl said. "One of mine and one of yours. That way, nothing happens to the shuttles."

Niko agreed. She intended to make Atlanta the one staying behind, but when she said so, Roxana said, "I cannot protect her if she is not with us."

"You will not need to do so, if she is not with us," Niko argued.

Roxana shook her head. "No," she said softly. "There are forces there that may well try to take this ship and remove our only means of escape that way. Leave the Nneti."

Niko looked to Milly, who shrugged. "Your call, Captain."

"I trust you," Niko said, eyes locked with Milly's.

"Do you?" Milly said, stretching her neck out to its fullest, the feathers half raised in emotion. Her heart raced as fast as though they were about to duel. "*Do* you?"

"Enough to do this," Niko said.

Milly eased. "It's a start," she said. Then: "Thank you."

Niko only nodded, wondering if yet again she'd done the wrong thing. Lassite had been of no real assurance. He'd said that the moment could have come in different forms, and this was only one manifestation. She'd have made more of that if she believed in any of it, she thought with a touch of anger, but she knew she'd come to pay attention to the Sessile in the war, when he'd proved uncannily accurate in knowing when raids and counterstrikes were about to manifest.

"Ready to roll the dice?" Jezli Farren said softly from beside her.

"This isn't a game," Niko said.

"All of life is a game, and a joyous one." Jezli Farren's tone was oddly formal. "That is the core of my existence. Come, we will play this round together."

They left Milly and one of the bodyguards behind and then their tiny shuttle entered the moth.

31

You Sexy Thing was *anxious*. It chose to assuage that anxiety by doing something. Niko had not forbidden this particular action yet, but the ship thought she would, once she returned and thought harder about that clone. There was a very strong chance that she might have the clone never wake up, but simply continue sleeping in its space, or else even jettison it. It would be much harder for her to jettison it if it had already been decanted, the ship decided. That way it could plead its own case.

The ship would not have done it, perhaps, if Atlanta had not insisted on spending time with the servitor and ignoring the ship. The indignity of being ignored in favor of a part of itself was too much to bear. If she was too obtuse to understand its clever sarcasm about her ear, then it would find something else to be its pet.

And there in the chambers, there was the person who would be Thorn but also not Thorn. The ship was still very unclear on the whole question of identity, but as mentioned, it also was very anxious about those who had gone to the space moth. This may have contributed to its decision as well.

There was a point of no return when the fluid levels would change and could not be reversed. Those microseconds were nearing. The ship considered possibilities, spun out paths, and considered its options. And then the fatal second came, and it started the process of waking up the clone.

The first thing they knew was contentment. There was darkness and bland warmth, and floating, and while they had no words for any of these things, they felt them.

And then these things ebbed away, and there was HEAVY and then there was COLD and then there was harsh LIGHT and then all the words for these things came strong and bright—too strong! too bright!—into its head.

Words in the air—a voice, a voice speaking—

"Happy birthday!"

Dabry knew only when the ship said, "If you are preparing a meal, then I believe there are six to feed instead of five."

"What?" he said blankly, setting down the spoon he had been using while his mind fanned out a hand of possibilities and considered it.

The ship said, "The clone has woken."

It had spent a great deal of time preparing that phrasing of the statement, which took no responsibility for the action.

Dabry cut straight to the core of things in a way that dismayed the ship. "What clone?"

"The clone of Thorn."

"Who . . . no, that can wait. What is the clone's status?"

"It has woken," the ship repeated.

"Who woke it?"

The ship considered the phrasing of possible answers. In the end, it said, "I did."

"And the clone is awake and who has been tending it?"

"Talon is there with it and I have several servitors in attendance. I have installed basic language and skills packages already while it was still in vitro," the ship said proudly. It was quite pleased with how quickly it had mastered the clone sac's technology in order to install and monitor it.

Dabry moved to the door with uncharacteristic haste. "Tell Skidoo to meet me in the cloning chamber."

As he ran toward the chamber, he said to the ship, "Have you taught him how to shapeshift yet?"

"I lack the technology for that," the ship said. "It will be something that Talon will teach him."

"That's one small mercy," Dabry said, thinking of how much damage a panicked were-lion that found itself cornered on a spaceship might wreak.

Talon could hear Dabry in the former warball chamber, footsteps thundering in a way that meant Dabry was serious, and probably angry.

"The sergeant will be here in three minims," the *Thing* said.

The clone was not his brother.

When he'd fallen out of the sack into Talon's arms, his first action had been to push himself out of them and away, away from his brother, scrambling to the wall to stare at Talon. He even held himself differently. But it was the cold indifference in his look that was the most convincing, that froze the excitement racing through him and stopped it dead.

Still. It was done. And hope still surged in him. Even this confusion and fear was better than grief.

"You have to pretend," he told the stranger Thorn.

The clone had been awake for two minims total now, but it had preinstalled knowledge and skills to draw on. It understood the basics of the universe in which it now found itself and had been given knowledge of three languages, the last of which he spoke much better than Talon, or would, once he'd had a chance to sort out all this newness.

"Pretend?" he said.

His voice was wrong, pitched differently than Thorn's, just one of a hundred little differences that made it clear just how badly Talon had fucked up this time. But he *smelled* right, he smelled like the absent Thorn. That had to mean something, after all. That had to be a good sign.

"Your imprint went wrong," Talon said. "You have to persuade them that you remember being my brother or they won't believe it."

"Why pretend?" not-Thorn demanded.

"You're an illegal clone," Talon said urgently, and watched as the clone processed and understood. Its preinstalled knowledge included a basic understanding of the legal system that held sway through most of the Known Universe.

"Who pretend?" he demanded.

"My brother," Talon said, trying to hope that all of this could be salvaged somehow. "All you have to do is say you know somehow that I'm your brother and that will be enough to convince them you're him."

The hatred that smoldered in the other's eyes surprised him.

"Not him," not-Thorn said flatly. But before Talon could deny it, the door had opened and Dabry was upon them, Skidoo at his heels. Startled, the clone screamed, flinching away from the sight of Dabry's towering, angry form.

Dabry went to his knees a meter away from him, holding a hand out, not close enough to touch. Talon held his breath, willing things to go the way he wanted and desperately, achingly afraid that they wouldn't.

"Sssshhh," Dabry said. "It's all right. You are with friends. I'm sorry you were awakened suddenly and without preparation. It's all right."

It did look exactly like Thorn, although a Thorn two or three years younger than the one they had lost. A Thorn unscarred and shiny as new metal. Dabry noted that it would be easy to tell the two apart at first. Later, it would be a problem, he suspected. If there was a later.

So many things about this creature—person, he reminded himself—would be a problem.

Skidoo stepped forward and the clone flinched, re-curled into its ball.

"Steady," Dabry said. "I'm Sergeant Dabry. This is Skidoo."

"You are not," the clone rasped. He flinched again at the sound of his own voice, cowering back as though unsure where the noise had come from. "You are. I am not."

He repeated, his voice filled with terror as he tried to pick and choose among all the concepts that had been forced into his mind in the last hour, "I am not! I am?"

Dabry was perplexed, but Skidoo said, "They is being requesting their name."

"Name," Dabry said blankly. His mind was racing. This complicated things enormously. They would have to fake documents for this clone, good enough to pass most places, and as long as they stuck to the edges of Known Space, everything should be fine enough, but this complication was most unwelcome. He'd seen Gnarl's ship earlier, but all Niko had disclosed over the comms was that Gnarl would be accompanying her party and that they'd talk about it once they were out of the moth.

He cast about in his mind. He said, "I will give you a name, a name from my people. Is that acceptable?"

The clone nodded, his eyes calming a little, but only a grain or two.

He said, "Your name is Rebbe, which means the lost has been found. Do you like that?"

The clone nodded eagerly, as though seizing on the concept. He said, "Rebbe," and his shoulders sagged as though some weight had been lifted.

"Rebbe," Dabry repeated. "We are friends. Will you let us take you elsewhere, to feed you and get you used to things?"

The trust in the clone's eyes as he held out his hand gave him pause. He knew that trust. It was the same trust that had always filled both twins' faces, a sunny serenity unshakable in its faith that all would be well eventually. He had missed it lately in Talon's face. Even now Talon was hanging back, as though frightened to push too close.

Would this creature lose that trust as well, given time? Or would it bring the expression back to Talon's face? This wouldn't be Thorn; that was impossible.

Instead, the clone would be his own person, although Dabry had his doubts that Talon would be able to resist at least trying to force his expectations on Rebbe.

And after all, didn't everyone grow up with expectations forced on them by those around them? Would it really be any different here, even with the accelerated development that the clone had experienced?

32

The opening on the side of the moth was, Niko was relieved to note, nothing like a waste sphincter. It was vast enough that their tiny ship was just a blip within the immense ring that could have swallowed up a ship five hundred times the size of their shuttle.

She looked over her comrades. Milly and Atlanta stood at the ready, both with helmets down. Milly's attention was on Niko and Niko nodded at her. Atlanta was at one of the windows, watching the approaching debris. Jezli and Roxana stood prepared as well; Jezli with her attention on Niko in that attitude of maddening politeness and Roxana watching beside Atlanta.

One of Gnarl's crew, a lean knife blade of a humanoid, was piloting the shuttle. Gnarl and the other were across the chamber, watching Jezli Farren as though ready to shoot her down at the slightest move. Farren appeared utterly unfazed by their attitude.

If it weren't for Gnarl's contingent, it was not a bad crew to be going into the darkness with, despite her doubts about Jezli.

By now, they were all watching out the windows.

As they passed through the great aperture, they could see the blend of organic and inorganic on the walls: irregular spirals laid with more regular patterns, odd horns and other protuberances, all the same dead white, the color of bone or ash that has burned away anything inorganic. Nothing stirred in the shadows, and their light passed over the surfaces, the features ticking by like clockwork.

"There," said Jezli. "There's the dock, just ahead. Once we're fully inside, our comms won't work to connect us to the *Thing* anymore."

"This is the last you'll hear from us for now," Niko told the ship. "Link me to Dabry so I can check in before we lose link with him."

"Perhaps this is a bad time to bother the sergeant. He has been cooking."

In the past half hour, the ship had continued to explore the boundaries of the idea of lying. It was uncertain whether this was a good tactic or not, but something about the thought of Niko finding out everything it had done in terms of waking the clone made it feel what was definitely *panic*.

"Perhaps it sounds to me as though this is the best time imaginable to bother the sergeant," Niko said ominously.

The ship refrained from further comment and opened a channel to Dabry.

"Sergeant, status," Niko snapped.

His voice was cautious. "Nothing to report at the moment, sir, but I would request that we confer on your way back to the ship."

Something had happened, something that he did not want broadcast to the rest of those in this ship. Niko considered and decided that it had to be something about Jezli and Roxana. Had he discovered something about them that she should know before they were all back on the ship together? But if that were the case, surely he would have said something now in one of the codes they had arranged, if it affected the trip together on the space moth.

All she could do was trust him.

She said, "I believe I understand, Sergeant. I look forward to speaking with you about this."

The ship tried to decipher exactly what she meant by this but was unable to fully figure it out. It experienced *worry* mixed with *resignation*.

They disembarked from the tiny shuttle and clustered on the vast shelf inside the opening leading into the moth's dark interior.

Gnarl and his two guards followed them out and the small group huddled together as though allying against the darkness.

By preference, everyone had left their mic live. Atlanta found the collective sound heartening, the breaths of the others reminding her that they were there with her.

Most important, Roxana was there.

It was clear that Jezli had spoken at least some of the truth. Something in the vast structure recognized the paladin, or some quality in turn about her. As she stepped from the shuttle, light bloomed where her foot touched, spreading outward. Although it dimmed as it went, finally dying some hundred meters away or so, it was easier now to see, and when Roxana took another step forward, it rebloomed, the light spreading out, strengthening.

Above them, the cavern's ceiling was furred with shadows and indiscernible ripples.

"Here we go," Jezli said lightly, as though they were embarking on some pleasure excursion.

"Stay close," Roxana said to Atlanta. "A step or so behind me but where I can see you." Atlanta did, and they pushed forward.

They walked. As they did, Roxana switched to a private channel and spoke to Atlanta. She told stories of her past as they moved through the darkness, and Atlanta did not speak, only listened, trying to fix the stories in her memory to the best of her ability.

Roxana talked about what it had been like to be reborn, to be called into the armies of the Cauldron-born, and how she had escaped that existence to become a paladin.

"I knew myself claimed by the universe," she said, "but it could not have made that claim to me if I had not opened my heart to it in the first place. That was the hard part, and I still do not know how I did it."

She shook her head. "I suspect I owe a great deal to some piece of me from before, something which survived long enough to give me that quality. If I had not had it, I would have met the fate my fellows who did not fall in battle faced, destroyed for being made things. But I was long gone before their final battle, and when the forces that had destroyed them came after me, the other paladins intervened and vouched for me."

They walked farther a few silent paces before she said, "That was decades ago, and I have wandered since then. It has been lonely at times, but what is life if not loneliness? And of late, Jezli has brought some light and levity to it all."

"You seem unlikely friends," Atlanta said.

"There are depths to Jezli that cannot be guessed," Roxana said. "I knew that since I first saw her, and it is one of the two reasons that I have followed her."

"What is the other?"

"I knew that she would lead me to something I had been seeking awhile," Roxana said.

Atlanta wanted very badly to ask what that something was. But she kept silent. If Roxana wanted to tell her, she would. The fact that she hadn't yet probably meant she had some reason for keeping that information to herself. But curiosity burned in her.

At first, as they moved from one tunnel to another and then another, she thought Roxana was telling her all of this in order to keep her mind off their journey. But as the stories went by, she realized each one held a truth that the paladin had discovered over the course of her existence, and that she was giving each of these to Atlanta in turn.

And so they went on. Behind them walked Jezli, her quick interest flickering over everything, caught by a sparkle here, a glint there, a trace of pattern that she would pause to record. After her were Niko and Gnarl walking side by side, with his crewman behind them bringing up the rear but taking care to remain within the circle of light that moved with Roxana.

Gnarl was no conversationalist, nor was Niko of a mind to spend time swapping pleasantries with him. Instead, she counted through possibilities and probabilities as they went, trying to build plans out of them, unable to come up with anything that did not seem too flimsy, too chancy. She chewed her lip.

The air inside the suit already smelled like sweat, and Niko knew it would only get worse with time. They should try to get wherever they needed to go as quickly as possible. They all knew that.

Roxana, walking ahead of them with Atlanta, had unslung her weapon from her back and held it easily in both hands, despite its massive size. Niko thought surely that it would be of little use against missile weapons. But who knew what they would encounter deep inside the winding tunnels that filled the moth?

An abundance of things. There were archways and doorways and round slots that perhaps a child could have wriggled through. There were passageways and catwalks across stretches of empty space. It was a labyrinth and Jezli guided them through it, her fingers dancing over the necklace at her throat, information pulsing from the dance, telling her which fork to pick, which stairway to ascend, which hole to crawl through.

Sometimes the hallways were cavernous voids that could have held hordes, and sometimes they were so small that they could only walk single file.

Niko had been in many strange places in her life, between her existence as a Free Trader and her time with the Holy Hive Mind, but this was surely the strangest. And there was something oppressive about the interior of the moth, some sort of psychic malaise that seemed to accumulate on them like ancient dust or moss, layer after layer, as first almost imperceptible, and then heavier and heavier until she thought she might stagger under the weight of that unknown force.

Roxana paused to let the others catch up. When she touched Niko's arm, some of the oppressive weight lifted. Startled, Niko looked at the paladin's serene face and felt her cynicism melting away despite herself. The face could have been carved from gray stone, but it was not the deathly white that surrounded them. It was a gray that held a thousand other colors in it. A gray that said life rather than sterility, joy rather than sadness, purpose rather than the void.

They pushed on.

Later, Niko would have said, if she had been questioned about it, that they walked those hallways forever.

Gnarl walked beside Niko, but he didn't want to talk to her. He didn't need to. He should have felt smug, should have felt like he had it all in the bag, but the truth was that all he felt was envy.

What was it about Niko that made her crew stick so tightly to her? That big one—Dobby, was it?—would have died for her, and he suspected most of the others would have too. Maybe not this one she had with her, that Nneti that was all white feathers and surprising curves under all of that. Moved like a dancer too. Just as well that one had stayed back at the shuttle. She had looked like a fighter, and the fewer of those Niko had with her, the better. He grinned to himself.

Niko didn't notice. She was frowning at Jezli Farren's back, and that, he liked. That pleased him because he didn't like either of them. If they were at odds, that lessened the chance that they'd be teaming up on him. No, it was good that Niko didn't trust Farren any more than he did, because that meant Farren had no incentive to be loyal to her.

Farren. She'd tried to defraud so many, and he'd be the one to catch her and take her skull back because she was too slippery not to kill. Let her live and she'd wriggle away, and that would be intolerable.

No. He had them both, and that meant he was the best and people would acknowledge—finally—that he was the best. Best captain, best pilot, best trader, best everything, or at least, best anything that mattered.

He flicked a look over his shoulder at the bodyguard, who walked so quietly that Gnarl had been unable to hear him and had to reassure himself. But the man was there, dark and tall and thin as a spear blade. He could trust that one; the man knew better than to cross him.

That was why Gio had escaped. Gnarl hadn't learned how to break someone without destroying them yet, or at least any time he succeeded, it was pure accident. No, now he knew how to do it, and he itched to do it to all of them. Would there be enough time to do it to Farren? Or would that give her too much of an escape window? But, oh, it would be sweet to have all of them set beneath his heel, bowing their heads. He could barely wait for that.

His brain was seized with possibilities, plots and plans and schemes, so busy that he barely saw anything around him. To some of them it was a world of wonder and terror.

To Gnarl, it was simply another place.

They hadn't explained the entirety of things to him, but he thought he understood well enough. The secret to getting into the moth was the paladin, and that was good to know. How hard would it be to persuade such a person? Everyone had their price. He would have to speak with her, find her soft spots, the vulnerabilities that he might be able to exploit.

Because a base like the one the moth would make—well, that was a base a man could do all sorts of things from without worrying too much about interference. The paladin wouldn't take to piracy, per se, but there were all shades of things that could be accomplished.

33

"Explain it to me again," Dabry demanded. "How is he awake?"

"It was time," the ship said. "So I did it. If you leave a clone in the sac too long, it can die."

"*Too long* meaning days, not minutes. You should have asked before doing it," Dabry said testily. He was looking at Rebbe, who stood dropping sac fluid that plastered his fur to his skin, making him look thin and frail. He wobbled like a baby bird.

"Sit down," Dabry said. As the clone continued to stand, he said, "How much does he understand?"

"He has been instructed with multiple languages," the ship said. "I gave him the basic educational package. But it is still in the process of self-installing and unfolding. He will remain disoriented until that process is complete."

"You had no soul chip," Dabry said to Talon. "You understand that without that, he is not your brother, doesn't have the memories and soul fire that makes him what he is?"

"He remembers," Talon said. "Ask him! He knows I'm his brother."

Everyone looked to the clone. Rebbe blinked at their expectant faces and said, "I don't know who any of you are."

"But I feel familiar, don't I?" Talon demanded. "Doesn't it seem like you know me even though this is the first time you've seen me? My voice, surely you recognize my voice. I spent all that time talking to you while you were in the sac."

"I don't remember any of that," the clone said with polite chilliness, and Talon sagged as though he had been punched in the gut.

"No putting him back," Gio signed. He shrugged. "Let's make coffee and talk."

"I do not want coffee, whatever that is," Rebbe said. "I am tired. I am new and tired, and you are all looking at me." The rawness in his voice made them all wince.

"Take him to your room for now, then," Dabry said to Talon. "Let him sleep. He will want to sleep every few hours for his first few days. It is to be expected."

"Thank you," Talon said fervently. "Thank you, thank you."

He tugged at Rebbe's hand. "Come on," he said in urgent tones, as though fearing that Dabry might change his mind and order the other pitched out of the airlock at any moment.

Rebbe followed the stranger along the hallway. The stranger was a stranger, no matter how much he might pretend otherwise, and the frustrating thing about him was the way he pretended, which made Rebbe (he centered that name, *I am Rebbe, Rebbe am I*) feel as though he were summoned to act in a play whose lines he did not know.

He hated this other person more than a little as he followed him, this other person that looked like him and claimed to know who he was. This other person who was, he gathered, somehow responsible for this whole situation.

And it was a situation, no matter how much Talon might act otherwise. Rebbe (*I am Rebbe, I am Rebbe*) had read the tension in the other bodies in the room. Dabry had not approved of his presence, and the others had not looked him in the eye, had spent all their time watching Talon.

"What happened to him?" he asked.

Talon kept moving along the hallway. "Who?"

"Your brother. The one you thought I would replace."

He saw that statement hit home in the way the shoulders in front of him slumped. "He died," Talon said.

"I understood that already. How?"

"Someone killed him."

"Murdered him, you mean?" The thought shocked him. It made him realize, for the first time, how orderly his thoughts on such things were, how they came in the same pattern every time, *it is wrong and against society to murder.* It was the result of his preprogramming, but he did not understand that yet, just felt, somewhere in the depths of his gut, the wrongfulness, the artificiality of it, the constraints imposed on him by it.

"Yes."

He pushed harder. "But what happened?"

Talon came to a door and shoved it open. He gestured Rebbe inside without answering.

Rebbe stepped in. The room smelled like Talon and someone else, not quite himself but close, so close. It was a relaxing smell above all, and that and the dusk-lighting of the room, easier on his keen eyes, did drain a little tension from him. Just enough that he realized how much he held, how his shoulders ached from keeping himself at high alert without realizing it.

He went to the cot closest to him, tested the surface and found it welcoming, sank into it, starting at first to sit, then giving up and swinging his legs up to lie back. He closed his eyes. "How was he murdered?"

"Ask Atlanta," Talon said. "She's the only one who was there."

"So she killed him?"

"What? No." Rebbe had succeeded in startling the other into more words. "A man named Tubal Last did it. But she was there. The only one of us that was."

Talon still hated her for that, even now that he had someone who might be—oh, how desperately he wanted that—his brother.

Rebbe read nothing of this in the silence. He gave up on pushing for more information. He would come back to it later. There would be time, apparently. "Where are we? Where is the ship, I mean. I know we're on one."

"My name," the ship interjected, "is *You Sexy Thing*."

"Stop listening!" Talon roared.

There was abrupt silence in the room.

They waited in that silence for three breaths. Then Talon went on, in a conversational tone. "The others are exploring, and they're going to come out with what they find. It's a way to kill Tubal Last."

Rebbe lay there quietly, absorbing it.

Talon gave him another three breaths before he said, "I know everything is scary for you right now, but I'm glad the ship woke you. I'm glad."

But Rebbe was fast asleep and heard nothing.

34

As the group progressed deeper and deeper into the moth, they came across unexpected things.

The light continued to bloom beneath Roxana's step, but it changed color from time to time. Sometimes a purple or blue so deep it seemed almost black; other times, taking on several colors, ethereal lacy pink against eggshell and amber. It was beautiful, and Atlanta paused from moment to moment, taking thought pictures to save for later. The two had fallen to the rear of the group, oblivious to the others.

"Do they always look like this?" she asked Roxana.

"I do not know," the paladin said. "This is the first time I have been in one." She smiled at Atlanta's startled look. "Did you think I made a habit of this?"

"You said that it was a place the gods listened, so I thought you had been in one, to know that," Atlanta admitted.

"Whenever you find Forerunner technology in great masses, the gods are near there, listening," Roxana said. "Why that is, I do not know, and there are plenty of guesses, each as good as the last in terms of being proven by evidence."

"Perhaps Jezli has some explanation," Atlanta said, and Roxana's smile cracked a little wider.

"The suspicion in your tone is warranted. But I will tell you that she has put more time into investigating such things than most. At least to hear her account of things, and it is an account that I have only a little cause to doubt. No, when Jezli says she is a scholar of matters like that, she speaks the truth."

"Why, thank you?" Jezli said, and Atlanta realized the two in front of them had stopped. The tunnel was perhaps two meters in diameter here, and Roxana's head stooped under the occasional lamp fixture. Before them, the tunnel branched, leading in two directions.

"Which should we pick?" Roxana said to Jezli.

Jezli's fingers danced over the crystals, but she frowned. "That I was hoping you would have some sense of," Jezli said.

Roxana pointed right. "That one."

"Is that a guess?" Niko demanded.

"Everything is a guess, only some guesses are more informed than others," Jezli said. "My artifact has played itself out, and cannot lead us further. But she is an artifact herself."

Niko looked to Roxana, but the paladin only gestured them forward.

Now, as they moved along through the cramped tunnels, the light beneath Roxana's feet began to increase. Now, whenever her foot landed, coruscations of brilliant light burst forth. Now, there was music throbbing through the material around so they could feel it underfoot, even though there was no atmosphere to bring it to them. The vibrations grew and grew, pressing in on Atlanta. She felt as though her bones were vibrating, as though she were shifting into some new plane of existence. The air tasted of light.

When had she started walking by herself? She looked around the glittering chamber for the others, but they were nowhere.

Each of them had their own moment of realization that they walked alone. Roxana and Jezli both simply continued walking forward as they had, though Jezli hummed something under her breath.

Niko scowled but pressed on. She remembered her testing

back in the days of the Holy Hive Mind, and there was something reminiscent of its illusions and mental chamberings in this journey.

The bodyguard hesitated, every instinct telling him to flee. But he kept moving. Gnarl had told him to do so, and disobeying his captain's orders brought pain. He had learned that long ago.

Gnarl's pace quickened till he was almost running, a predatory lope. There was something challenging him up ahead, he knew in his heart. It called to him, *Come face me*! And he could not resist that challenge.

The bodyguard was the first to fall, overwhelmed. To him it had seemed that the tunnel narrowed and narrowed, pressing in, and that he had Gnarl at his back, shouting at him in anger, urging him to move quicker.

He had been a stoic sort but, fiber by fiber, his nerves frayed, stretching tighter and tighter with the blinding, deafening forces around him until finally, they snapped. He fell to the ground, biting and clawing at the walls, ignoring the weapons at his belt.

The walls tore at him in turn, reaching out with jagged fingers, at least in his mind. White froth accumulated around his mouth. He breathed out in quick gasps and his eyes bled as his mind shredded.

He kicked out twice, coughed something unintelligible, and died.

Atlanta had not realized Roxana had rejoined her until the paladin spoke. "This is the place I have brought you in order to pass on what I am."

"What?" Atlanta said. Panic grabbed her stomach, flipped it inside out.

"It is still your choice," Roxana said, her voice cheerful. "If you don't want it . . . but if you do, I will carry your petition to the gods."

"Carry it how? By dying, you mean!"

"That is the usual way of it." Roxana smiled at Atlanta. "I have lived a very long time now, and I am ready to move on to the next stage."

"But I just met you!"

"I do regret that," Roxana said, "but I am very glad of the time we have had together."

"Did you know this was coming?"

"Of course I knew. How could I not?" Roxana's face was calm as a still pool. "In your turn, you will know when you have found the right one to pass your legacy—our legacy—on to."

"And if they say no?"

"Then they are not the right one, and things will move along as they are supposed to."

"So you won't die if I say no?"

Roxana outright laughed. "A clever plan!"

It occurred to Atlanta that the paladin was almost giddy with some emotion. How could it be joy at dying? There must be something else. "No, if you say no, I will pass, and all that I have been here will vanish, but it will still have been part of things at one time. I do not care anymore."

There was an inner light to Roxana's face, an impatience as though all of her being were tuned to a wavelength they could not hear, but one that she could, and all she wanted was to listen.

"Roxana, I don't understand!"

"You understand enough. Now I will tell you one more thing. You have accumulated enough luck to get the others out of here. All you have to do is spend it."

"I don't know how to do that!"

Roxana did not answer but took Atlanta's face between her

hands and regarded it solemnly. Leaning forward, she pressed a kiss into the girl's forehead and warmth bloomed where her lips touched.

"Love and be loved," she said, and released her. She glanced behind her as though someone had called her, then turned back to Atlanta for a second.

"Tell Jezli what I said too," she said. And then laughed again out loud, as though delight were consuming her from within. "Tell them all!" Light converged on her, swooped on her, outlined her in brilliance, and then tore her to pieces.

The paladin was gone.

Atlanta found herself in an empty chamber, and her eyes were so full of tears she could barely make out the glowing line on the ground leading out of this place.

How did they exit? Later, Niko would never be able to swear to what it had been, but it seemed to her that she finally walked Lassite's Golden Path, step by step, leading upward to some immense plateau and crowds of people awaiting her there. But no matter how she climbed, how she pressed forward, she could not reach them. She almost despaired, almost thought to give up, but that was not her habit.

She had been leading by example for so long that it was impossible to do otherwise.

Gnarl escaped and it seemed to him that he sheltered beneath his fallen crew, that he pulled the body to him and interposed it between himself and a fearful, golden light that threatened to encompass and devour him.

He felt as though he were being taken apart from the inside and studied, and he tried to cling to the pieces of him that were being removed and all he could cling to was the anger, because that was the part of him that he knew the best.

What remained after the process was not precisely Gnarl, but it believed itself him.

Only Atlanta would later remember the moments at the heart of the moth. How the light washed over her. How the light interrogated her, merciless and loving all at once. How the light took her soul where it spun out of kilter and recentered her.

Do you want this thing that you have come for, truly? the light demanded.

"Yes," she said. "It's how I'll save my friends."

This is a thing of death; is it just?

She thought about Tubal Last, kidnapping Petalia and poisoning them against the person who loved them most. Of his careless murder of Thorn, just to make the rest of them more frightened. Of his throne room, full of captive things stolen from across the Known Universe as well as prisoners. Helpless creatures, trapped under the weight of injustice.

"Yes," she said. "It is just." She felt the import of that statement. If she had been lying, she somehow knew, she would have been found unworthy.

She felt the luck leaving her, the light taking it away in an exchange she did not entirely understand, and no longer wondered why Roxana had not instructed her in how to do this. This was more than knowing her place in the world as she had as an heir. This was being it through and through, to the very core.

I am a paladin now, she thought, and then, terrifying and giddying all at once, *and I will spend the rest of my days figuring out what that means.*

Milly was beside Niko, somehow, even though she was also back at the shuttle, and when Niko staggered, Milly put up a hand and caught her, more than once. Until finally it was the two of them walking up together, like one thing, a single entity moving single-mindedly upward.

Niko found herself standing in front of the shuttle with Milly, and Atlanta, and Jezli, and Gnarl.

The last of these lunged at Jezli as though to attack, and Milly and Niko both interposed themselves. Niko wondered for a moment where the other crew member was, then caught sight of the body. *He must have attacked Milly while we were gone,* she thought, and then, *I made the right choice,* with a touch of relief.

Atlanta was carrying something, and Gnarl fell back in her direction and tried to snatch it, but she was too quick.

Then all of them were scrambling for the shuttle, and then the four of them were gone, and what was left of Gnarl stood in the void within the moth, screaming silently after them while in the shuttle, Jezli shouted angry questions at Atlanta, demanding to know where Roxana was, while all Atlanta could do was cry.

She pushed what she held forward at Niko, and Niko took it, knowing it was the artifact they had sought.

"Roxana?" she said, echoing Jezli's demand, but more softly, and she did not press when Atlanta shook her head.

"Then we will go home," she said, and took the helm.

35

Dabry met them in the ship bay, his eyes moving over the group to count the missing, widening as he noticed Roxana's absence. To Niko, he looked worn. She thought wryly that perhaps his duty had been even harder than hers, having to deal with those that had been left behind.

She said, "What happened?"

"There was . . . there is a clone. The ship decanted it. I've talked with him. I named him."

"Ah, I might have learned that from Gnarl and forgotten to tell you," she admitted, and received a startled flicker from him. "But I thought things were safely in stasis. Why did the ship decant it?"

"I believe," Dabry said, with grim irritation, "that the ship was bored."

"No," the ship protested.

She sighed. "We don't need to assign blame quite yet," she said. "You said you named it already."

"Rebbe."

"Which means?"

"The lost has been found."

She nodded. "And right now, where is he?"

"I had the ship take him to Talon's room for now. Talon has been told to prepare him a room but when I checked it was evident that he has put it off and not done it yet."

"He gets worse and worse," she said. She glanced upward. "I understand it was the ship who aided him. We'll have to have a talk about that."

Dabry nodded. "But it is we who lead him," he said. "As ever, we are the ones responsible for what he does."

"Lately I am thinking that we have not done a very good job of that."

"We have tried, and we have put time and thought and work into it. Can anyone ask for more than that?"

"Talon can, apparently. And has."

"How did you manage to get this aboard?" Niko asked Talon, staring at the discarded clone sac.

"Gnarl sent it, in a shipment. The *Thing* had everything else that I needed to do it. And it wasn't the ship's fault, Captain. I tricked it."

The ship wavered between indignation at the thought that it could be tricked and a sense of relief that its behavior might be excused. Had Talon really deceived it? Was that a friendly act? It decided to say nothing. For now.

"How did you trick it?"

He focused fiercely on the floor. "I told it if we had a secret, it meant we were friends," he muttered.

Niko blinked in disbelief. "Could you tell me that again?" she said.

"I thought. I mean . . ."

"You mean that you took advantage of the fact that it wanted to be friends with you. What if you found that we had done that to you? Picked you and pretended because it was because we were family but the truth being that we wanted to use you in some way?"

There was no way his whiskers could have sagged even lower.

Dabry exchanged looks with the captain. "Ingenious manipulation, at any rate," he said.

"This is really not the time for complimenting him on how

well he's managed to do something utterly, absolutely against the law, and not to mention selfish."

"Selfish?" Talon protested. "All I wanted was Thorn back."

"That is not Thorn. That is not even a copy of Thorn. It is their own person, and they do not deserve to have you trying to make them into a replacement for someone they cannot be. Thorn is gone, Talon. Thorn. Is. Gone."

He fell to his knees, fists gathered. He said, "I didn't even get to see his body after his death! He died and then there we were fleeing the pirates and we didn't take his body with us, and now it's just floating out there somewhere! All alone somewhere!"

He took a deep, shuddering breath. "I know it's not him. But it will look like him. It will smell like him, sound like him."

He was crying now, he found. When had he started doing that? He wasn't even sure, he was so lost in this storm of emotion tossing him every which way that he couldn't find himself anymore, wasn't sure who he was without the existence of Thorn to give him context.

Niko chewed her lip, watching Talon's grief. She knew that she had to see him through this passage, but this was the most that she could do—could hope to do.

She said, looking at Dabry, "Before it was decanted, it had no consciousness yet."

He said, "And now he does. Will you destroy that?"

"No," Talon cried out, catching their meaning. "You can't just kill him."

"According to law, it is not a being and has no rights. If the authorities find out, it will be executed out of hand. Is that what you want, Talon? To condemn someone to a short lifetime of hiding and fleeing?"

He said, "He can step into Thorn's identity."

"Can he? Will he *want* to?"

Listening to all this, the *Thing* was not happy that Niko was angry with it. It had never experienced quite this mix of emotions, and while it blamed Talon in part, it was also aware that it had made choices rather than simply doing what it was told. It resolved in the future to tell Niko everything.

Well, everything that it thought she needed to know. Otherwise, how could she appreciate the twists of *hourisigah* to come?

"Will you destroy that?" Dabry said more urgently, as though calling Niko back to her senses.

"No," Niko said and rubbed at her eyes. She looked at Dabry. "I'm going to regret this," she told him.

"Frankly, Captain, I don't know that there is any decision that can be made in this case that will not lead to some form of regret or another." Dabry looked at Talon. "This is disappointing, Talon," he said. "But I rather think you have created your own punishment."

"All right, *Thing,*" Niko said and turned away. "Make quarters for our new acquisition. It's Talon's and your responsibility to make sure they're taken care of, and you will treat them with courtesy and respect." She looked at Dabry again. "I'm going to talk to Lassite," she told him.

Dabry arched an eyebrow. "Why?"

"Because I want to make sure none of this is due to some terrible act committed in a previous existence."

Despite her facetiousness, she did want Lassite to reassure her. That this was part of his Golden Path—well, she didn't really believe in it, she told herself—but some of the rest of the crew did, and so it was important to keep that under consideration.

The dry air sucked at her as she entered. He was sitting in the middle of the room, cross-legged, his hands resting on his knees. His red velvet hood had been pushed back to his narrow shoulders, exposing his hairless, snakelike skull, the divots of his nostrils, his flat, scaled face. A Derloen ghost was flowing on the flooring in front of him, a shape like a sigil, repeated again and again.

He opened his enormous dark eyes to regard her.

Before she could ask her question, he spoke. The ghost left off its tracing and fled as though startled, disappearing into the wall.

"It will be all right, Captain. It will not turn out anything like he expects, but it will be all right."

It was a reassurance, but somehow not as reassuring as she had hoped. There was an eerie implacability to his tone at these times when he was uttering prophecies that made her skin crawl, made her feel like an animal in a trap.

She ignored it, as she always did.

"Very well," she said, and went about her business.

Lassite stared after her. Despite what he had said, he was not sure this particular thing would go very well. It was simply that it didn't matter much to the overall shape of things.

The truth was that it could go very badly indeed.

Talon waited and waited to hear what his punishment would be. He could not imagine it. He had disobeyed Niko in the past but only in small ways. This had been an act of major rebellion, the sort of thing that got a crew member turned away.

The thought of that made him feel weak, as though his bones had been replaced with melting ice. What if he had betrayed Niko so thoroughly that she no longer wanted him in her crew? What would he do if he was out in the universe, utterly alone? What would happen to the clone? The thought surrounded him, terrified him.

It was what drove him, finally, to go to her rather than waiting for her to come to him. He went to her in her cabin, where she was reading. She looked up from the tablet and said, "Yes, soldier?" Her tone was businesslike and matter-of-fact.

He said, "I wanted to find out what my punishment is."

"Your punishment. Ah." She laid the tablet down. "What are your thoughts on it?"

"You could make me do scrub work for a long time."

She raised an eyebrow. "Oh, I thought that was a given."

He faltered, then went on. "I don't want to be sent away but if you had to, maybe only for a while?"

She sighed. "Oh, Talon. I will not send you away. You are my responsibility. When you do something like this, I am the one that the law will punish, you know. Because you did it while under my command."

He hadn't known that and it shocked him. He had been willing to take the risk on his own, but to think that he had made her liable . . . "No! That's not fair!"

"The laws of the Known Universe are more known for being inflexible than fair," she said. "No, here is your punishment. You are responsible for that clone. You will oversee him."

His heart leaped for joy. But she went on.

"You will never tell him that he is a replacement for your brother. You will never treat him as anything but his own person. Like a cousin you have never met before, freshly arrived, who you have to take under your wing. Do you understand me?"

He opened his mouth and closed it, then swallowed and said, "Yes, sir."

"Never. Do you understand? You will never make him feel that he is obliged to you in any way. If he asks where his genetic material came from, you will say your mother. Do you understand what I am saying?"

"To let him be his own person, without pressure," he said easily, but his heart was starting to sing again. No matter what, surely it would be like having Thorn back, the smell of him at least, the sense of him in the air.

And while the clone would not be as close as a twin, if he

were watching over Rebbe, then there would be a reason that they would be together all the time. He didn't need to be lonely anymore. He caught himself smiling and made his face somber. He didn't understand how Niko would think this was actually a punishment, but that was all right. He said, "Yes, sir."

"*Thing* has prepared quarters for him. Take him to them and show him how everything works."

"Quarters for him? But he will share mine."

She shook her head. "No. That is not letting him be his own person. If that is what *he* wants, certainly you can change to that later. But you will not invite him or try to sway him or imply that it is expected of him or anything like that. You will let Rebbe become whoever they want to become. Perhaps that person will resemble your twin, a little. But I would not count on it, I would not set my hopes on it, because I know—not guess, not suspect—I *know* that will lead to heartbreak."

She could see that he still wasn't listening and understanding fully. And that broke her heart in turn.

After Talon had gone, the ship said, "Am I to be punished as well?"

"What do you think would be a suitable punishment?"

"I will give up artistic expression for a month."

"All artistic expression? Including tourwhatsit?"

"Yes."

"Very well. But *Thing*, you understand what I will have to do if you keep acting in ways that are harmful? We will give you back to Takraven and say goodbye."

Panic seized it. "No! You can't do that!"

Niko rubbed her nose to avoid smiling. As she'd thought, this was the best lever to use. "Just keep that in mind," she said. "I'd hate to have to do it."

36

The Gun was made of cold blue glass and colder glints of silver, a tangle with a hole in one side, sized for a hand. It had no visible way of projecting anything. Atlanta thought that she could tell where its name had come from: The cold, rapacious quality that seemed to exude from it attested that it was not a thing of peace.

Niko had kept the artifact away from Jezli, refusing to let it out of her hands. "Are you sure it's a weapon?" she said dubiously, inspecting it.

"It is perhaps the most dangerous thing you have ever held," Jezli said mildly.

Niko put the Gun down on the table in front of her, taking care not to make the action seem overly hasty, but also doing it as quickly as possible.

"What next?" she demanded of Jezli. "How do we shoot it?"

"Ah," Jezli said. She was still subdued from Roxana's death, her face paler than usual, her movements not as animated. "That requires a specialized individual."

"You're saying that you can't?"

"I'm saying that there was a reason I was seeking your Florian friend." She nodded at the Gun. "Forerunner tech, and it can only be manipulated by one of the species the Forerunners created. I know of only one of those that is left, and now it is extinct, and only one of its members remains. We'll need to find them, and then move to someplace unobtrusive to fire the Gun. I have no idea what that will look like; no text describes it, but the Forerunners never did anything on a small scale."

"Why didn't you tell us all this before?" Niko said.

"I play things one step at a time," Jezli said. "And I was not entirely sure we'd be able to pluck it from the moth." More quietly, she added, "And I might not have gone chasing it, if I knew the price was so high.

Their eyes met and Niko said nothing more on that subject. Instead, she said, "We parted ways at Montmurray. That's where we've been headed all this time. Who knows where they went from there, but it's the best place to start."

"Agreed," Jezli said.

She started to reach for the Gun, but Niko forestalled her. "I'll be finding a safe place for this," she said. "But for now, we have to consider certain things." She glanced around at the assembled crew. "Our friend here has been claiming to be able to open Gates that have died. Last will have heard that, or at least rumors. We'd heard some of them even before we met."

She looked directly at Jezli. "If we had power over the Gates, that is something that we could trade for substantial resources, enough to be able to go hunting for him and wipe him out with confidence. The Gates are key to the way the Known Universe currently works, a vital part of its infrastructure. The threat of taking them out of it is a game changer. If something like that fell into his hands, he would be able to use it at his whim and change life as millions of people know it."

"That certainly would," Jezli said. "If I had something like that."

"I knew it!" Niko said. "What's the trick?"

Jezli sighed, stroking the crystal. "This lets me know when a Gate is due to go down."

"Gates never go down," Atlanta said.

"Well, now, you yourself have seen that is not so. Truth is, we're about to enter a cycle where all of them die and rekindle, one by one, and I know where and when for each. It's a maintenance cycle. I simply got lucky with the timing at the first one, and then

I thought, why not play it a little?" Jezli shrugged. "The con couldn't have lasted much longer, I don't think. Gnarl would have seen to that."

"Could still see to it, if his crew picks him up," Niko said.

"I give that fifty-fifty," Jezli said. "All of them seem more used to him than fond of him."

"So we are, once again, off to Montmurray," Niko said. "And who knows what we will find there?"

The others had come back, but Talon didn't care. Thorn—no, Rebbe—had moved into another room and would not speak to him, even when he sat and sat and sat outside the door. It was unendurable.

"Come out and play warball," he said. "You're angry, and that helps when you're angry."

The door opened and the other was there, looking at him.

They played in silence, no matter how much Talon tried to start a conversation, and Rebbe picked the game up quickly enough to play to hurt. He shoved and pushed, he slammed into Talon, and once, his claws flickered out and left a line of blood on the other's skin. He did not apologize.

Talon didn't mind. He didn't mind at all.

37

Niko stared at the console. Almost to Montmurray, and what then? She had acted to the others as though tracking the Florian would be easy, and Dabry, even though he knew better, had not contradicted her. He knew despair was bad for morale. He stood beside her now; they'd be through the Gate soon. After that exit, Montmurray was two and half days' distance.

She said, "What if we can't find them?"

"Then we will have a weapon that we can wave around but not fire," he said. "We don't usually operate on the premise we'll fail, sir. At least we never have before."

She looked up at him from the console.

She said, "I figure we'll send in a small group, those of us good at gathering intelligence, and find out what we can, while you and the ship pick through the outgoing records and look for any trace of Petalia. If there's no sign, we'll try Ydll."

"Why Ydll?"

"It's the closest big Gate within a reasonable timeframe," Niko said. "If they left Montmurray that way, either they've gone there or they've done something else that I would consider smart—they've hired a slowship and gone on a very long journey, figuring that heat dies while you're in coldsleep."

"Mmmm," Dabry said.

"What?"

"You are here thinking about what-ifs, and meanwhile, Atlanta was apparently with Roxana when she died but will not speak of it, we have acquired a crew member whose face we know but not his mind, and we have lost someone we knew a little while, yet another death after so many." Dabry's face was somber.

"Sky Momma dance me true," she said. "I'm groping, Dab."

"And that's all we ask. That you keep doing it."

The words steadied her, so much so that she realized how off-kilter she had been until that moment. She breathed in, feeling her feet on the floor's solidity, the chair holding her up, the warmth of Dabry beside her.

It was enough. It was enough to continue on.

Jezli sat in her cabin, tightly curled around her core, green eyes closed. She made no sound, and after a while, the ship grew tired of watching her.

Gio and Milly were both working in the kitchen. Milly was making cookies while he cleaned out a frothing apparatus. She'd told him about her time on the moth; most of it had been waiting once Gnarl's crewman had come at her and been suitably disposed of.

"What about this question with Talon?" she said.

"I understand why he did it," Gio signed. He picked up a cloth and ran it along a crevice, removing an accumulation. He had been thinking about Talon, and friendship, and loneliness. He turned back to Milly and signed, "I'm glad you made it out."

"Are you?" she said.

He looked down at his hands, then back at her. "Yes," he said. And then added, "I'm sorry."

Nneti do not cry, but he could smell the swell of emotion in her. "I am too," she said.

"Still friends?"

"Always," she said.

Atlanta had gone to the ship's gardens, unheeded in the hubbub after their return. Everyone was in shock from Roxana's death, herself included, but the sorrow that pulsed in her was matched by joy. She was alive, and she had come back with a purpose, a role that the universe had for her. She didn't know what it was, but she was filled with assurance that it existed, that she'd be shown it in due time.

That joy kept surging in her, at least until she tried to talk with her counselors, to tell them their efforts had somehow brought her luck. And how wonderful was that, that she had somehow worked actual magic with their aid, as she understood it?

But when she entered the room within her mind, it lay in ruins. The window was smashed and rain poured into pools across the floor. She saw the counselors standing there, but when they saw her, they fled through mental corridors she had not known existed.

She chased one, then another down those endless halls that billowed and swooped in their dimensions, dizzying, stomach-lurching. But she could catch none of them until, somehow, she cornered the Happy Bakka.

It was happy no longer. Panicked froth garnished its muzzle, its fur was sweat-matted, and its button-black eyes rolled wildly in its head as it cowered, scrabbling at the wall in a futile attempt at escape.

She went to her knees, held out a hand. She said, "It's me! What's going on? Why are you frightened of me?"

"I don't know you," it screamed in a voice full of agony. "Who are you? How dare you come here?"

"It's me! It's Atlanta. You know me! Stop this!" Its fear could not help but spread to her; she felt it clinging persistently to her, attaching itself with spidery hands.

The Bakka panted as though it could not catch its breath, desperate gulps of air.

To her horror, she realized it was shriveling before her eyes. The plump flesh dimpled inward, shrinking, and the thinning fur hung in folds.

"What's going on? Stop!" she wailed and tried to touch it, but it flinched and shrieked a thin, brain-addled wail of pure terror, and she withdrew her hand.

"What's going on?" she asked it again. "What's happening?" But it did not speak again and she sat there in the echoing, decaying space, watching it waste away, go thinner and thinner, fur stretched over bones, black eyes dulling and hazing with white.

It crumpled. It curled in on itself. It died.

Around her, the space was collapsing. She did nothing to stop it or escape, just sat there as it shattered and the shards fell away and she was back in the ship's garden, sitting beside the rack of laseriabells. No matter how she tried, she could not access the counselor space again.

Rebbe hadn't meant to snoop through Talon's things, but the other had asked him to get something for warball. And there he was, pawing through the drawer, and out fell the recording cube.

Even then, he wouldn't have deliberately played it, but it slipped from his hand as he tried to put it back and when it fell on the floor, it activated. There was an image of Talon looking into the cube. He looked so sad.

He said, "I know you won't have any of Thorn's memories, and that's okay."

Rebbe kept listening, even when he knew it was long past

when he should have returned to the warball room. He heard the door open and Talon come in and his inhalation when he saw that Rebbe was listening to the cube.

The cube was almost done. Rebbe could see the green dwindling. Just an edge of it was left.

From it, Talon's voice said, "The captain said I'm never supposed to try to make him be Thorn. And he doesn't act like you. I mean, like Thorn. I don't know. I guess since I'll never give this to him, it's really for you, Thorn. Maybe. I don't even know who I'm talking to anymore. I asked Lassite if it's possible that you could become a ghost. But he shook his head and said no, and a bunch of stuff about how there would have had to have been certain preparations."

A sigh. Then the recorded voice continued.

"I don't like him. I'm going to keep pretending he's you and maybe if I pretend hard enough, he will be. Lassite said that's what magic is, thinking really hard about something sometimes. Anyhow. I love you. I miss you. I'll keep trying."

Rebbe put the cube down very carefully, very precisely, lining it up with the corner of the table. Then he rose, feeling anger boiling through every inch of him, snakes in his muscles, poison in his blood. He demanded, "You think you can make me into your brother?"

"The captain said not to!" the other—his brother, not his brother, his twin who was a stranger, his supposed cousin, but above all the person who was not him, was not anything like him—protested. "She said to let you be your own person. And you are, you're Rebbe." He faltered over the name.

"Rebbe, who someone else named. Rebbe, who you don't like. Rebbe, who you wish didn't exist, so he could be your lost brother instead."

"It's not like that. I understand that he's gone. I don't hold it against you."

That was even more the wrong thing to say. Anger flared in him, bright as a star, fierce as its fiery heart. "Oh, you don't, do you? That's very kind of you. You, to whom I owe my entire existence."

"I know what I did was wrong," Talon said. "I understand that now."

"Why should I be the thing that's used to teach you!?" he cried out.

"You're misunderstanding on purpose. It's not like that."

He picked up the cube. "That's not what you say here!" He did not replace it this time but threw it down so it bounced across the floor, rolled to Talon's feet.

He did not lean over to take it. He kept staring at Rebbe as though he had never said he wished he didn't exist, that he was someone else instead.

"It's not like that," he repeated.

But Rebbe did not stay to find out what it was like. Instead, he fled, going along the maze of halls in the ship, moving downward into the lowest passageways where it was warmer and darker.

"What is this place?" he demanded of the ship.

"It is a place where the others do not come," the ship said. "It seemed to me that you did not want to be speaking to anyone at the moment."

He kept moving but considered the ship. It was his only ally, really. He had known it ever since he had been decanted. It had always been there to explain things as soon as he needed them explained, and it explained things in words that were understandable, unlike Talon, who kept scattering everything he said with in-jokes, trying to summon back the person who would have understood them.

He slipped into the doorway it opened for him and found what he wanted: a small, dark space into which he could curl himself, his shoulder firmly against the warmth and reassuring solidity of the ship.

He folded his knees to his chest and wrapped his arms around them, feeling anger in him, and sorrow, and helplessness, and almost-panic.

He was supposed to be someone other than he was. He was a failed experiment. He was an interloper in a space that had been made for someone else.

Sure, the captain had acted as though he were still welcome here. As though he could continue along with them, but how could he do that, knowing now what he did? Feeling Talon fucking yearning after him the way that he did. Feeling that he didn't know anything, because he didn't. He had a total of a week of experience of life and a bunch of preloaded knowledge he had no reason to trust.

What was he to do?

Concerned, the ship alerted Niko.

She could have sent Dabry to deal with Rebbe. He was better sometimes with the people side of things. But the truth was that the boys were her responsibility, had been since she had first met them and their mother, even without that mother entrusting her with them.

And now here was another one, unasked for, unlooked for, but still her responsibility.

The ship told her where he was. She rapped gently on the door, expecting a "Go away!" of the sort that would have come from either Thorn or Talon, but instead, he said, "Who is it?"

"Niko," she said.

He palmed the door-pad and it slid open. He was in half form, his face wet with tears.

She stood there. She did smell right to him, somehow, although he couldn't have said why, in a way that very few of the others did. And because of that, he said, simply, "I don't know what I am supposed to do or be."

She did not reach out to him for reassurance. But she said, "You are a member of my crew until you decide you no longer want to be."

"And what will I do in it?" he demanded, sudden and fierce in a way that was Thorn-like.

She shrugged. "You'll figure out your place. And you won't be the only one. Atlanta is still trying to figure out her role. You may find the two of you have a lot in common."

"I hate him," he said.

She didn't object to the sudden leap to another topic, but followed him. "Talon, you mean."

"Yes," he said, almost hissing it. "He did all this. Made me without asking me. Made me not a person, just a replacement for something I can't be."

She considered this. It reassured him somewhat that the answer was not immediate but thought out.

"He was grieving," she said. "You don't know what that is like yet, but it is as hard as what you experience right now. If you could do something to relieve how you feel, how much time would you spend second-guessing it before you acted?"

He thought about this in turn. She could see him thinking about it in a way she didn't expect, as though he were considering the statement from all sides. How could he be so different from Talon mentally? She filed that question away to contemplate later.

"I don't want anything to do with him," he said.

"You are fellow crew, so there is some inevitability to your coexistence," she said gently. "But you do not have to share quarters and I will not make you share duties unless it is unavoidable. Is that acceptable?"

She refrained from adding "or shall we drop you off at the next station?" knowing it would come across as more threat than reassurance.

His eyes met hers, frank and thoughtful. "For now?" he said. "Is that all right?"

She nodded at him. "But you will tell me if it changes, and we will readjust things together. Understood?"

She wasn't sure it was, but she had to make the effort nonetheless.

38

Montmurray Station was its usual bustle of activity, hanging against the stars with a sheen of activity, ships going back and forth, most of them to one of the two nearby, settled stations.

Atlanta had seemed abstracted since coming back, clearly processing what had happened with Roxana on the moth, so Niko figured she would send her with Milly to buy trade goods. Milly's luck had proved so good with the Velcoran goods that Niko was willing to trust her with that, at least. Gio seemed to share that attitude; Niko had found them playing music together in the lounge the day before.

Dabry would stay aboard with Talon and Rebbe, the latter of which Niko planned to keep very much under wraps. She and Dabry had discussed what to do if Gnarl had survived.

Niko rather thought he had. "We just don't get that lucky," she said wryly. "But if he tells the authorities what Rebbe is, he's as implicated in it as Talon, and he won't risk that. He was counting on panic to keep us from figuring that out, and I will admit that it did for a while."

Skidoo, on the other hand, was their best intelligence gatherer. Privately, Niko considered her their best hope of finding where the Florian had gone. As she had told Dabry, she had little hope. Petalia could have gone anywhere from here, and they knew enough to cover their tracks in doing so.

But Niko kept these thoughts to herself. She accompanied the others into the station, submitting their Keinlot papers and getting them stamped. But after she had nodded them on their way and made sure they had enough credit on them to do whatever they needed to do, she herself went down to one of the deep-deck bars, where the booze was cheap and the corners were dark.

The special was something called an Arranti Comet, and part of the gimmick was that you rolled a ten-sided die and got a shot of whatever was indicated. Niko rolled and got a purple circle. "Tengu fortified," the bartender, an Ettilite like Dabry, said and added a deep purple dram to the golden drink. The two liquids did not mix, but curled together in an intricate pattern. He slid it across the counter to Niko. It tasted like fiery violets, not unpleasantly so.

She liked this place. The music was just a trickle of soft, slow notes over the intercom, and they didn't allow hassa smoke the way the rest of the deep-deck establishments did. And everyone kept to themselves, and let a person sit quietly by themselves in the dim light and drink alone.

Or so she thought until someone slid onto the stool beside her. Irritated, Niko turned to say something, then halted at the sight of pale white hair, ornamented with tiny blossoms, and icy eyes.

"I thought you promised you were never coming back," Petalia said.

39

Sometimes you find yourself in a moment that you have dreamed of more than once. And yet the words, the same ones you have spoken so suavely so many times in your head, never come out.

Niko stammered, "What? How are you here?"

Petalia said, "You look terrible."

Niko gathered her wits long enough to signal the bartender for another drink, indicating the new arrival. He gave off wiping the counter with a dirty rag in his lower hand and switched to the upper to offer Petalia a special. They declined to roll the die and he shrugged and poured in a measure of clear liquid before handing it to them.

They took it and put it in front of them without sipping from it. "I am here because it seemed likely you would return once you also discovered Tubal Last is alive."

"So you waited for me," Niko said giddily.

Petalia's face did not warm. "I may know you are my best chance against him, but don't think that is welcome knowledge."

"We have something . . ." Niko started, then broke off, coming to her senses. Who knew what sorts of ears might be listening, even here? Instead, she said, "Come back to the ship with me, and we'll talk."

She gulped her drink down before they left. Petalia's remained untouched on the bar and the bartender drank it himself when he realized they were not returning.

"How does it work?" Petalia asked, staring down at the machine. "You said it is called the Devil's Gun, and that would imply it shoots something."

"A metaphorical gun," Jezli said tersely. She and Petalia had disliked each other on sight, like fire and water introduced for the first time. Niko might have enjoyed seeing her discomfited, but it was clear Petalia felt the same, and the constant squabbling was getting annoying, even though the two had been coexisting for less than an hour now.

"Then how do I metaphorically shoot it?"

"When we are well away from the station, so they do not sense any fluctuations that might come from it, you will hold it and think of the person you want dead."

Petalia scoffed. "It cannot be that simple!"

"You go through a Gate and come out elsewhere, and that is simple enough, but you do not question that!" Jezli snapped back.

Dabry looked to Niko.

She cleared her throat. "Enough," she said. "Dabry, are the others back on board yet?"

He nodded.

"Are you sure you don't need to get anything from the station?" Niko asked Petalia.

They shook their head. "I travel light," they said.

40

Not too hard to find an isolated spot, a full day away from a Gate, a star system with little to recommend and less to profit from.

Not too hard to pause in the shadow of a small moon and prepare to fire the artifact.

Not too hard for Petalia, standing with the others clustered around them in the lounge, to take the Devil's Gun gingerly in their hands. There was hesitation on their face. Artifacts like this could be—often would be—deadly.

As their fingers closed around the Gun, it lit with a deep blue light from nowhere, a light that could not help but remind those who had been aboard the space moth of the light that had greeted Roxana's steps. It gave everyone in the room an unearthly cast, as though the light were battling natural color and extinguishing it. Odd patterns were visible on Skidoo's skin, a thermal lacework revealed for the first time.

Tendrils, fine as whiskers, extended from the glittering tangle, sank into Petalia's skin, making them gasp with a sensation more like the bite of frost than fire.

"Think of your target," Jezli said. She had insisted on taping all the enterprise and was standing by the camera drones, watching intently, her fingers straying restlessly over the necklace around her throat from time to time.

Moments stretching endlessly. Their faces, full of light from the Gun's illumination.

A sequence of sound, singing in their ears, at first soft, then louder and louder, making everyone press their hands, their arms over their ears, Skidoo retracting hers fully but still feeling her flesh battered by that sound, because it was *wrong* somehow, repeated over and over till they could hardly bear it.

It battered Lassite but he stood fast, prepared for the moment. Atlanta, too, found herself less shaken than the others, although she was not sure. Had Jezli reacted at all?

Then it stopped with staggering suddenness, and the Gun fell clattering from Petalia's hands.

"What was that?" Niko demanded.

"It was an error message," Jezli said, shaking her head as though to clear it. "Give me a second to decipher it." Her fingers strayed over the crystals at her neck.

Then she blinked in surprise.

"It says it cannot be fired because there is more than one target."

"More than one target?" Niko said.

"What does this mean?" Atlanta asked.

"It means," Niko said, eyes meeting Dabry's, "that Tubal Last is not just alive but even more so than one might think."

She looked out the window at the stars, chewing her lip, before turning back and continuing.

"It means that now there is more than one of him."

ACKNOWLEDGMENTS

Writing is a solitary game, but we depend so much on those who supply the encouragement in between our solitudes. I couldn't do what I do without that encouragement.

Early readers and encouragers included Anastasia Mayette Draper, Kel the Best Purveyor of Gay Books Ever, Wayne Rambo, and Alice Swanberg. Influences and abettors included the Griffon Bookstore, Ken Peczkowski, and the cheerful baristas of West Seattle.

Special thanks to the Rambo Academy for Wayward Writers' Patreon and Discord community, a major source of support both mental and financial, and to all my amazing students, mentees, and fans. You are all well-loved and appreciated. I hope you enjoy some of what I produce.

And last but never least, many thanks to my agent, the ever-awesome Seth Fishman, as well as editor Chris Morgan, editorial assistant Mal Frazier, publicist Desirae Friesen, and all the other wonderful support staff at Tor.